KU-790-282

THE HOUSE HUNT

Also by C. M. Ewan

A Window Breaks

The Interview

Writing as Chris Ewan

Safe House

Dead Line

Dark Tides

Long Time Lost

The Good Thief's Guide series

The Good Thief's Guide to Amsterdam

The Good Thief's Guide to Paris

The Good Thief's Guide to Vegas

The Good Thief's Guide to Venice

The Good Thief's Guide to Berlin

THE HOUSE HUNT

C. M. EWAN

MACMILLAN

First published 2023 by Macmillan
an imprint of Pan Macmillan
The Smithson, 6 Briset Street, London EC1M 5NR
EU representative: Macmillan Publishers Ireland Ltd, 1st Floor,
The Liffey Trust Centre, 117–126 Sheriff Street Upper,
Dublin 1, D01 YC43
Associated companies throughout the world
www.panmacmillan.com

ISBN 978-1-0350-1068-4 HB
ISBN 978-1-0350-1070-7 TPB

Copyright © C. M. Ewan 2023

The right of C. M. Ewan to be identified as the
author of this work has been asserted by him in accordance
with the Copyright, Designs and Patents Act 1988.

All rights reserved. No part of this publication may be reproduced,
stored in a retrieval system, or transmitted, in any form, or by any means
(electronic, mechanical, photocopying, recording or otherwise)
without the prior written permission of the publisher.

Pan Macmillan does not have any control over, or any responsibility for,
any author or third-party websites referred to in or on this book.

1 3 5 7 9 8 6 4 2

A CIP catalogue record for this book is available from the British Library.

Typeset in Celeste by Palimpsest Book Production Limited, Falkirk, Stirlingshire
Printed and bound by CPI Group (UK) Ltd, Croydon, CR0 4YY

This book is sold subject to the condition that it shall not, by way of
trade or otherwise, be lent, hired out, or otherwise circulated without
the publisher's prior consent in any form of binding or cover other than
that in which it is published and without a similar condition including
this condition being imposed on the subsequent purchaser.

Visit **www.panmacmillan.com** to read more about all our books
and to buy them. You will also find features, author interviews and
news of any author events, and you can sign up for e-newsletters
so that you're always first to hear about our new releases.

This book is dedicated to my agent,
Camilla Bolton, and my editor, Vicki Mellor,
with deep appreciation and thanks.

You have one new voicemail message.
Message left: Today, 3:36 p.m.

Lucy, it's Bethany. I'm running late, stuck on another viewing. Crazy day. And listen, I know you said you weren't keen to show people around your place by yourself but would you mind just starting the tour before I get there? The buyer's name is Donovan, he's highly motivated and I think your house could be perfect for him. And in this market . . . Well, if you do want to sell . . . So . . . Call me if you have a problem with this and I'll try to reschedule with him but if I don't hear from you I'll get there as soon as I can. OK? OK. Good luck!

1

Paranoia stalks me when I'm vacuuming the house and Sam is out. I get spooked that I'm not alone – convinced a stranger is creeping up on me when my back is turned.

My spine prickles. I tense.

And then I turn.

I *always* turn.

Even though I know nobody is there, or can be there, because I watched Sam leave, heard him lock the front door behind him, waved him goodbye when he paused and smiled back at me from the gate at the end of our path.

And there never is anybody there.

It's always just me, on my own.

And so I go back to the vacuuming and the cycle begins again. The deafening roar of the vacuum. The tingles down my spine. The niggling fear that if I don't look, well . . .

It's not rational. I get that. And I've talked it through with Sam, of course. Not that he's in any way surprised. We've spoken about what happened to me so many times – too many times, I sometimes think. Sam likes to joke that it's an occupational hazard for him.

I stopped the Hoover. Held my breath. Straightened my

back – and yes, checked behind me again – then sighed with relief and glanced up at the skylight overhead.

I was in the rear attic bedroom, which was one of my favourite rooms in the house. It was nearly always flooded with light, even on a dreary and windy day like today. And with the off-white walls and the thick, pale carpet, I felt like I could think better up here. It gave me a sense of calm and clarity I couldn't always find.

A safe space.

Shaking the nerves from my body, I tucked the vacuum away into its spot in the cupboard under the eaves before taking my phone from my jeans pocket and checking the time.

I was planning to go to a nearby cafe while the viewing was on. I'd take my book, order an Earl Grey tea with lemon, try to relax. When the viewing was over, Bethany would call and tell me how things had gone. If we were lucky, maybe today would be the day when we received an offer we could accept.

That's when I saw the voicemail that was waiting for me and a twist of anxiety corkscrewed inside my gut.

Even before I dialled, I had a bad feeling about it, and when I listened to Bethany's message, it grew worse.

I hung up, a sticky flickering in my throat, my hands beginning to buzz and hum.

Easy, Lucy.

Fifteen minutes until the viewing.

I couldn't cancel now.

Or maybe I could, I supposed, but it would be rude and I knew we couldn't afford to put a potential buyer off.

My mouth had gone dry. I pressed the heel of my hand to my head and tried to keep the panic at bay.

Our debts were spiralling. There were the loans Sam had taken out to cover the renovation costs, and when those capped out, the credit card bills that increased every month. Sam hadn't been sleeping because of it. And there was so much more wrapped up for both of us in the idea of selling this place and leaving London for good. A clean slate. Starting again.

Bethany.

I liked her, even if she was your typical estate agent in most respects. She could be pushy and brash, and she'd lie as easily as breathing, but at least she was open about it, which was a kind of honesty in a way.

At night, when Sam tossed and murmured and I listened in the ringing darkness to the brittle click of the lock on a bathroom door – the metallic rasp of an unknown voice – what saved me was remembering the way Bethany had arrived at our house that very first time in her expensive coat and statement spectacles, sweeping inside to talk valuations, telling us how tastefully we'd decorated and how desirable we'd made No. 18 Forrester Avenue.

I trusted her – in as much as it's possible to trust any estate agent – and lately I'd found myself hoping that we might stay in touch after we'd sold our house, but it was hard to shake the suspicion that she could have warned me earlier that she was running late; that she'd ambushed me knowingly.

And? You have to make the best of it now.

Hurrying downstairs, I rushed along the first-floor landing

and down again into the main living area, my gaze darting around, searching for anything I'd overlooked.

The lights were on throughout the house. I'd brought home fresh lilies from our local florist and arranged them in a ceramic vase on the marble coffee table. The honey-coloured floorboards gleamed. Only this morning I'd dusted every single blade of the pale wooden shutters we'd fitted in the bay window.

OK. All good.

I spun and looked towards the kitchen area, which was sunken and lowered by several steps. I hadn't brewed coffee. Bethany had warned us it was too much of a cliché. But I'd made sure everything was spotlessly clean.

During the renovation process, we'd knocked through most of the downstairs walls to create one large, open-plan space that ended in a set of industrial-style Crittall doors giving access to the modest back garden. We'd done nearly all the work ourselves, swinging sledgehammers, plastering walls, but the kitchen had been professionally installed and it was sleek and high-end. Expensive cabinetry, top appliances. The granite on the countertops and the expansive kitchen island had cost as much as a new car.

It'll be worth it, Sam had told me, looking up from his spreadsheets with red-rimmed eyes and a coating of dust and grime matted in his wayward hair. At the time, I hadn't been sure which of us he was trying to convince. *It's expensive now but it's what buyers of a place like this will expect. It's the best way to protect our investment.*

My head swam.

I wondered what Sam would say now if I could tell him I was considering showing a stranger around our home by myself. He'd probably fall silent, think carefully, then wrap me in a gentle hug, rub my back and tell me that perhaps it was time to confront my fears.

Not that I could ask him. Sam would be finishing up a lecture and getting ready for his support group. His phone would be switched off.

And anyway, Bethany had said she was definitely on her way. I wouldn't be on my own for long.

I chewed the inside of my cheek and glanced at my coat and scarf – I'd draped them over the back of the green velvet sofa ready for my exit – then swept them into my arms, carried them upstairs and hung them in the walk-in wardrobe we'd carved out of what had previously been the spare room next to our bedroom.

When I stepped out, I drifted towards our bed, smoothing my hands over the pleated throw I kept to one side especially for viewings. There were multiple pillows and cushions at the top of the bed, resting against the oversized headboard I'd upholstered as part of a days-long project.

The headboard was bolted to a privacy wall that shielded the en suite bathroom, and taken together, it created the impression of a fancy suite in a boutique hotel. I hoped it looked like a restful and calming place to sleep, even if it hadn't always been that way for us.

Please be the one. Please be the one.

I caught sight of my reflection in the full-length mirror by the doorway. A pale, undeniably frazzled woman in her early thirties. Hair loosely tied back. Baggy Aran sweater and comfortable jeans. Worry lines around my eyes and mouth.

Perhaps I should change, give a different impression?

But before I could act on the impulse, the doorbell rang.

2

He was early.

Not by much but it was enough to throw me.

The doorbell app on my phone pulsed and buzzed.

I could dismiss the notification from the app. I knew that. I could go downstairs, open the front door and welcome him inside with a forced smile.

But instead I hesitated, took my phone out of my jeans pocket and stared at the image of the man on my doorstep.

My fingers trembled. A coppery taste flooded my mouth.

I couldn't see him clearly because his face was down. All I could really see was the crown of his head – he had wavy grey hair, neatly styled. The collar was up on his dark woollen overcoat. His hands were loosely clasped together in brown leather gloves. He had broad shoulders and looked athletically built.

I wish I could see his face.

I glanced towards the shutters that were tilted open in front of the windows, then made a quick decision and hit answer on my phone.

'Hello?'

I said it as casually as I could, as if I was expecting a parcel delivery, and the man looked up into the doorbell camera with an easy smile.

Not someone I recognized, though that hardly helped.

He was handsome in a roguish way. A prominent brow over startlingly blue eyes. Jaw shaded in stubble. He had on a fawn turtleneck jumper under his coat.

He looked a little jaded, and for a second it made me think of him as a lounge-room singer, tired and possibly hung-over after a long night of crooning.

'My name's Donovan.' The skin around his eyes crinkled as he moved to one side and motioned towards the 'For Sale' sign in our front yard. It had been fastened to the painted metal railings running along the top of the low side wall we shared with the neighbour to our right. The rest of our front yard was shielded by the formerly scrappy box hedge we'd tamed and kept for privacy, itself hemmed in behind more barbed metal railings. 'I'm here for the house viewing.'

'One second.'

Snapping a hasty picture of him on my phone, I quickly attached the image to a message to Bethany.

Just checking this is the man who made the appointment with you? Mr Donovan?

I knew Bethany would probably think it was a strange, possibly neurotic, thing to do, but right then I didn't care. I needed reassurance if I was going to show him around by myself.

Three dancing dots appeared, and while I waited for Bethany's reply to reach me, an anxious ache bloomed inside my chest and I swiped back to the video feed from the doorbell again.

The man had stepped back and he was leaning sideways,

inspecting the stonework around our bay window, glancing up towards the roof.

Behind him, I could see a fish-eye view of Forrester Avenue. The terrace of painted and red-brick Victorian villas opposite our own. The wizened old plane trees that lined the road. Cars and tradesmen's vans were parked bumper to bumper along both kerbs with drifts of autumn leaves scattered across them. Nearly all the cars were BMWs and Range Rovers. A few were Porsches.

There was no passing traffic but a young girl in the red and grey uniform of the local primary school was rolling along the nearside pavement on a scooter, pursued by a woman in a raincoat who was striding after her while staring at her phone, the girl's school bag banging against her hip.

Bethany's reply popped up at the top of my screen.

Yum! Donovan is his first name. Feel free to mention that I'm single and . . . enjoy!

I let go of a lungful of air as I tapped out a fast reply.

OK, thanks. How long until you get here?

But this time, she didn't respond.

Slipping my phone away in my pocket, I closed my eyes for a dizzying second and told myself I could do this, that everything would be fine, then I curled my hands into fists and moved towards the stairs.

I was halfway down when I heard the shriek from outside.

3

I opened the door to find that the man who'd introduced himself to me as Donovan had vanished.

But only for a second.

When I slipped on some shoes and ventured beyond our box hedge I found him kneeling on the pavement in front of our house. His back was to me. I moved closer and that was when I spotted the schoolgirl lying on the ground.

She'd fallen off her scooter and she was howling in pain. Her scooter was toppled over on its side nearby, its wheels still spinning.

'Hey,' Donovan said to her softly. His voice was deep and gruff. 'Hey, it's OK.'

He was gently cradling the girl's wrists in his gloved hands. She'd skinned one palm and the bloodied graze was pebbled with grit, her upper body shaking. One knee of her grey school tights had been torn through and her shoe had come off. Her face was a tangle of tears, eyes huge and trembling.

'Where did you learn to do a stunt like that? Because I have to tell you, that was impressive.'

She blinked up at him, lips wobbling, breath hitching. The air was so damp and chill that her breath formed misted plumes.

'Oh, darling,' cooed the woman crouched beside them, who I took to be the girl's mother. 'I told you to be careful.'

'I don't think it's broken,' Donovan told her. 'Just a bruise.'

I wondered if he was a doctor. Close up, his eyes looked puffy with fatigue, his movements slack and weary. Perhaps he'd just finished a shift at Charing Cross Hospital, or Queen Mary's. Maybe that was why he was hoping to buy in this area.

He must have sensed my presence because he looked up at me with a slow but spreading grin and I felt myself blush.

'I'm from number 18.' I pointed towards my open front door. 'Lucy.'

'Hi, Lucy.' A flash of concern crossed his face as he looked at the girl again. 'I don't suppose you have a clean cloth, or some tissues, or . . . ?'

'Of course. Let me fetch something.'

I hurried inside and removed the first aid kit from under the sink, taking out a couple of wrapped antiseptic wipes and a sticking plaster. By the time I was back outside again he was fitting the girl's shoe back onto her foot and the woman was thanking him profusely, placing her hand on his arm, fixing him with a lingering look.

'Here.' I thrust the wipes and the plaster at her and she took them, seemingly irritated by the interruption.

She had long blonde hair, recently styled. Immaculate make-up. She was slim and fashionably attired in a close-fitting dress over knee-length boots. I'd seen a lot of women dressed just like her dropping their kids at the school gates, driving by in luxury SUVs.

Not for the first time, I felt mismatched with the area –

out of keeping with the otherwise wealthy residents of Putney.

Sam had inherited the house we lived in from his grandparents on his mother's side. There was no way we could have afforded to live here otherwise. We'd had to stretch ourselves and dig perilously deep to modernize the place for sale.

As the woman tore open one of the wipes and used it to swab the girl's knee, I folded my arms across my chest and looked up at our house. It was three storeys high with a mansard roof and a pair of French doors set into one of the dormers on the top floor that opened onto a small balcony concealed behind a triangular parapet. The brickwork was painted lemon yellow, the windows a crisp white. The front door was a deep, glossy red.

'Thank you again,' the woman said to Donovan. Her voice was husky and soft. 'You're incredibly kind.'

'It's nothing, really.'

Donovan helped the girl to her feet and righted her scooter, and as she hopped and winced, he stepped clear, cupping a hand to the back of his head, suddenly sheepish.

'Well, take care.'

'Oh, we will,' the woman said. 'It was *so* lovely to meet you.'

We watched them go – the woman still hadn't really acknowledged me – and as she glanced back at Donovan one more time, the awkwardness built between us until he finally broke it by saying, 'Sorry about that.'

'No, you did the right thing.'

He gazed closely at me, as if my opinion genuinely

14

mattered to him, and for a second I felt the full force of his charm, his looks, everything.

'You're the owner?' he asked.

'My boyfriend is.'

'Ah.' Another slow smile. 'And is Bethany inside?'

I frowned. 'She didn't call you?'

'About what? Oh, no!' His eyebrows shot up and he patted his coat pockets, as if searching for his phone. 'Has she cancelled on me? Have you already accepted an offer?'

'No, it's nothing like that,' I told him, and then I explained about how Bethany was running late and had asked me to begin the tour in her absence.

There must have been something in the way I said it – some hint of my reticence or the discomfort I was trying to conceal – because he paused, then angled his head to one side.

'And are you OK with that?'

'I'm—'

'Because if you're not, I can wait. I don't mind. I should probably warn you, though, that I have to be on my way in about half an hour. Did Bethany mention how long she'd be?'

She hadn't. And my phone hadn't pulsed from a reply to the text I'd sent her. I hoped that meant she was almost here but it was getting late in the afternoon, the October light was beginning to dim, and I knew that traffic in the area could be bad.

Instinctively, I went up on my toes, as if I might spot her racing our way in her branded company Mini, and that was when I felt a twinge in my chest.

There were two other 'For Sale' signs in our street. Sam

and I had looked both properties up online the moment they'd come on the market. The first house had a fancy glass extension. The other had an extra bathroom and was competitively priced. There were also a number of other houses surrounded by scaffolding and plywood screens where teams of builders and tradesmen were at work. It was an easy guess that some of them would go on the market before long.

I sensed Donovan tracking my gaze, perhaps reading my thoughts, and in that moment I knew what I had to do.

'No, don't wait,' I told him. 'Please. Come inside.'

4

Sam

The distance from No. 18 Forrester Avenue to the London School of Economics – located between Covent Garden and Holborn – was close to six miles. It was possible to walk there in a little under two hours, though today Sam had taken the Tube. The District Line from Putney Bridge to Temple. A ten-minute stroll after that. He'd delivered his foundation lecture on perception and memory to a group of half-awake and semi-interested first-year undergrads and now here he was, contemplating the four strangers seated in front of him.

The first-floor seminar room was unremarkable in most ways. It had the same grey hard-wearing carpet, whitewashed walls and suspended ceiling tiles as nearly every other seminar room in the university complex. There was the same interactive whiteboard. The same stained board rubber and pens. The same U-shaped arrangement of tables and chairs.

With two main differences.

The first was outside the room, where beneath the number fitted next to the door – 22A – was a small screen on which Sam had input the words PRIVATE MEETING.

The other was inside the room, where Sam had placed six chairs in a circle in the middle of the space. Six for now, because there was no predicting how many more people might respond to the ads he'd posted online and around the university complex.

Do you have a crippling fear or phobia?
Would you like to talk about it in a
supportive group environment?

'How is everyone feeling about being here?' he asked.

The strangers smiled nervously, exchanged hesitant looks, glanced down at their hands. A short silence passed before a stylish woman in a denim smock, colourful necklace and dark leggings broke the ice.

'A bit nervous?'

'I'd have to say it's the same for me,' agreed the tall, muscular young man dressed in athletic gear who was seated next to her. He had a cut-glass accent, excellent posture and a full head of curly blond hair. The long-sleeved training top he had on over a pair of gym shorts and leggings featured the insignia for the LSE rowing club over his left pectoral.

'I'm just hoping for some help,' said a willowy girl with dark eyeshadow, purple lipstick and jet-black hair, whom Sam guessed was probably a final-year student. There were multiple piercings in her ear, a ring in her lip. The black leather bag on the floor next to her was open with binders and textbooks spilling out.

'I don't really know what to expect.'

This last answer, spoken almost inaudibly, was from the gaunt and bug-eyed guy in the slim-fitting V-neck jumper and skinny grey jeans who hadn't stopped fidgeting since he'd arrived. Sam recognized him and felt a tug of sympathy. He'd seen him working behind the main counter in the university library, although it was no surprise that he'd removed his staff lanyard before coming here today.

'OK, good.' Sam nodded and smiled, as if they'd said exactly what he'd expected them to say. 'The first thing I want you all to know is that this is a safe space. You'll have submitted your consent forms, which I myself don't see, and you don't need to tell anyone here your names. You don't need to give any identifying details.'

Aside from the crippling anxieties and fears you've come here to share.

Because, let's face it, Sam could recognize the signs. The edgy restlessness. The dry skin and haunted eyes and cracked lips. The pained smiles and the wary reluctance to meet his gaze, as if they were each burdened by something shameful.

This wasn't the first support group Sam had organized. Over the past three years he'd run similar groups that had helped him to meet the community engagement requirements the university imposed on all academic staff, as well as offering him an opportunity to give back.

And – being honest – the groups had also uncovered some interesting research opportunities, which is where Sam's real passions lay. With the way his career had begun to stall, not to mention his heavy teaching load, his opportunities for pure research were getting fewer and fewer, and that was one of the reasons he could feel a frisson in the air. The neat thing about phobias was you never quite knew what you might be presented with. And if some of the participants here today were willing to consent to further assessment down the line . . .

'No names at all?' the well-spoken young man asked, bringing him back to the room.

'For now,' Sam said, and as he scanned the faces in front of him, he could detect clear signs of relief. 'This is our first session. Let's see how everyone feels next time around.'

If everyone turned up, which Sam also knew from experience not everyone would.

The anonymity would help with that, though. And not just because it encouraged the group members to relax. Truth was, Sam also had to be careful not to become too invested in the lives of the people who came to him for guidance. It was vital he kept some scientific distance, where possible, aiming to think of them as potential case studies, not people. And sure, part of that was because he needed to maintain some academic rigor, while the rest was pure self-preservation.

Not that it stopped him from assigning them all his own private labels. The librarian could be, well, the Librarian. The woman in the denim smock and colourful beads could be the Artist. The female student with the pale skin, dark hair and piercings could be the Lost Girl. Which left the young man in the athletic clothing and pristine training shoes to be the Athlete.

'We'll give it another minute,' Sam said, taking his phone out of his pocket to check the time and seeing the little aeroplane icon in the top corner of the screen. 'If you could all turn off your phones or switch them to airplane mode, I'd appreciate it.'

There was a rustle as they reached into pockets, backpacks and handbags to comply.

That was when the door to the room swung open and a balding, ruddy-faced man thrust his head inside. He was thickset with a crumpled nose that had obviously been broken at some point in his youth.

'Is this the place for people going out of their minds with crazy thoughts?' he asked, in a voice that was deep and hoarse.

The Boxer, Sam decided.

'That's not quite how I'd put it,' he told him. 'But come on in. Sit down.'

5

'Wow!' Donovan said. 'This is incredible!'

A tentative buzz of relief pulsed behind my breastbone. I eased the front door closed behind me, then turned and kept my back to the wall as Donovan stepped forwards into the open-plan living area, unbuttoning his coat with one hand.

I was alone with a strange man in my house.

I was having difficulty wrapping my head around that.

My heart began to race. I could feel the knot in my stomach beginning to tighten.

Taking a slow, deep breath, I glanced again at the front door. It was still right there. Still within reach.

I could let myself out any time I needed to, even if my brain was right now doing everything it could to convince me otherwise.

'Do you like it, then?' I asked.

'It's stunning.'

I tore my gaze away from the door, my scalp tingling not unpleasantly despite my anxiety, the same way it sometimes does when I'm in the salon having my hair cut and styled.

It was a nice thing to hear. Bottom line, we *had* to sell, but secretly I wanted whoever bought this place to love it as much as we did. I knew we couldn't afford to be picky, but it would mean something to me if we could find a buyer who appreciated all our hard work.

'This colour?' He pointed to the walls and for the first time I took a small step forwards, circling my thumb and forefinger around my left wrist to stop myself from scratching nervously.

'It took us ages to find the right shade of white.'

'It just . . . lifts the whole space.'

'We like to think so.'

That had been one of the biggest challenges of the renovation process. The house had been so dark before. The sash windows were cracked and grimy. The walls were covered in layers and layers of dark floral wallpaper. The coving and cornices were crusted and damaged, and had been painted a strange mottled brown that had the appearance of nicotine stains.

I'd wanted to change all that. Breathe fresh life into every room.

'Is this fireplace original?'

'Yes.' Another small step forwards. 'I really love the veins in the marble,' I told him.

'And the tiles?'

'They're replacements. The original tiles were too damaged to keep but I took pictures and sourced the ones you can see in a reclamation yard. We wanted any changes to be as sympathetic as they could be.'

'Original floorboards?' he asked, flexing on the balls of his feet.

'Yes. Every one of them.'

And didn't I know it. The floorboards had been a true labour of love. I'd lifted the tattered carpets that had concealed them, then sanded the boards back, cleaned them, varnished them, filling every crevice of the house with dust. I'd worn safety goggles and a mask for the sanding work but it hadn't stopped me from being plagued by a dry cough for weeks afterwards.

Donovan squatted and smoothed his gloved fingertips over the finish before looking up at me for a lingering moment.

'Listen, if I don't end up buying this place, will you give me the name of your builders? The care and workmanship that's gone into this is really something.'

I teetered.

'I could,' I told him, 'but it wouldn't help you. We did nearly all of it ourselves.'

'Seriously?' He looked amazed. 'Is your boyfriend in the trade?'

'No.' I actually laughed. 'Sam's a lecturer in psychology and behavioural sciences at LSE.'

And he would be the first to admit he wasn't a natural at DIY. Sam was tall and gangly with a head of spiky, permanently unruly dark hair. I loved him, but he was much more suited to ordering smashed avocado on toast and an oat milk macchiato at our local hipster cafe than he was at putting up a set of shelves. It had sometimes been excruciating to watch him struggle to heft bags of damp plaster and rubble out to one of the many skips we'd had deposited in the street outside.

'And you?' Donovan asked.

I lifted my shoulders. 'It's amazing what you can learn by reading books.'

'Why does something tell me you're being too modest?'

'Well, I do have a bit of a background in interior design.'

'Ah. That explains it.' He glanced around again from his crouched position, the soles of his tan brogues squeaking against the floor.

'But we didn't cut any corners, if that's what you're thinking,' I said quickly. 'Refurbishing this place has been my life for the past couple of years.'

There was more truth to that than he knew. Probably more than I wanted to admit. For a long time I'd felt bad that I wasn't earning a wage and paying my way because my fledgling interior design business had failed to take off. Gradually, though, Sam had convinced me I was the one doing him a favour. I could oversee all the renovation and design work for him and I could help him save on labour costs. And when we were finished, he could apply his photography skills to take shots of the finished house for a design portfolio I could present to future clients. Supposing I could ever summon the courage to put myself out there again . . .

'Did you buy the house as a project?'

'No. It belonged to Sam's grandparents before us. They lived here from the early sixties, but obviously the house is Victorian originally.'

'Right.' Donovan rose up and advanced towards the bay window, carefully separating the shutter blinds we'd installed and analysing the sash units they concealed. 'May I?'

'Please.'

He unscrewed the security bolt holding the nearest window shut and eased the sash upwards. It glided freely on the hidden counterweight system until it hit the buffer about two-thirds of the way up.

'You had these replaced?' he asked, rubbing the timber.

'In the end we did. We went backwards and forwards on it, but ultimately we decided it would be better to have double glazing installed rather than keeping the original single-pane glass. We paid good money for authentic frames.'

A rush of noise swept in from the street. The drone of a passing car engine. A shout from one of the builders nearby. The repetitive chirp of a warning signal on a reversing vehicle.

The backbeat to the city.

It was always reassuring to me that there were so many people and so much going on around us. But even so, it was gratifying to hear how muffled the sounds became when Donovan closed the window and retightened the bolt.

I watched him gently swing the shutter blinds back into position, tilting the blades, admiring the mechanism, humming to himself. His eyes seemed to go inwards for a second, as if his mind was elsewhere.

'All this work.' He turned to face me, adjusting the fit of his gloves. Perhaps I should have set the thermostat a degree higher. 'Why are you selling, if you don't mind my asking?'

Because we have to.

But instead I summoned a smile and gave him the prepared response – the one we'd given to Bethany.

'We love the house, and it's been tough to put it on the

26

market, but we made the decision that it was time for us to leave London as a couple.'

He nodded slowly, his lips parting slightly, as if he was about to ask more, then he drifted towards the shelves beside the fireplace. He leaned closer as he looked at a framed photograph of Sam and me.

Sam had snapped it using the timer on one of his old cameras. We'd been sitting at a picnic table outside our local pub last summer. In the image, Sam had his arms wrapped around me. I was leaning back against him wearing a Breton top with my sunglasses on top of my head. I looked happy and relaxed but it was easy for me to remember how shattered I'd been.

There were other photographs, too. Most were candid black-and-white shots of me around the house, carrying out different projects in my decorating gear. There were pictures of me tiling the bathroom, painting our bedroom ceiling, hanging wallpaper. Sam had been a keen amateur photographer since he was little. It was a passion he'd picked up from his grandfather, whose equipment he'd inherited along with the house, later adding to it with several more expensive cameras and lenses of his own. I felt a twinge of guilt as I thought about how Sam had been forced to sell everything on eBay six months ago to help fund the new bathroom suite we'd installed.

'Where are you heading once you leave London?' Donovan asked.

I held off on answering, my pulse fluttering in my throat. When he glanced at me for my answer, he gave no indication that he might have overstepped the mark.

'We haven't decided yet. The current plan is to go travelling for a year. See the world. Sam is set on Canada. I mostly want to lie on exotic beaches and swim in the ocean.'

A muscle twitched in his cheek. 'Sounds like an adventure.'

'Would you like to see the kitchen?'

6

Sam

'So listen,' Sam said, looking at each of the five people in front of him in turn, 'I thought I should begin by telling you a bit about me. The first thing to say is that I'm an Assistant Professor here in the Department of Psychological and Behavioural Science. Some of my main research interests are in how we quantify happiness and how we can help people to change their behaviour and make positive choices to lead happier and healthier lives, but – and this is where you all come in – I'm also fascinated by phobias. And yes, I get my kicks from the really weird ones.'

The Artist and the Lost Girl humoured him with smiles. The Athlete straightened in his chair, alert and attentive. The Boxer scowled, scratching at his swollen belly, while the Librarian kept glancing towards the door as if he was contemplating leaving.

'What I'm really saying is you can relax. Or try to relax. Because whatever fears you've come here to share today, I will probably find you super interesting. But more than that – and I hope you'll all see this as reassuring rather than a challenge – you should probably also know how unlikely it is that you'll tell me anything that will surprise me. There are a whole host of recognized phobias, and numerous recurrent and recognized patterns with phobias, and over the years I've probably heard them all.'

Sam paused to take the temperature in the room. Most of them seemed to be with him so far. He would have guessed the Boxer would be guarded and hard to win over, and he wasn't altogether surprised by the Librarian's skittish vibe. But experience had taught him how vital it was to lay out his credentials and his expectations in order to build a foundation of trust.

Leaning forwards, he rested his elbows on his thighs and pressed his fingertips together. A little stagey, but it worked.

'A quick primer on phobias,' he continued, 'because you may be wondering if you really have one, and if you do, if it's even that big a deal. And it may not be, but it could be, and if it is, I want you to know that I am here to help you. I can give you some strategies to think about, some exercises to try at home, and I can also recommend specialist therapists if that becomes appropriate.'

'What kind of exercises?' the Boxer asked.

'I'll explain more a bit later, if that's OK?'

'What if they don't work?'

'Odds are they will. In fact, the odds are very good that they'll work comprehensively. A lot of the people who have come to these support groups in the past have found them hugely beneficial.'

'Well, that's reassuring.' The Artist smiled, hunching her shoulders.

'Good,' Sam said. 'The other thing I think it's important to make clear early on is that we all have fears and stresses in our lives. That's perfectly normal. For example, right now

I have a house that I've inherited and am trying to sell, and while that should probably be a good thing, it also comes with a lot of baggage. Financial worries. Stress. Guilt. Will I be able to sell it? When will I sell it? How? But even though it's keeping me up at night, that's really a regular worry. It's part of the stresses and strains of normal life. With phobias, what we're talking about is a persistent, unreasonable and excessive fear that can become all-consuming, sometimes overwhelming.'

He paused again, aware of the watchful silence in the room, the way all five of them were now hanging on his words as if maybe – just maybe – he really did hold the key that could unlock them from the mental cages they were trapped in.

'Left untreated, as I'm guessing some of you have been finding, any phobia can make going about your normal life increasingly challenging.'

The Boxer grunted. 'Try impossible.'

'Then why don't you go first?' Sam said to him. 'Can you tell us about what you've been experiencing?'

7

Donovan went ahead of me down the trio of steps towards the vast kitchen island. We'd had bookshelves built into the near end and there was a sink in the middle. Three wooden bar stools were arranged along the right-hand side, facing across the island towards the range cooker that was fitted amid the run of grey Shaker-style cabinets butted up against the opposite wall.

I hung back, keeping my distance.

'I can see you went all-out on this,' Donovan said, bumping his fist on the granite countertop.

'We did.'

It was almost embarrassing that the kitchen was so grand when most of the meals we ate in it were modest. Sam and I rarely cooked anything fancy. And not simply because we couldn't afford it right now. Our tastes were pretty basic, which was something Sam liked to joke about. Only last week he'd made a big, goofy production out of serving me soup and a sandwich by candlelight.

'When was it fitted?'

'Just under three months ago. There are still some cupboards we haven't put anything in yet. It was one of the last jobs we completed. They're all top-quality appliances.

There's a steam oven. The American fridge-freezer. A built-in coffee machine. Sam talked me into getting two dishwashers.'

'Two?'

'When one is working, you stack the other one. It keeps the surfaces clean and uncluttered.'

'Huh. And is that important to Sam?'

A flicker of irritation.

'To me as well.'

He nodded as if that made sense and reached out to release a steaming jet of water from the brass boiling-water tap over the sink. When he switched the tap off again, he hummed in appreciation.

'This whole place is immaculate.'

'We like to keep things neat.'

'Wish I could say the same about my place. Is it always like this, or have you styled it this way for selling?'

His tone was casual but I sensed the real question lurking beneath it. I got the impression he was trying to gauge how eager we were to sell.

Careful now.

'Honestly, it's a bit of both.'

'I noticed that nearly all the photographs you have on display are of you working on the house. Is that something Bethany suggested?'

I felt my guard go up. I thought I understood what he was driving at. Common wisdom had it that you should remove personal touches, such as photographs of family and friends, if you wanted a buyer to be able to picture them-selves living in your home. But the reality was our decision to feature photographs of the renovation process had nothing to do with Bethany or any advice she might have given us.

Unsurprisingly, though, I wasn't about to tell a complete stranger that the reason I had no wider family photographs up was because I had no family to appear in them. Or that when I'd moved to London a few years ago, it was shortly after I'd discovered that my ex had been sleeping with my best friend. I'd cut myself off from them and nearly all the people back home who reminded me of my past life because I'd been determined to make a fresh start in the city.

It was a similar story for Sam. Seeing pictures of his parents around the place would just cause him pain. They'd died when he was a teenager, long before we'd met. His grandparents had taken him in. It was another reason why this house meant so much to him.

'Sorry,' Donovan said, waving a hand. 'Not my business.' He moved on to the end of the island, where he ducked and looked under the counter. 'Nice wine cooler.'

'Thanks.'

'Who's the Sauvignon Blanc fan?'

'That's mostly me.'

As it happened, Sam was generally a lager drinker on the rare occasions when he drank at all, whereas I had a glass of wine most nights. Sometimes, when the fear and paranoia got its hooks in me, I secretly drank in the afternoons, too.

'What can you tell me about the neighbours?' Donovan asked, straightening up and crossing towards the Crittall doors at the back of the kitchen space, next to the wall of brickwork we'd exposed and the oak dining table and the benches that I'd draped with sheepskin throws.

I watched as he put his face towards the glass, craned his

neck and gazed up at the terraced properties on either side of us.

'One side is a couple with teenage kids. They're lawyers in the City. The kids are out at school most of the day.'

'They don't play the drums, do they?'

'Luckily, no. They're away right now on holiday. The kids are at private school, so it's half-term for them. They have a second home in Cornwall.'

'And the other side?'

'John. He's retired.'

'And them?' He pointed to the rear of the terraced house that overlooked our back garden. It faced onto the next street along.

'No idea, I'm afraid. London.'

For a second, it was as if he hadn't heard me. His attention remained locked on the back of the house and I realized I should probably say something more if privacy was important to him. In my head, I tried to think what Bethany might say.

'But I can tell you they're hardly ever out in their back garden. You'll see from upstairs that it's a bit of a mess, so they don't use it often. And really, it's only the bathroom window and that one bedroom window that overlooks us, so we've never had any concerns.'

He remained silent, weighing that up, before pointing to the key in the lock by his hip.

'Can I take a look?'

'Of course.'

He turned the key quickly and pushed the door open, stepping through into our back garden. My little oasis.

The space was only modest, so I'd kept everything as simple as possible. The porcelain patio tiles were a modern bluish-grey that shimmered like ice on a rainy day. We'd laid them at the exact same height as the floor inside to give the impression of a seamless transition between inside and out, and we'd hired an electrician to wire in some discreet uplighters. I'd whitewashed the brick walls and then Sam and I had worked together to fit contemporary slatted fence panels along the tops. In the far corner I'd designed a seating area with a shade sail above it. It was surrounded by raised beds and pots with a collection of topiary, lavender and kitchen plants to give some greenery and structure.

As Donovan took it all in, I ventured towards the open doorway, seizing hold of the metal frame for support and leaning my upper body out into the cool, damp air.

Another recent memory came back to me. Late at night and not so very long ago, I'd slow-danced with Sam out here to the music playing on our kitchen radio. Sam was a truly terrible dancer, but he'd slowly relaxed into it and I'd relaxed into him. It was a reminder that it wouldn't only be our blood, sweat and tears we said goodbye to when we sold this house. It would be a lot of sweet moments, too.

'What do you think?' I asked Donovan.

He was gazing up at the neighbouring properties again, eyeing them carefully. 'There's no rear access?'

'None. Our neighbour's back garden is the other side of that wall. There's no alley running between us.'

'Has that been a problem?'

'Not for us. It's better for privacy. And security.' I instinct-ively raised a hand to my throat, then covered up the move by pointing towards the cafe table and chairs in the corner. 'It can be a really peaceful spot. Lovely in the spring and summer.'

'Mmm.'

It bothered me that he wasn't showing much interest in the seating area. I'd been really pleased with how it had turned out. Instead, he tipped his head back, cupping his hands around his eyes as he studied the back of our house.

'The roof is new,' I told him. 'Getting the tiles replaced was the first job we tackled.'

'You're saying all the right things, Lucy.'

'Am I?'

'When Bethany gets here, I'm going to have to tell her she's in danger of being out of a job.' He dropped his arms and gave the rest of the garden a cursory once-over. 'Did she say when she was hoping to make it?'

'No. Just as soon as she could.'

He stared at me without breaking eye contact – almost as if he was looking *through* me – and that was when I felt it. The tingles in my spine. The prickles on my skin. The strange and nervy sensation that someone was sneaking up on me.

Not now.

But I couldn't resist.

Using his question about Bethany as an excuse, I spun around, making a show out of leaning to one side and gazing through the kitchen towards the front door.

A flush of relief.

Nobody was there.

'Basement next?'

I startled and whirled back to find him standing right next to me.

'Sorry,' he said. 'I didn't mean to make you jump.'

8

Sam

'With me, it's about being sick,' the Boxer said.

'Actually, I have the same problem,' the Athlete cut in. 'I'm a hypochondriac, too.'

'Nah, not like that. I'm talking about being *sick* sick. Like . . .' The Boxer stopped himself and raised a closed fist in front of his mouth. His cheeks and eyes bulged. He was wearing a faded polo shirt and Sam watched with some concern as he cupped a pudgy hand over the emblem of an alligator that covered his heart.

'It's OK,' Sam told him, aware of the others in the group backing away. 'Take your time.'

The big man nodded and bowed his domed head, keeping his fist clamped to his mouth, looking down at the ground. He blew air through his cheeks some more. The back of his neck was flushed. When he looked up, his complexion was florid, his eyes damp and blurred. He wiped his lips before speaking.

'Sorry. It's just . . . *vomit*,' he rasped quickly, covering his mouth once more. 'Can't stand it.' He shook his head. 'Can't stand the thought of it. I'm afraid of puking all the time. Lately it's got really bad.'

Sam empathized, nodding his understanding, though

39

inwardly he couldn't deny a small stab of disappointment. He'd heard this one before. It was a long time now since he'd come across anything truly unique. Not that the Boxer needed to hear that.

'Can you remember when this started for you?'

The Boxer licked his lips and fixed him with a haunted look. 'I suppose it's always been there but then, earlier this year—' He broke off, raised a hand, did the ducking-his-head-and-blowing-air-through-his-cheeks thing again. It was another few seconds before he was able to continue and Sam was careful to give him the time he needed. 'I'm a cabbie, see? And this pregnant lass was in my cab and she, well, she just, you know . . .' He grimaced. 'And I couldn't deal with it. Not even close. I had to stop my cab and get out and call a mate to come and help me. In the end he had to drive the cab to a valet service. Sort it out. And even *then* I could smell it afterwards.'

'That can't have been easy.'

'It was a nightmare, pal. And now every time I pick a ride up, it's always there. The door closes and I'm like, are they going to . . . ? Am I going to . . . ?' He waved his hand in front of his face as if wafting away an imagined scent. 'And then because I'm *thinking* about it, that makes me feel ill and I have to stop driving, because if I—'

'We get it, thanks,' said the Lost Girl, with a look of disgust.

'Yeah? Well go on, then,' the Boxer shot back. 'What are you here for?'

9

I backed up into the kitchen, circling around and behind
the island unit, my body shimmery with embarrassment and
unease. Bracing my hands against the edge of the countertop,
I summoned a watery smile as Donovan closed and locked
the door to the garden. When he turned and saw me, I felt
myself shrink.

'Lucy? Are you OK?'

The door to the basement was just a few metres away to
my left, at the end of the run of kitchen units against the
far wall. We kept the pedal bin in front of it because we
rarely had any need to go down there. It was where Sam
now stored most of the DIY tools we'd used during the
renovation.

But that wasn't the only reason the bin was there. It was
also a kind of safety barrier for me. A psychological one.

'You're going to think this is strange,' I said.

'Try me.'

He sounded so composed. So calm and patient. Again, it
made me ask myself if he had a medical background. A good
bedside manner.

'I can't go into the basement.'

I said it fast, like ripping off a plaster.

'OK,' he replied slowly.

'I'm claustrophobic,' I explained.

'Oh, right. So when I mentioned going down into the basement just now . . .'

He indicated the door and I pulled a face, bending slightly at the waist and clutching my side as if I had stomach cramps.

'Sorry. It's just, even thinking about it freaks me out.'

'That bad?'

I nodded, cringing, but the reality was even worse.

I could already feel a dimness seeping in from the corners of my vision, shadows invading my mind. I knew from the decorating work Sam had done and the photographs he'd shown me that it wasn't dingy and unlit down there. I knew there was ample light and air, and that Sam had spent days clearing the space out, painting the walls, sweeping and vacuuming the tiled floor, installing a tool bench and storage. I knew all that, but somehow a part of me didn't believe it. When I thought of the basement, all I could picture was blackness and dampness and fear.

'I'm the same with lifts. Or tunnels. Even underground car parks. It's just the idea of no windows and being confined and—'

'It's OK. I get it.'

But he didn't get all of it. I wouldn't tell him *that* much.

It's all in your head.

You can control this.

These are just thoughts you're having and these thoughts will pass.

I could almost hear Sam saying those words to me. He'd coached me through enough fledgling panic attacks in the past, rubbing my back, stroking my hair. One of the things I loved most about our relationship was that I could be vulnerable with him, trust him to be there for me in a way I hadn't been sure I could trust anyone again after what happened with my ex, though sometimes it made me worry that I wasn't much fun to be around.

I'd said to Sam more than once that it had to be frustrating for him that his fixes had never quite stuck with me. I knew they'd worked for lots of the people who'd attended his support groups because I'd seen the thank-you cards and gifts in his study that many of them had sent him.

Sam, though, just smiled and told me it was fine. My case was just more complex and stubborn than most. And while I knew that on one level he was right – I understood probably better than anyone that my phobia was compounded by the trauma I'd suffered – I still couldn't help feeling as if I'd let him down.

It took me a moment to become aware that Donovan was stroking his jaw, looking between me and the basement.

'So here's the thing,' he said. 'If I'm honest, one of the big selling points for me with this place is the basement I saw on the plans. I have some gym equipment and weights that I wouldn't want cluttering up any house I buy, and the details said your basement is finished, so . . .'

'It is finished.'

'Right. So really, it's sort of perfect for me. Down there. And I would like to see it if I can.'

'Oh, absolutely! But would you mind waiting until Bethany gets here?'

'Sure, I guess. Why not? Are you OK to show me the upstairs instead?'

10

Sam

'Since you ask, my problem is sleep,' the Lost Girl said.

'How so?' Sam asked her.

She slipped her hands into the pockets of the hoodie she had on – it was black with an anime character on the front – then drew her shoulders inwards, making herself small.

'It scares me,' she said, immediately looking towards her lap, concealing her face behind her hair. 'I'm scared that if I fall asleep, I'll die. That I won't wake up again. Or that someone will attack me while I'm sleeping.'

'Christ,' said the Boxer.

She glanced up at Sam hesitantly and he nodded, encouraging her to go on. Now that he was paying close attention, he could identify the puffy skin around her mouth and eyes, perhaps even a faint trace of jaundice.

'What you're describing is more common than you think,' he assured her. 'It's called somniphobia.'

'Yeah, I googled it. But it's like . . .' She shrugged. 'I don't know where this came from.'

'It may not have come from anywhere. Or rather, it may not have originated from one simple source. Many phobias can have multiple causes and complex triggers that combine or overlap.'

45

'I used to sleep OK, but then I got this idea in my head that I was going to die in my sleep and it wouldn't go away and . . .'

She stopped to pick at a speck of something in the corner of her eye, and as she did so the sleeve of her hoodie rolled up slightly, exposing what appeared to be some small cuts and abrasions on the inside of her wrist. From the way the Artist caught her breath, Sam gathered she'd noticed, too.

'I'm just so tired.' Her voice cracked. 'All the time. Like, sitting here right now I'm not even sure how much of this is real or even if it is. I have headaches. I can't eat.'

'I'm sorry to hear that,' Sam told her.

'You poor thing,' the Artist said.

'Have you tried sleeping pills?' the Librarian asked.

'*No.*' She shuddered. 'They'd just make it worse.'

'Exercise?' the Athlete suggested.

'Sometimes.' A fragile smile. 'If I have the energy, which isn't often.'

'What happens when you do sleep?' Sam asked her. 'You must sleep sometimes.'

She tugged the sleeves of her hoodie down over her hands, gripping the material under her fingernails. They were chipped and painted the same dark purple as her lips.

'It's horrible. I have this thing where I keep sort of choking when I'm drifting off. And I'm never really sleeping properly because I'm all clenched up and scared and sort of trying to keep one eye open and . . . I just want it to stop.'

She stared at Sam, pleading, the room falling still and silent around her.

This is what they all wanted, he knew.

For their phobias to just stop.

The challenge for him – perhaps the most difficult part of all – was to help them with that without promising more than he could deliver.

'Coming here is the first step towards making it stop,' he told her. 'Admitting your difficulties, seeking help. You need to give yourself a pat on the back for doing that today. Really, you do.' He waited until she nodded and smiled faintly, then he allowed another few seconds to pass before turning to the Athlete. 'You said you're a hypochondriac?'

11

Donovan glanced back at me from partway up the stairs, giving me an encouraging smile until I felt myself reach out and take hold of the banister.

Baby steps. You can do this.

It wasn't easy. My legs felt deadened. My instincts screamed at me to keep my distance. But even if I couldn't quite believe I was doing this – even if it didn't feel entirely real – I knew I had to make an effort here.

That was another of Sam's sayings, something he'd repeated with a knowing grin over and over during the renovation process: *You can only achieve change by making changes.*

And not just because we needed to sell the house. For me, as well. I knew that someday I was going to have to be strong and push past what had happened to me. Maybe that day was today.

'It's actually Sam's specialism,' I blurted out.

'Excuse me?'

'Irrational fears. Like my claustrophobia? It's one of Sam's main areas of study. He's written papers on it. He teaches it as part of an undergrad course.'

'And is that how you two met?'

'God, no.'

I forced a laugh as he reached the top of the stairs where he paused and looked back at me again, awaiting my instructions.

'If you keep going towards the rear of the house, you'll find the guest bedroom,' I told him.

'Got it.'

He moved onwards and I climbed further.

'We met when Sam came into a furniture shop where I was working,' I called after him. 'That was before he'd started on the renovations here. He seemed a bit lost.'

'And you took pity on him?'

'Pretty much.'

I reached the landing myself, then hesitated. The main family bathroom was ahead on the right and Donovan was close to it.

I wobbled.

Don't.

For an alarming second, it was as if the hallway was squeezing in around me, compressing me, while Donovan loomed monstrously larger, his features becoming smudged and indistinct.

With his back to me he could have been almost any man at all, and that was a problem for me.

Steady now. Breathe.

'So this place brought you together?'

'You could say that.' My voice sounded OK to my own ears. 'Sam explained that he was about to tackle an entire house renovation, but he didn't really know what he was doing. I must have mentioned I had some design experience and that's when he asked me if I had time for a coffee in my lunch break. It started there.'

Though even now it was all a bit of a blur for me. Most things had been back then. I hadn't been in a great place. I wasn't sleeping. I was depressed, scared, barely socializing. My business was failing; hence why I was working in the furniture shop in the first place.

Ask Sam, though, and our first meeting was like something out of a rom-com movie. It was a story he'd told me many times. How he'd known from the very first moment he saw me that I was *the one*. How he'd felt like he was tripping over his tongue all the way through our first conversation. How, even as I'd begun to make rough sketches and had suggested areas for him to focus on when it came to developing a coherent design scheme, all he'd really been thinking about was how he might see me again.

Six weeks later we'd moved in together and our preparations for the real work on the house had begun. It had been fast, reckless even, but as Sam liked to say, sometimes you just *know*.

'Back here?' Donovan asked, pointing ahead of him.

'Yes.'

The tails of his woollen overcoat swept behind him as he paced forwards and I realized with a jab of guilt that I should probably have invited him to take his coat and gloves off downstairs, offered him a drink.

Secretly, I knew I hadn't done any of that because I'd been waiting for Bethany to arrive and take over from me, and also because I hadn't wanted to do anything to prolong the viewing. I just wanted to get through this and put it behind me. Besides, Donovan still having his coat on was a reminder that he would be here and gone before long. He'd said he had to be going in half an hour and he'd probably been here ten minutes already.

For the first time, it struck me that he could have *another* viewing scheduled. And of course that made sense, because Bethany had told me he was a highly motivated buyer . . .

You're screwing this up. Letting your anxieties get the better of you. He wants to buy a house. Make it this house.

'It's a lovely room,' I said, trying not to get hung up on the note of desperation that had crept into my voice. 'It's the smallest bedroom but still a good size.'

He stepped inside and stood in silence for several seconds as I moved into the doorway.

'Thoughts?' I asked him.

'Honestly?' He turned and contemplated me. I was a bit taken aback by the intensity of his gaze. 'I think it's a bedroom.'

'That's a working fireplace.'

'Right.'

'And that's a standard double bed, though you could squeeze a queen or a king in here if you wanted to. Or a single bed or bunks if you have kids.'

He looked away without responding. It was difficult to tell if he was ignoring my prompt deliberately or not.

I imagined he was shrewd enough to know that I was trying to gauge him in the same way he'd been trying to get a read on me. This was the first time I'd met any of the potential buyers who'd viewed our home and I knew that, later, Sam would want all the details.

Did he seem interested? I imagined him asking me. *How interested? Did he strike you as the type of person who might make a good offer?*

Knowing if Donovan had kids might help me to answer some of those questions. The local primary was rated 'outstanding' by Ofsted and lots of professionals with young families had paid a premium to move into the area.

Children were a subject Sam had touched on when we'd been finishing this room. I'd been up on a stepladder, hanging the rattan lampshade from the ceiling pendant, when he'd cleared his throat and said, 'You know, this would make a perfect nursery for us.'

I'd wobbled a bit on the ladder and he'd rested his hand on my leg to steady me.

'Easy,' he'd said.

'We can't afford to stay here,' I'd told him, keeping my attention studiously on the light fitting.

'No. But sometimes I like to pretend we can. It's nice to dream.'

I'd finished lining up the shade and Sam had flipped on the bulb, then he'd helped me down the ladder.

'What do you say?' he'd whispered.

I'd looked up into his face to find that he appeared nervous but also hopeful.

'A baby?' I'd hedged.

'Why not?'

Deep inside, I'd felt a trill of exhilaration.

'What about travelling?' I'd asked him.

'What about afterwards?'

'You're really serious?'

'Nothing would make me happier.'

The memory comforted me as I thought about it now. Our whole future was ahead of us, just as soon as we found a buyer for our home.

'That's a specialist wallpaper,' I told Donovan, speaking a bit louder.

'What makes it a specialist wallpaper?'

He'd got me.

'Well, mostly the price, I think. But it's a period design.'

'Not hiding anything, is it?' he asked, bumping a closed fist against the wall.

'Sorry?'

'I mean like damp. Rot. I'm not accusing you of anything but some sellers would paste up wallpaper to try and hide something like that.'

I felt my brow furrow slightly. I resented the suggestion, but I knew I had to be careful not to show it.

'Then no. There's no damp or rot. We took this room back to bare bones. Same with all the bedrooms. We replastered them. Rewired them. In case Bethany didn't mention it, the whole house has been rewired and replumbed.'

'You didn't do that yourselves, did you?'

'Not the wiring. We did tackle some of the basic plumbing and we got a professional in for the rest.'

He hummed and glanced up at the ceiling, then crossed to the sash window that looked down over the side return at the back of the house. Resting his hands on the sill, he twisted his body sideways and looked out.

'I see what you mean about your back neighbour's garden. Bit of a dumping ground, isn't it?'

'We can't help that, I'm afraid.'

He kept looking for a short while longer, as if he was searching for something that was eluding him, then he turned away from the window, digging his hands into his trouser pockets, staring at me again.

'Look, I'm sorry,' he said. 'It's done really nicely, and you probably don't want to hear this, but if I moved in, this room would likely become my home office.'

'You might want to reserve judgement on that until you see Sam's study upstairs.'

'Ah. A surprise.'

It was hard not to be aware of how handsome he was, how confident he seemed in his own skin. I always envied other people that.

He obviously spent a lot of money on his clothes and his appearance. I was fairly sure the fawn sweater he had on was cashmere. It clung tightly to his chest, tapering down to his trim waist. His shoes looked handmade.

And compared to Sam – not that I *should* have been comparing him to Sam – he had a tangible physical presence. Strong arms. An athletic bearing. Maybe he was a rugby player, I found myself thinking. Lots of medics were.

That's when it dawned on me that we hadn't moved and I'd been staring at him a little *too* openly.

Say something, you idiot.

'What is it you do?'

A beat. His smile tightened by a fraction.

'I've just got back from working overseas.'

It was hardly an answer, and he showed no inclination to expand on what he'd said.

Why so obtuse, I wondered, but the vibes he was giving off told me that pushing him for more would be the wrong move to make. I could always ask Bethany about it later. Right now my priority was to not offend him. I wanted to sell him this house.

'Listen,' he said, plucking a smartphone out of his pocket. 'Do you mind if I take a couple of pictures? I know I can check the details online but this way I'll have them with me. And some of the images estate agents use, well, don't tell Bethany I said this, but they're not always totally accurate, are they?'

'OK.'

He prodded and tapped at his phone screen. His gloves were obviously the expensive touchscreen type.

'You really don't mind?'

'Why would I mind?'

He smiled as if I'd said exactly the right thing, then he turned and fired off a couple of photos towards the corner of the room as I retraced my steps back along the landing.

12
Sam

'I suppose with me it's actually quite similar to what you just described,' the Athlete said, casting a gym-honed arm in the direction of the Lost Girl.

He could have been the lead in a Regency romance. He had the chiselled jaw, the curly hair, the refined looks. When he'd walked into the room he'd towered over Sam by several inches.

'I'm basically convinced I'm going to die all the time. But from a heart attack, not sleeping. My father died of a cardiac arrest when he was fifty-two.'

'I'm sorry to hear that,' Sam told him. It was a loss he could all too easily relate to.

'I was twelve. It happened completely out of the blue. I was the one who found him.' The Athlete blinked rapidly, glancing away towards the whiteboard for a moment to compose himself. 'I loved him very much. We all did.'

'That's awful,' the Artist said. 'You were so young.'

Sam didn't think it was his imagination that the Artist was looking at the Athlete with something more than sympathy, nor that the Athlete appeared to be responding in kind, nodding gratefully, holding her gaze.

'In many ways I'm incredibly fortunate. My family is well

off. My father ran a successful business and my mother and uncle continued it after his death. Everyone keeps telling me to get out of my own head. My brother and sister are always urging me to look to the future, but I really can't help myself. I'm terrified and convinced it's going to happen to me. A hundred per cent. And even when people tell me it's not going to happen, I don't really *believe* it, because I can't.'

'Same for me,' the Lost Girl whispered.

The Boxer scrubbed a hand across his balding scalp. He looked dubious. 'Have you had tests?'

'Lots, yes.'

'And?'

The Athlete frowned at the Boxer. Sam could tell he was irritated by the Boxer's question but he also believed that could be a good thing. Part of the reason for the support group was for the people who came along to have their phobias challenged. In Sam's experience, it could be a powerful factor if the challenge came from somebody else who was suffering in a similar way.

'It doesn't matter,' the Athlete said. 'Because that's the whole thing with a phobia, isn't it? For all of us, I'm assuming. That's why it's this kind of mental torture. I eat healthily. I don't drink. I go to the gym every day. But you could have a hundred doctors run a hundred negative tests on me and I'd still think they'd missed something and that I'm going to have a fatal heart attack any second.'

'You're young,' the Librarian spoke up. 'Statistically speaking—'

'Yes, statistically speaking,' the Athlete agreed. 'But what do statistics really mean? They deal in averages and no statistic would have predicted my father would die young. He didn't have any underlying health conditions. So I'm afraid they bring me no comfort. And I imagine it's similar with you, isn't it? What's your phobia, by the way?'

13

I had got almost as far as the top of the stairs again when Donovan emerged from the bedroom behind me, pointing at the doorway on his left.

'Is this the main bathroom?'

'That's right.'

'OK if I go in?'

I nodded, knowing it wouldn't be a good idea for me to try to say too much.

There was no way I could be in there at the same time as him. It would be even worse than the thought of opening the door to the basement.

'Wow, stylish.'

I didn't reply. I couldn't.

I leaned sideways, resting one hand on the radiator behind me and using my free hand to pinch the bridge of my nose.

Dread churned inside.

Something bitter rose up in my throat.

'I like the rainfall shower.'

Say something.

'That was Sam's idea. He wanted a "wow" factor.'

'Well, it worked. You can tell him I said, "Wow!"'

If I focused hard I could just about conjure Sam's voice,

his slow, calming tones. Telling me to inhale, then exhale. Talking me through a meditation exercise. Reassuring me I was in a safe place. Holding me until I calmed.

But as hard as I tried, his voice began fracturing and whistling out like a bad radio signal as the harrowing memories crashed over me, bringing with them all the distress and upset and terror of . . .

Another bathroom. Another time.

The swell of party music and laughter, a raucous shout and the clink of glasses.

A door closing behind me.

—click.

A lock engaging.

A small space.

Four walls.

'I've been watching you.'

'Lucy?'

I snapped back so fast that for a horrifying moment the memory flickers of my trauma were partially overlaid on top of the scene in front of me.

I was seeing Donovan lean his upper body out of our bathroom, his knuckles wrapped around the door frame, but at the same time I was *also* seeing a gauzy, unknown figure closing the distance between us, thrusting out an arm, until he was so close that he passed through me like a ghost disappearing through a wall.

'Lucy? Did you hear what I said?'

'Mmm?' I rubbed my hand around my shoulders and stretched my neck to one side, as if I was freeing up a muscle kink.

'I asked if I could run the shower? I just want to check the water pressure.'

'Fine.'

There was a brittle scratch as my nails flaked away some of the paint on the radiator.

'Terrific. Thank you.'

He ducked back into the bathroom and I immediately turned the other way, staring down the stairs towards the front door.

Where was Bethany? Why wasn't she here yet?

From the bathroom behind me I could hear the twist of a tap.

A ragged splatter.

The hiss and drumming of water pummelling the shower tray.

Oh God.

My skin seemed to be wired to a dangerous voltage. I could feel my pulse in my fingertips.

I shouldn't have done this.

I wasn't *capable* of doing this.

It was much too much for me on my own.

I fumbled in the back pocket of my jeans for my phone, my fingers slipping on the case in my haste, almost dropping it as I took it out, then catching it and swiping at my mouth and eyes, staring at the screen.

No new messages.

No missed calls.

The time read *16:19.*

Bethany had to be here soon.

You just have to hold it together for a little longer.

61

You can do that.

The shower stopped.

A few stray drips.

A taut silence.

I thought about firing off a quick text to Sam, letting him know what was happening. I knew he wouldn't read my message until later but the prospect of him picking it up after his support group, understanding how I was feeling and calling me the moment he was able to would be something for me to cling to.

But before I could act on the impulse, Donovan backed out onto the landing, wiping some wetness from his glove onto his coat before raising his phone in front of his face and lining up a picture of the bathroom.

'The pressure is great,' he said. 'I'm a fiend for a good shower.'

'Glad you like it,' I replied, surreptitiously slipping my own phone away again.

He didn't appear to notice. He was too busy adjusting the angle of the photograph he was taking.

'I'm starting to think this house could be my perfect match, Lucy.'

A tiny capsule of courage cracked open inside my chest, warm liquid oozing out.

I found myself taking a step away from the wall and the radiator.

You've got this. You mustn't let it beat you.

'Then let's go up to the attic,' I said before I could change my mind. 'I should show you my favourite room.'

14

Sam

'I really don't think this is the right place for me to talk about it,' the Librarian said in a soft, quiet voice.

He folded one leg over his thigh and hunched forwards with his arms crossed, scratching his upper arms with his nails. The top button on his skinny shirt collar was fastened so tightly that Sam could see it flicking up and down against his Adam's apple as he swallowed. His face was gaunt, eyes hollowed, his complexion greasy.

'I know this can be difficult,' Sam coaxed. 'But research has shown that voicing your fears can really help. It's also useful to get other people's perspectives.'

The Librarian didn't answer, choosing to shake his head rigorously instead. His lank hair danced around his forehead, revealing a cluster of pimples.

'Why don't you try? I think you'll feel much better once you've shared.'

'I'm sorry,' he said, barely loud enough for Sam to hear. 'I'm just not sure I'm comfortable doing that.'

'Oh, come on, pal.' The Boxer clapped his hands and rubbed his palms together, as if he were a weightlifter applying chalk before attempting a mighty clean and jerk. 'I've told you my thing. Yours can't be any more pathetic than that, can it?'

The Librarian scowled at him from his hunched position, something unpleasant slipping into his face.

Sam sensed it then. A shift in the air. A drop in the temperature in the room. The fine hairs on the backs of his hands rising upwards.

'I could go first?' the Artist cut in, apparently sensing something, too. 'I don't mind.' She was leaning forwards on the edge of her chair, smiling bravely at Sam. 'Is that OK?'

15

This time I went up ahead of Donovan, moving quickly, stepping into the attic bedroom before he'd begun to tackle the stairs.

A shimmer of relief.

The room weaved its magic on me again.

The white walls. The glass skylights.

I ventured forwards, blowing air through my lips, flexing my fingers and toes as I listened to his approach.

The walls trembled gently as he reached the half-landing, then his mouth gaped with surprise.

'I can see why it's your favourite room.'

I cupped my hands together in front of my waist, toying with my fingers as he moved towards the skylight nearest to him, bracing his hands on the framing, going up on his toes. The darkening sky meant that I could see a reflection of him in the glass.

Donovan rocked backwards, his heels sinking into the dense carpet, looking past me towards the daybed. It had a white metal bedstead, taupe cushions and a knitted throw.

Across from it, an egg-shaped wicker chair was suspended from a ceiling rafter, its insides lined with another sheepskin rug. Low bookshelves were nestled against the eaves. A stereo, a lamp, some candles and a number of plants were arranged on top of the bookshelves.

'What is this? Your chill-out space?'

'I read here. When I have the time.'

Which wasn't often.

During most of the renovation process I'd worked late into the night, sanding and prepping, painting and wall-papering. And when that was finished, I'd waged a relentless campaign against the endless build-up of dirt and dust. Usually, I was so tired at the end of the day that I'd have little energy to do anything except collapse into bed, where Sam would have his research papers spread out across the duvet, his reading spectacles on, his bedside lamp burning away on an old cardboard box on the floor until the small hours of the night.

Throughout the hard times – the days and weeks when it felt like we would never complete the renovation – this room had sustained me because I'd carried a vision of it in my mind. I'd viewed it as a perfect haven where I would sit in my swing chair, study my design books and wait for Sam to come home with a bottle of wine and a takeaway.

In my heart, I knew that's what I would miss most when we sold this place. Not the room itself, because I hadn't had nearly enough time to use it, but the *idea* of it. The future it had once seemed to promise.

My heart skipped over something, a stone skimming across a lake.

'You don't get claustrophobic up here?' Donovan asked me.

I pointed upwards. 'Windows.'

'Right.' He approached the bookshelves, pushed back the tails of his coat and squatted with his elbows balanced on his thighs. After glancing at some of the spines of my books, he straightened and moved to the far wall, smoothing his hand over the finish before turning and looking past me to cast an appraising gaze towards the wall opposite. I sensed he was sizing up the angles and dimensions of the space.

'Quick question. Would you throw me out right now if I told you I was likely to turn this into a home cinema?'

I laughed. 'Can we pretend you didn't just say that to me?'

I felt a crackle in the air between us again, a renewed awareness of his confidence and charisma.

'Didn't you say there's a study up here?'

'Next door. It's on the other side of the landing. I'll follow you in.'

16
Sam

'**I sometimes get afraid I'm being followed,**' the Artist said, and raised her palms in the air, as if she was confessing to something simple and ridiculous when it clearly wasn't either of those things to her.

She was late twenties with the appearance of a mature student, possibly, or perhaps she worked somewhere nearby. Pretty, with delicate features. Her hair looked recently cut and blow-dried. Look closer, though, and you could see the patches of dry eczema on the backs of her hands, the strips of raw flesh where she'd picked at the skin next to her nails.

'I get scared when I go somewhere. When I'm coming home. It's as if I can feel it. This sense that someone is following me.'

'Nasty,' the Lost Girl murmured.

'It's made me really isolated. I live alone and I haven't been going out as often because of it. A few of the people at my job have asked me to go out with them, but I keep saying no because I'm scared about getting home afterwards, especially after dark.'

'Are you concerned about someone in particular?' the Athlete asked.

'No, that's not it.'

She smiled at the Athlete as if he'd asked the very question that got right to the heart of her phobia. As if she sensed that he understood her better than anybody else.

Sam waited, gratified to see the group beginning to interact with each other. In his experience, the support groups that functioned the best were the ones where he ended up speaking less and less.

'Ever see anyone?' the Boxer asked.

'Never.'

'OK, but if you haven't seen anyone—'

'That's not what this is about,' the Athlete told him, then immediately glanced at Sam, as if he was afraid he'd overstepped the mark. 'Sorry for interrupting.'

'No, that's OK. Why don't you explain your thinking?'

The Athlete looked at the Artist for a go-ahead, who smiled and nodded at him. 'Please. It helps hearing someone else talk about it.'

'Well,' he said, sitting up in his chair, the fabric of his fitness top clinging to his muscular torso. 'It's not really about evidence, is it? Because it's the same with my worries about having a heart attack.' He motioned to the Lost Girl. 'Or her worries about sleeping.'

'They're more than just *worries*,' the Lost Girl told him.

'You're right. I apologize. What I suppose I'm trying to say is that you don't have to see something to believe it's happening. You can believe it in spite of a lack of any evidence to support what you believe.'

He peered at Sam again, as if waiting for his opinion, but instead of giving it, Sam raised his eyebrows as he looked around the rest of the group, inviting their input.

'I agree with that,' the Artist said, picking up the thread. 'I know I need to make more effort to meet people, go out and about, make connections. I don't want to let this beat me.'

'Well, I had that one lass who was ill in my cab,' the Boxer grumbled.

'And how long ago was that?' the Athlete asked him. 'A while, didn't you say?'

'He is right, though.' The Artist touched the Athlete's hand in a gesture that seemed intended to thank him for defending her while at the same time letting him know that she could defend herself. 'I don't have any *real* reason to think someone could be following me. I've never been stalked, to my knowledge. Or threatened. It's just that lately it's nearly all I can think about. And when I do find myself outside on my own I keep having these panic attacks where I can't breathe. Can't think clearly. I hate getting home because I have the sense that someone has been there before me. It's terrifying.'

'Same,' the Lost Girl said. 'About the panic attacks, anyway.'

'I sometimes want to bang my head against something,' the Athlete said. 'Just to stop the thoughts.'

'Been there,' the Boxer agreed.

'Me too,' the Librarian whispered, looking up from his hunched position.

They all turned to him, almost as if they'd forgotten he was there.

'Well, then.' The Artist smiled at him encouragingly. 'Will you tell us all about it now?'

17

Donovan was standing behind Sam's desk with one arm folded across his chest and a finger pressed to his chin when I joined him inside the study.

'Does your boyfriend chase aliens?' he asked, nodding towards a framed poster on the wall.

The print was a blurred image of an alien spaceship with the slogan 'The Truth Is Out There!' written across it. It was a replica of the poster that had featured in Fox Mulder's office in the television series *The X-Files*. It was one of Sam's favourite shows. Early on in our relationship, we'd binged our way through a rewatch together, cuddling under blankets on the sofa.

'Birthday present,' I said. 'Sam is a big fan of *The X-Files*.'

'Is he always this tidy in here?'

'He's *never* this tidy in here.'

'So this is you?'

'Mostly. But I have to promise to keep everything in the order he had it in.'

And even then, it wasn't *that* tidy. There were papers and files stacked everywhere. Textbooks piled on the floor. We'd bought a small filing cabinet for some of Sam's research materials, but it had quickly been filled to overflowing.

'If we weren't selling the house . . . Truthfully, I doubt you could see the carpet.'

Donovan toed a stack of textbooks on the floor. Among them was a book on repressed memories that I'd slipped out once and flicked through when Sam had been out. I hadn't learned anything Sam hadn't already told me about my condition. Certainly nothing encouraging. In some ways, reading about it in such stark and clinical terms had just made it more upsetting. It probably hadn't been the healthiest approach, but I'd put the book back before I'd got more than halfway through.

It could have been worse, I supposed. There were books on all kinds of rare and unusual mental conditions, ranging from studies on schizophrenia to extreme narcissism and psychopathy, PTSD to ADHD, insomnia to self-mutilation. For a nice guy, Sam was fascinated by some of the darkest things.

'I don't know many academics who could afford to renovate a house in Putney,' Donovan said.

I got where he was going with it, but I didn't bite. He was obviously fishing for information about our finances. So far he hadn't mentioned anything about the house he didn't like and if he was looking for an angle to make us a low offer, I didn't want to be the one to give it to him.

'Now that you've seen in here, do you think you could make this room your home office?' I asked him.

'Maybe.'

'Sam likes it up here because it's quiet. He can shut himself away and focus. And when he comes downstairs, he can close the door behind him and completely switch off.'

'Can he?' He gave me a quizzical look. 'I'm sorry. It's just that working from home, I'm not sure you can ever fully leave your job behind.'

Speaking from experience, I wondered? But then again, my attempts to find out what Donovan did for a living had already hit a brick wall.

I smiled neutrally, unwilling to engage on the subject of Sam's working habits, though in truth I knew he was right. I loved Sam. We'd built a life together. We'd pushed ourselves to the edge doing up this house to give us a platform for the future, and he'd cared for me and nurtured me after what had happened to me.

But one thing I'd had to learn to accept was that a part of Sam was never fully present. His mind was always turning on other things, preoccupied with his teaching or his research. Sometimes I thought that he spent so long analysing behavioural theories and striving to understand other people's tics that he left no space to truly be himself.

It didn't help that his professional life had been so stressful lately. I'd heard that academia was fiercely competitive and that it could be a dog-eat-dog working environment. But some of the tales Sam had told me about the internal politics in his department had shocked me.

One of the reasons we were looking to take a break and go travelling for a while was that Sam's career prospects at LSE had become unfairly stymied. Even now, there were colleagues who queried the value and efficacy of the support groups Sam ran, but I admired Sam for not backing down on his belief that psychological research programmes could and should have positive real-world outcomes. That said, he still had to cover his back, which was why anyone who took part in his support groups first had to file an online consent form with his department secretary.

Donovan swivelled on his heels, taking in the rest of the room. I wondered if he was picturing his own belongings up here, asking himself how it would feel to occupy this space, in this house, if it was the right fit for him or not.

'What about a landline phone?' He pointed to a socket down near the skirting board. 'Is that connected?'

'It can be. Sam and I don't use a landline. We both just use our mobiles.' I pointed behind him towards the pair of French doors that had been fitted into one of the two dormer openings in the roof. 'Did you see on the details that there's a small balcony outside?'

'Mind if I take a look?'

'Go ahead.'

He strolled over, reaching out with both hands to take hold of the handles and test the security of the doors, then unlocking them with the key, opening them outwards and stepping through.

It was growing steadily dimmer outside. Donovan's outline was grey and sketchy in the ambient glow of the street lighting showing through the tree branches below.

From my position over by the doorway, I could have been looking at Sam out there, and for a second I was reminded of the first time I'd caught Sam vaping. He'd been sheepish when I'd stepped out and clocked the smell of weed, but then I'd held out my hand and taken a drag myself. I didn't smoke with him often but it sometimes helped us both to wind down in the evenings. Especially before sex.

'Nice spot.' Donovan leaned forwards over the brick

parapet and briefly surveyed the drop, then ducked his head as he returned to the room, closing the doors behind him.

'Do you have any questions?' I asked him. 'I'm trying to think what else Bethany would be telling you that I'm not.'

'Some, but they can wait. What's next? Your bedroom?'

'The master bedroom, yes,' I told him. 'I'll show you.'

18
Sam

The Librarian let go of several fast breaths, as if he was psyching himself up to talk.

'So, the thing is, I'm scared I'm going to attack someone,' he said quickly, then wrapped his arms tightly around himself, rocking on his chair.

Silence in the room.

The Librarian probably weighed no more than nine stone when he was dripping wet. It would be hard to think of someone who could be less physically threatening.

And yet . . .

There was that intensity about him. A sense that he was wound so tight he really might snap.

'Have you ever attacked anyone?' Sam asked carefully.

He kept his tone level and calm. It wasn't an uncommon phobia, but if he betrayed any concerns now he knew they would spread in the room like a contagion. These were people who were wired to be scared, after all.

'N-no,' the Librarian stammered.

'Ever tried?'

He shook his head.

'Ever verbally or physically abused anyone?'

The Librarian shook his head a second time. He seemed

to be growing smaller, coiling tighter. His clothes were so fitted he could have been shrink-wrapped.

'So to clarify, these are thoughts that you're having,' Sam suggested.

'But I'm having them all the time!'

'Like, how?' the Lost Girl asked. 'I mean, are you thinking about hurting one of us?'

Sam watched as the Librarian gripped hold of the sides of his chair, curling his fists around the moulded plastic as if he was having to hold himself back from vaulting forwards.

'Shit,' the Lost Girl murmured.

The Athlete and the Boxer stiffened, adjusting their poses.

'Most of the time it happens where I work,' the Librarian babbled. 'I work in—'

'A public space?' Sam volunteered.

'Y-yes. A public space.' He was tipping forwards and backwards on his chair so fast it was as if he was sitting on a rocking horse. 'Sometimes I start thinking about, I don't know, picking up a pair of scissors and stabbing someone with them. And then once I *start* thinking about it, I can't stop thinking about it, and that makes me think I'm definitely going to do it, because why else would I be thinking about it and—'

'But it's just thoughts?' the Artist asked, in a tone that made it sound as if she was seeking reassurance as much as trying to soothe his pain. 'I suppose what we're all saying is that we're tormented by bad thoughts.'

'I . . . don't know?'

'Then let's try something,' Sam suggested. 'All of you, take just a moment and think about it. Then raise your hand in the air if you've ever given some thought, however fleeting, to actually hurting someone.'

19

Our bedroom was large and spacious. It extended across the full width of the front of the house. I crossed it quickly to take up a position by the cast-iron fireplace in the end wall and when I spun back Donovan was lingering by the doorway, giving me an intrigued look.

'It used to be two separate bedrooms in here,' I explained. 'We knocked the wall down. Created one large space.'

He whistled. 'Big risk.'

'But worth it, we think.'

He entered the walk-in wardrobe to his left, placing his hands on his hips and contemplating the brightly lit shelving, fitted drawer units and hanging rails.

'You don't have many clothes in here.'

'We won't need them when we're travelling.'

Another white lie. A harmless one, I hoped. The fact was a lot of my clothes had been ruined by paint flecks and rips and tears from all the decorating and DIY I'd been doing, and Sam pretty much lived out of the same handful of chinos and plaid shirts that he rotated beneath a battered sports jacket for teaching. It wasn't as if we had any spare money to buy new outfits.

As Donovan sized up the wardrobe, I took the opportunity

to move towards the nearest of the three windows in the room, tilt the shutter blades down and peer outside. There was a small white sofa underneath the window and my leg pressed against it as I leaned forwards.

I couldn't see Bethany.

The pavement was empty. The road was still.

For a second, I pretended to myself that the room was as it had been for much of the last year. Exposed walls and bare floorboards. Dust sheets and ladders and decorating gear stashed everywhere. Sam and I had slept amid the mess. Some nights we'd eaten takeaway pizza together on the bed with our travel guides and maps spread out before us, planning where we'd go when the work on the house was finally complete and the place was sold. Back then, it had been our own private world. I hadn't given much thought to who might inhabit it after us.

I was about to pull away from the window when I caught sight of a blur of movement from the corner of my eye. It was the headlamps of a car reversing into a tight space further along the street. I stared harder, but when the headlamps switched off and the interior light came on, I recognized the driver as a woman who lived nearby.

'Are you looking for Bethany?' Donovan called to me.

'I thought I saw her car, but I didn't.'

'I'm starting to think she's not going to make it.' He took out his phone and contemplated the screen. 'She hasn't messaged me.'

'She'll be here soon, I'm sure.'

I wasn't sure, but for reasons I couldn't fully articulate, I didn't want Donovan to know that.

He weighed my answer along with the phone in his palm, then he crossed the room and stepped closer to me – so close that I heard my breath catch in my throat – and gazed over my shoulder to peer outside.

20
Sam

There were six hands in the air. All of them, including Sam.

'How does that make you feel?' Sam asked the Librarian. 'Seeing that we've all experienced what you're talking about. At some point in our lives, we've all thought about hurting someone.'

'I don't know.' The Librarian licked his cracked lips, his tongue flicking out fast and lizard-like. 'I suppose . . . I know what you're saying. And I probably used to be like that. Like all of you.'

'Yes?'

'But I keep thinking that if I can't stop myself *thinking* about hurting someone, that has to mean I'm going to do it at some point. And maybe the reason I'm here right now is because I'm cheating. It's like I just want to justify it to myself or make myself feel better about it even though part of me knows I *am* going to hurt someone. It could be I'm looking to exploit the way I've come here today, because it makes me think that I could argue I came here to get help *after* I'm caught hurting someone. Because I was secretly planning it.'

Sam was aware of the Lost Girl and the Artist shooting each other nervous glances. Of the Boxer becoming impatient. Of the Athlete looking towards Sam for guidance.

Which was something he needed to provide right away.

'What you are talking about is called Harm OCD,' he said. 'It's a form of obsessive–compulsive disorder where the recurring fear is of causing someone harm or doing something illegal, committing a crime. We all have thoughts along these lines from time to time. Flashes of them. But here's the thing. I've spoken to lots of people going through the exact same thing as you are. People who thought about hurting people in all sorts of terrible ways. And do you know how many actually did?'

Again, the Librarian licked his lips. 'How many?'

Sam raised his hand in the air with his finger and thumb joined to form a circle.

'Zero,' he said. 'None. It's an irrational fear. A textbook phobia. I want you to know that I don't believe you're going to hurt anyone. At all.'

21

'It's quiet out there,' Donovan said.

I froze.

It was difficult for me to think clearly.

The panic was crowding in again. I was uncomfortable with how he was invading my personal space.

'We keep the lower half of these shutters closed most of the time,' I told him. 'More privacy that way. And it makes sense with the en suite.'

I used the opportunity to squirm out from behind the sofa and step away from him, drawing his attention towards the opposite end of the room, past our bed and the privacy wall with the headboard attached to it.

I thought he'd be impressed when he saw the en suite. It was even more luxurious than the main bathroom. Concealed behind the privacy wall was a sleek walk-in shower, a wall-hung toilet, a pair of 'his and hers' sinks in front of a large mirror and two terry-cloth dressing gowns hanging from some hooks next to a freestanding copper bath.

As with the wardrobe, there were no doors to access the en suite. To get in, you just walked through the gaps at either side of the bed and the partition wall.

I'd pitched the absence of doors as a quirky design feature

to Sam and, even though we both knew the real reason why I was keen on the concept, he'd been understanding enough not to say anything.

I blinked away the train of thought and became aware that Donovan was staring at me as if he was waiting for me to say something more.

'Um . . .' For a bewildering second I felt a chill at the back of my neck, as if an ice cube had been pressed against my skin. 'Would you like to see it?'

'Sure,' he said, and then he gave me a curious look – almost as if he thought he was rising to a challenge I hadn't intended to set for him – before he strode away from me, past the bed, behind the partition wall.

The moment he was gone, I went up on my toes and gazed out at the too-quiet street again, rubbing my left forearm through the material of my jumper.

Something rippled across my skin. A chemical murmur. An instinctive response to a discomfort I couldn't readily explain.

A warning?

No. Don't think like that.

It doesn't matter that Bethany's not here.

It's almost over now anyway.

'That is one classy bathtub,' Donovan called.

He hadn't stepped out from behind the partition wall.

A stiffness seized hold of my body as I gazed out of the window, a slow ticking in my bloodstream.

It was unnerving to think of Donovan being back there while I was standing so close. Stranger still that I couldn't see him.

Not that I was worried about anything he might see. I'd cleaned and tidied. I'd polished the glass screen in front of the shower enclosure. I'd mopped the tiled floor. I'd even replenished the soap dispenser and wiped away the toothpaste residue that sometimes collected in the dish underneath our electric toothbrushes.

There was nothing that I should feel embarrassed about, and in any case—

I jerked at a sudden bright sparkle followed by the crackle of a simulated camera shutter.

When I spun around I found Donovan stepping out from the other side of the partition wall with his phone held in front of his face, the flashbulb light shining. He took another two quick photos. One aimed towards the walk-in wardrobe. Another in the direction of the fireplace and the window where I was standing.

'Oh, I—'

I blinked away the haze of bright sparkles that were cascading before my eyes.

'Problem?' he asked.

I didn't know quite what to say to that. He'd asked for my permission to take photographs and I'd agreed, but I hadn't said he could take any with *me* in them.

'No.' I plastered another smile onto my face. 'No problem.'

He gestured towards the bed. 'Is this where you sleep?'

'Excuse me?'

'I'm asking because I'm interested in street noise. If it keeps you awake, or disturbs you in any way.'

'Oh,' I said. 'Then, no. Or I mean, yes I do sleep here, but no, the noise doesn't keep me awake.'

'And Sam?'

'He's the same.'

He nodded as if that was all he needed to hear, then glanced down at his phone and pulled a face. 'Listen, I'm sorry but I can't stay much longer and Bethany's not here yet so . . . What do you say? Can I take a look at the basement?'

22

Sam

'**Have any of you heard of NATs?**' Sam asked.

'You mean like the insects?' the Boxer asked him.

'Actually, I do. But we'll come to that in a second. Right now I'm talking about a simple acronym. N.A.T.S. It stands for Negative Automatic Thoughts.'

The five members of the group traded looks, frowning, shaking their heads in bemusement, perhaps even mild embarrassment, too.

The Boxer looked uncomfortable, as if this was just the kind of nonsense he was afraid Sam might spout. The Lost Girl seemed almost embarrassed that Sam could have used something as tragic as an acronym. The Artist waited patiently to hear more while the Athlete inspected his pristine white training shoes and the Librarian remained huddled on his chair, scratching his elbow.

'Some negative thoughts can be good,' Sam told them. 'When they're working effectively, they can be like a sort of early warning signal that protects us. For instance, I could be near a cooker and I might think to myself: "That stove could be hot." And if it *is* hot and I don't touch it, I've protected myself. But when negative thoughts become *automatic* – or when they recur and we ruminate on them – they can be harmful.'

He locked eyes with the Artist and for a second he thought he saw a tremor pass behind her expression, as if he'd read her mind.

It had to be difficult for her, he imagined. Everywhere she went, feeling watched and vulnerable. Constantly on alert. Hearing imagined footsteps pursuing her.

'That's where the insects come in,' Sam continued. 'I want you to think of them as GNATS with a silent "g".'

'And then what are we supposed to do?' the Lost Girl asked, sweeping back her curtain of hair, her lip ring twinkling in the glare of the overhead lights.

'Then you have a choice. You can swipe at them – just like you might swipe at a real swarm of gnats – and by that I mean you can challenge your negative thinking. You can apply a set of reasoned questions and ask yourself how likely it is that the thing you're worrying about could genuinely happen or not.'

'What's the other option?' the Athlete asked.

'The other option is just to acknowledge them. Just to stand back and notice that a bunch of negative thoughts are massing around you – a swarm of them if you like – and then to just . . . let them be. Because just as a tiny flying insect might irritate you but can't do you any real harm, neither can the thoughts you're having. They're just that. Thoughts.'

23

I couldn't say no to Donovan's request. Not without seeming unreasonable. And I didn't want to blow any chance that he might put an offer in.

But the basement . . .

They're just thoughts, I heard Sam's voice telling me. *And since they're your thoughts, you're also capable of controlling them.*

And anyway, the basement was the last thing Donovan needed to see. He'd said it himself. If I let him take a quick look around, he could leave afterwards and I would have made it through this. It would be over. I'd have done it.

'I'm not expecting you to go down there with me, you know.'

I pretended to wipe perspiration from my brow. 'Phew.'

'So are you OK with it?'

There was a rapid knocking in my chest. An urgent pulsing in my head.

'Yes,' I lied. 'I'm OK.'

'Great.'

He took one last look around the bedroom, then spun and set off along the landing, running his hand along the balustrade.

And . . . breathe.

His glove slid against the polished timber. I'd sanded down every spindle by hand, carefully applied undercoat, then added two coats of eggshell white. It had taken me nearly a week, all told.

I caught sight of my reflection in the mirror by the doorway again. It was impossible to say if I looked as unmoored as I felt.

Get it together, Lucy.

Launching myself forwards, I flitted by my reflection, then closed my fingers around the banister and walked woodenly down the stairs.

At the bottom I cradled the newel post and stared wide-eyed at the kitchen, aware of a dry clicking in my throat.

'Am I OK to move this bin out of the way?' Donovan asked me.

'Yes.'

Letting go of the stairs, I made it down the steps towards the kitchen island, grabbing for the countertop, craving the feel of something solid and cool underneath my hands.

'I'm just going to stay over here,' I told him.

'Understood.'

The base of the bin scraped against the floorboards as he slid it to one side. He then flicked aside the metal bolt on the outside of the door and opened it.

Blackness blazed out.

All of a sudden, the floor I was standing on felt much too flimsy, as if it might collapse and give way and I'd find myself down there.

No.

'Light switch?' he asked.

'On your left.'

A second later the stairwell sprang into light. The whitewashed walls glowed. Bracing his hands on either side of him, he began to descend.

A coolness seeped up my legs from my ankles as I watched his torso, shoulders and head disappear.

Then he was gone and I looked away towards the other corner of the room, fixing my attention on the dining table, allowing the vision in my peripheries to blur.

In a few hours' time Sam would be home and we'd be eating there together. Something quick and easy. Eggs on toast, maybe. Everything would be normal. Everything would be OK.

But right now the house felt oddly silent and cold. My senses seemed strangely desensitized.

Stupid.

It's fine. You're fine.

The fronts of my thighs and kneecaps pressed up against the kitchen island. For a second, I had the crazy idea that an invisible tide was dragging at me, sucking me towards the basement.

It's just a negative thought.

There's no logical reason to be afraid.

I waited.

The waiting was excruciating.

I was intensely aware of how my toes had curled inside my shoes. Of the dry rasping of my eyelashes when I blinked.

Slowly, I turned my head the other way and stared at the digital clock on the front of the range cooker.

It was almost half past four.

The green digits shone lurid and bright.

The first aid kit was on the nearby countertop, its contents spilled out from when I'd grabbed the antiseptic wipes for the schoolgirl. It looked so untidy against the rest of the kitchen.

This is something you can do.

This is a practical thing you can do.

I moved towards the first aid kit and packed the loose items away inside, zipping it closed.

It's OK.

Nobody expects you to go down into the basement.

You won't have to go down into the basement.

Steeling myself, I grabbed hold of the countertop and turned towards the open doorway again.

The air seemed to shimmy in front of me as I waited in silence for him to reappear.

24

Sam

'Is that it?' the Boxer asked. 'Is that all you're offering us?'

Sam leaned back in his chair, tipping his head to one side. 'No,' he replied, in a friendly tone. 'What I'm really doing today is giving you a sense of where we'll be heading as a group and the ways in which it might be possible for me to help you. A lot of what we'll be working on together is about training your mind to think differently, more calmly. You may have heard people talk about cognitive behavioural therapy and it has been proven to be a really effective treatment for phobias of all kinds.'

'And what if it's not?' the Lost Girl asked, immediately jumping to the customary response of anyone with an irrational fear that had taken over their everyday life. She looked with some concern towards the Librarian, who seemed to be possessed of an intense, fidgety energy, as if he couldn't sit still.

'Then there are other things we can look into. Immersion therapy, for one.'

'What is that exactly?' the Artist asked.

'Simply put, it's a way to confront your fears and test them in a controlled environment. Gradually to begin with, then more extensively.'

'Oh.'

'Don't be alarmed. I've designed lots of safe experiments that have led to really persuasive results. A simple example might be encouraging someone who is afraid of spiders to face their fear by having them observe a small spider in a Perspex box before steadily building up to a point where they can hold a tarantula in the palm of their hand.'

'Whoa,' the Athlete said.

'I do not like the sound of that,' added the Boxer.

Sam smiled his understanding. 'As I said, it wouldn't be our first option, but it is something that is sometimes worth exploring with a suitable candidate, particularly if their phobia has proven quite deep-rooted. But that may well not apply to any of you. For starters, we need to take things one step at a time.'

25

I waited a bit longer – as long as I could stand it – before calling out.

'Is everything OK down there?'

He didn't reply.

'Hello?'

No answer.

'Donovan?'

Had he heard me? Perhaps down there, under – *oh God* – the concrete floor and the rock and the earth, he couldn't hear me at all.

My stomach roiled. My palms were damp with sweat. My lungs felt achy and scratchy on the insides, as if I'd inhaled lint.

'Donovan?'

Still nothing.

A dark image flooded my mind of the basement walls folding inwards, like a collapsing deck of cards. And Donovan stuck down there. Pinned by fallen masonry. Pleading with me to help him, to tackle the staircase and—

'Shit.' I fumbled in my pocket for my phone. 'Shit.'

I prodded at the screen, my hands shaking.

'Can you please just say something to me?' I called. 'Just to let me know you're OK?'

Silence.

'Is this . . . a *joke?*'

Still nothing.

My phone had unlocked. Bethany's contact details were displayed on my screen.

You're acting crazy.

I wished Sam was here right now. I wished he was sitting on the kitchen stool, talking me down, offering to make me a mug of green tea.

But Sam's not here.

You're on your own.

'Shit.'

I prodded at Bethany's name and snatched my phone to my ear.

The ringing sounded tinny and distorted, though I knew it was only because I was pressing the phone so hard against the side of my head.

'Pick up. Pick up.'

The phone rang on.

Six seconds.

Eight.

I really needed to hear Bethany's voice. I wanted her to tell me she would be here soon, that I didn't need to deal with this myself.

Please.

My phone was ringing on, uselessly.

Answer it, Bethany. Just answer my call and tell me where you are.

The phone rang out, switching to voicemail.

I listened to Bethany breezily telling me to leave a message and she'd get back to me soon, but I hung up without saying a word.

Silence rushed in like a physical force as I stared towards the silent basement again.

'Listen, Donovan, if you can hear me, you need to say something. I'm beginning to freak out here. You really need to come back upstairs now.'

I paused and this time it was as if I could hear everything and nothing all in the same moment.

The hitching of my breath, the creaking of the kitchen pipes and the background hum of the fridge-freezer, but nothing at all from Donovan.

'This isn't funny.'

My palms were so slick, my phone case squirmed in my grip.

Then I heard something.

A scrape.

A low scuff.

Downstairs.

I waited again but nothing else reached me.

He *had* to have heard me calling to him by now.

I ventured forwards, then paused.

The stairs loomed before me.

I had a vision of my legs going out from under me, of falling down the stairs.

'No,' I said aloud. 'Not happening.'

Backing away from the doorway, I turned and hurried through the kitchen, up the steps into the living area and on towards the bay window.

26

I stared out of the window through the shutter blinds. I didn't have a very wide field of vision because of the box hedge at the front of our yard, but from the angle I was at I could see past the 'For Sale' sign on my right towards the road outside.

It had grown darker again. The street lamps glowed electric yellow. Tree limbs swayed in the breeze.

I could see a plumber's van parked on the other side of our gate and next to it the front nose of a small city car that had been nestled there for so long it had collected litter and leaves under the windscreen wipers, a patina of dirt and tree sap.

A handful of lights had come on in the windows of some of the houses opposite, but most people wouldn't be home from work for more than an hour yet.

I bounced on my toes, craned my neck and strained my eyes, but it made no difference. Bethany wasn't there.

I checked my phone again, willing her to call me back, then tapped at her name on the screen and dialled her once more. Placing the phone on speaker, I cradled it in my upturned palm as I stepped back from the window, turning to gaze at the open door to the basement.

A void opened up inside me.

The phone droned on.

I reached out stiffly and clicked on a floor lamp.

Better.

We'd had multiple ceiling lights fitted across the kitchen and they burned brilliantly, reflecting back off the counter-tops and the appliances, the butler's sink and the floorboards.

I half expected Donovan to hear the ringing of my phone from down in the basement. I thought he might call up to me, say he was on his way back up.

But he didn't say anything.

I had a funny thought then. I asked myself if he really *was* in the basement. I knew he had to be because I'd watched him go down there. There was no other way out. And he couldn't have snuck out without my seeing him.

Unless he did it while you were peering out of the window.

The thought got its hooks in me.

Irrational, yes, crazy even, but as I stepped carefully to my left, past the coffee table and the sofa, I found myself ducking and glancing up the staircase towards the landing above me, knowing I was being ridiculous listening for some trace of him up there, some hint of what was happening, but doing it anyway.

All I could see was the empty landing.

Leading to the bathroom.

'Shit.'

I turned swiftly towards the front door, paused for a half-second, then reached for the snap lock and put it on the latch.

I opened the door a fraction.

A draught of street air swept in.

Better.

It smelled of grit and soot, ozone and tarmac.

Part of me was tempted to open the door fully and go outside. I could wait by the gate for Bethany. Or for Donovan when he emerged from the basement. Or for Sam when he got home.

But if I was honest with myself, I knew that part of me wanted to make sure I could make a quick exit if it came to it.

Stop it. You're overreacting.

But was I? Hadn't I had a bad feeling since before the viewing had started? Since I'd first got Bethany's message?

But you always have a bad feeling.

Even on a good day you have bad feelings.

You get scared just vacuuming the damn house.

My phone stopped ringing and the connection quickly switched to Bethany's voicemail again.

I cut the call, weighing the phone in my hand.

From outside on the street I heard a shout from one of the builders followed by a reply from one of his mates, and it occurred to me that I could go out there and ask them to come inside with me. They'd probably agree to go down into the basement for me to check if Donovan was OK.

But should I?

Again, I worried how it would look to Donovan. Sam would be so disappointed if I let my paranoia screw up this viewing.

Donovan probably hadn't even been down there *that* long.

And he had told me the basement was important to him. He could be preoccupied with his own thoughts, inspecting the space, maybe picturing where his gym equipment would go, maybe asking himself if the house was right for him and what kind of offer he might be prepared to make.

You need to give him just a bit longer.

I reached out and touched the door behind me again, making certain it was still hanging slightly open, then I tightened my grip on my phone and walked slowly back towards the basement.

27

I wasn't going to go down there. I was perfectly safe if I didn't go down there.

'Hello?'

I didn't get quite as far as the basement steps. I stopped just short of them, towards the end of the kitchen units with the bin to my side. Wrapping my free hand around the countertop, I gripped my phone in my other hand.

'Do you need some help?'

That would be the worst thing, wouldn't it? If he was hurt. If he was unconscious or had collapsed or had suffered, I don't know, a heart attack or something.

My actions (or *inactions*) would be unforgivable then.

And yes, he'd looked fit and healthy, but looks could be deceiving and why was I wasting time up here when he might be hurt?

'Donovan?'

Or perhaps he really couldn't hear me.

Was that possible?

I supposed it could be. The basement walls and floors would be thick.

Or – and this I really didn't want to think about – maybe he was messing with me. I'd told him about my claustrophobia.

103

I'd told him how uncomfortable I was about the basement. He'd seen that I had a problem with it. I knew next to nothing about him and he could be exactly the type of arsehole who'd get a kick out of terrorizing a woman.

I went up on my toes and peered down the steps. They twisted to the right at the bottom and my stomach twisted with them.

I teetered forwards, stretching out my arm but unwilling to release the countertop just yet, then froze when I heard a vehicle blast by on the street outside.

A gust of wind must have followed it because the front door swung fully open and bumped against the hallway wall.

I swivelled and stared back at it.

The breath I was holding seemed to chill and condense in my lungs.

'Donovan?'

When he still didn't respond, I got that awful feeling again.

Could he be somewhere else?

Was the basement empty?

Angst crackled around me. A static charge.

I wrestled with what to do.

The front door is open behind you. You have fresh air and an exit. You are not shut in. You are not confined here.

I shuffled ever so slightly forwards until only the tip of my finger was still touching the countertop behind me.

I glanced back at it, then watched it drop free.

When I looked frontwards again I rocked precariously on my ankles, feeling as if I was balancing on a high wire that was trembling out of control, the wobbles getting worse, amplified by my own spasms of fear.

I paused for a second and took a fistful of my sweater in my fist.

'Donovan? I'm sorry, but would you mind coming back upstairs now?'

Nothing.

'Please? I know it sounds silly but this is making me uncomfortable and I really think—'

I was interrupted by a sudden, fast rapping on the front door behind me.

'Knock knock,' called a high, cheery voice. 'Lucy? Where are you hiding?'

28
Sam

'There's one thing I don't get,' the Boxer said.

He folded his hairy arms again, his generous belly swelling over his lap. From the way he was jutting his chin forwards and scoping out the rest of the group, making certain they were listening to him, Sam sensed he was trying to position himself in an alpha role.

'Go ahead,' Sam said.

'These negative thoughts you're talking about.'

'Negative *automatic* thoughts.'

'Right. You said some of them could be good for us? If there was a threat to us, say? Like with the hot stove.'

Sam nodded. 'They could be, yes.'

'OK. Then how can you tell? What I mean is, how do you know when a threat is something you're imagining and when it's real?'

29

Bethany stepped through the front door and into the hallway with her handbag balanced on her wrist.

Relief rushed through me. I placed my hand over my heart as she stepped in further, craning her neck to peer up the stairs.

'I'm over here,' I told her, moving away from the basement and out into the middle of the kitchen.

Bethany did an amused double-take when she saw my appearance. I realized I must have looked almost as stressed and crazed as I felt.

'What are you doing back there?' she asked. 'And why is your front door open?'

She was wearing a fashionable raincoat that was belted at the waist and a bright statement scarf, like a TV news reporter about to do a live broadcast. Her heels were killer. Her make-up looked freshly applied. She was mid-twenties but she acted older. She had the confidence and bearing of someone for whom life was working out exactly as she'd planned.

'Where's Donovan?' She removed her gloves, folding them in her hands, fussing with her hair.

'I've been calling you,' I said.

'Have you?' Her brow furrowed in a pantomime of surprise. She parted her handbag, delving inside to remove her phone. 'Oh look, I'm sorry, I think I had it on silent and—' It took her a second to process what she was seeing. '*Three* missed calls?'

I swallowed and glanced back at the basement.

'Lucy? Is something the matter?'

'Yes, something's the matter,' I said, keeping my voice low as I pointed behind me. 'He's gone into the basement and he won't come out.'

'Sorry?' Her laugh was stagey, tinkling. 'Are you saying that you've lost him?'

'No.' A kick of temper but I got it under control, taking a step closer, wanting her to understand the importance of what I was telling her. 'He went into the basement but now he's not answering me when I call down to him.'

'*Riiight.*' She said it slowly, infuriatingly. 'And you didn't go down with him?'

I didn't say anything to that.

'Well, have you been down to check on him, at least?'

'Not yet.'

'*O-kay.*'

I didn't explain why.

It was clear she already thought I was overreacting and I'd never mentioned my claustrophobia to Bethany before. It simply hadn't come up. Sam had been here with me when she'd valued the house, so he'd been the one to show her the basement. And the viewings she'd arranged since then had always been conducted when I was out.

'I'm sorry, but you're being very serious, Lucy.'

'Because it's odd,' I told her. I was still clutching my phone and now I became aware that Bethany was glancing at the way my knuckles had whitened around it. 'I don't know if he's trying to scare me, or if he thinks it's funny, or—'

'Bethany?' I jumped at the sound of Donovan's voice booming out from behind me. 'You made it.'

'Donovan!' Bethany opened her arms, breezing past me as Donovan emerged from the top of the basement stairs with a mildly puzzled look on his face. 'We thought we'd lost you! It's so wonderful we can finally meet.'

Bethany went up on her toes and air-kissed his cheek, her fingers gently stroking the sleeve of his overcoat as she pulled away, as if she was appraising the quality of the fabric.

Donovan seemed a bit taken aback by her greeting, but after checking her out in return he caught up to it soon enough. 'I was beginning to think you'd stood me up.'

She fake-gasped. 'I would never!'

Her hand returned to his arm and I was reminded of the way the woman had touched him outside, though Bethany was even more predatory. Donovan had to be at least ten years older than Bethany, but from the appreciative smile he was giving her he obviously had no problem with that.

And why should he? Bethany was beautiful. Single.

'So . . .' She twisted at the hips, finally removing her hand from him and tapping a finger to her lips. 'What do we think?'

'Of?'

'The house, silly.'

'I think it's everything you told me on the phone and more. Lucy's done a really terrific job showing me around before you got here.'

That was generous, and we both knew it, but we both also knew that something wasn't right here and I wasn't about to let it go.

'Bethany—' I began.

'Did she show you the back garden?' Bethany continued, talking over me.

'Yes, we covered that,' Donovan said.

'The kitchen has everything you need?'

'Everything for ordering in a takeaway, anyway.'

'Oh, you're one of *those* men. And upstairs?'

'I could make that work.'

'Mmm, I just bet you could.'

'I'm sorry,' I blurted. I knew I sounded rude. I also knew I looked angry and haggard and probably unhinged, but I really didn't care. 'I was calling to you,' I told Donovan.

'You were?' His face contorted with apparent confusion.

'Yes, when you were in the basement. I was calling down to you and you didn't reply.'

'Really?' He shot Bethany a mystified look. 'I didn't hear you.'

I should let it go now. I knew that, too. I clearly wasn't going to get anywhere with it. And yet . . .

'I was shouting pretty loudly.'

'Well, then,' Bethany said, clapping her hands, 'doesn't that just go to prove how solid your basement is?'

'It could have been my fault.' Donovan pulled a face and raised a gloved hand in a placatory gesture. His palm was about the size of a bear's paw. 'The truth is I get embarrassed about it, but I do have some trouble with my hearing. An old rugby injury. If I'd heard you, I would have come back up, Lucy. I did actually call to you at one point. Did you hear that?'

Something rippled under my skin. A feverish squirming.

I suspected he was lying, but he was looking back at me so casually, and Bethany obviously couldn't see a problem, that it was difficult for me to challenge him further without escalating the situation.

'Well, it's great that we've settled that one,' Bethany said, slipping her arm through Donovan's and guiding him forwards. 'Come on, I'm going to show you the bedrooms again. I don't want you leaving here with any doubts in your mind.'

They began to climb the stairs.

Again, I knew I should have left things, but again, I couldn't help myself.

'I thought you had an appointment?' I said to Donovan.

'Oh, please,' Bethany said. 'You'll make time for me, won't you, Donovan? Why don't you make yourself comfortable, Lucy? We won't be long.'

30

I remained where I was. Or close to where I was.

After gently pushing the front door shut, I lingered at the bottom of the staircase, my hand falling lightly on the banister rail, looking up towards the empty landing.

I could no longer see Bethany and Donovan but I could hear them. They were in the back bedroom, laughing and flirting.

But now I wondered – wasn't there a slightly unusual quality to Bethany's laugh? A vague artificiality?

As I thought about it more I began to think that perhaps Bethany's attraction to Donovan wasn't as genuine as she wanted him to believe. It could be she was a lot craftier than I'd given her credit for and she was actually much more focused on the commission her agency would take if she sold him our home.

Was that possible? I supposed so. I didn't know masses about Bethany but I knew enough to suspect she was a bit of a hustler.

And Donovan? How much did Bethany know about him, I wondered? She'd know he was searching for properties in our area and price bracket, but how closely would she have vetted him? I couldn't imagine any estate agent asking for proof that Donovan – or anyone else for that matter – could actually afford the places they wanted to view. And, sure, there were probably polite questions she'd asked, oblique strategies, though all of that could only go so far.

But still. I was finding it hard to shake the sense that there was something off about Donovan.

I leaned to my side, contemplating the basement again.

He hadn't closed the door.

He would have known that would bother me.

I shut my eyes for a second.

Swayed.

He'd claimed that he hadn't heard me calling to him down there, and also that he'd shouted up to me, but deep down I didn't really believe him. The part I didn't get was why he might lie.

—*click.*

That was when I heard it.

The noise in my head.

The one that would never fully go away.

—*click.*

Like the trigger being pulled on an empty chamber in a revolver.

It came to me whenever I got agitated. When I panicked. When I was in a state.

Not now.

—*click.*

And in my head I was in that bathroom again with the party music thrashing and pounding, then evaporating suddenly, sucked away into an absolute vacuum as the man who'd followed me inside and locked the door behind him stepped forwards, closing the distance between us, his face disintegrating into shadow as he flexed his hands, grabbed for me.

'I've been watching you.'

Sometimes I could almost get a fix on his voice, but only in my very worst nightmares, and afterwards when I woke, drenched with cold sweat and horrified, I was always amazed by how what had seemed clear and certain became so slippery and vague.

—click.

I flinched.

It got me every time.

I couldn't rid myself of it, no matter what I tried or how many of Sam's techniques I applied. I knew Sam sometimes got frustrated with himself that he couldn't help me more. When it came to my claustrophobia and my past trauma he'd speculated that there was probably a block further back in my psyche, perhaps from my childhood, something we hadn't yet figured out how to fix. He'd talked about other ways of helping me, more experimental strategies, but lately I'd begun to lose hope of anything working, fearing the *click* would always be there when I was faced with challenging circumstances, a strange sort of tinnitus, an unpleasant quirk, the same way some people get nervous coughs.

That was when Donovan laughed again, a raucous chuckle, and soon afterwards I heard Bethany mutter something in a sly and humorous tone before they moved along the landing, past the bathroom, with Bethany chattering away about the generous floor space in the main bedroom and the two of them giggling as if they were new lovers hurrying to a hotel suite.

I moved away from the stairs before they could see me . . .

—*click* . . .

. . . and strode into the kitchen, where I took down a glass tumbler from a cupboard and filled it with ice and water from the dispenser on the fridge.

Carrying my drink to the kitchen island, I dragged back one of the wooden stools and sat on it heavily, placing my phone on the counter in front of me, taking a sip of water.

The glass clinked against my teeth.

I stared at my phone, wishing I could call Sam so that he could tell me everything was under control and would turn out fine, talk me down. Maybe he'd even call me and tell me his support group had finished early and he was on his way back.

—*click.*

I drank more water, closing my eyes.

I shouldn't have tried to do this by myself, I realized. It was too much. Too soon.

It has been two years, I could imagine Sam saying. And not in a testy way. In a careful way. Soothing.

Two years in which I'd steadily tried to rebuild myself by sanding over my trauma and papering over the cracks in my psyche, just as I'd sanded and wallpapered this house.

My own form of therapy.

My own way of healing.

Bethany giggled again and I felt my hand tighten around the glass, the condensation cool and slick against my skin.

Because hadn't I been like that once, too? Heedless. Amused.

Let it go.

Move on.

This was a simple house viewing. Nothing more.

I was projecting onto it with my own experiences. I was making too big a deal out of nothing.

And yes, perhaps Donovan had misled me or fooled with me when he was down in the basement. Perhaps he'd enjoyed testing the limits of my neuroses. Perhaps he was – to put it bluntly – a complete dick.

But . . . so what?

It would be over soon.

He would be gone.

Bethany, too.

And if Donovan made an offer on our house then we could consider it and Sam could make a judgement call. It wasn't as if there was a rule saying he had to sell our house to someone I liked.

Bigger picture, the thing to focus on here today was that I'd taken a small step forwards. One I never would have envisaged when I'd woken up this morning.

I told myself all that.

I told myself and it made complete sense.

But, somehow, I still found myself picking up my phone and standing from my stool.

Because I was going to go up there anyway and make some excuse for joining them – it was where I lived, after all – and screw it if they didn't like it or thought I was interfering because—

I froze as a startled yelp interrupted my thoughts, funnelling down from our bedroom upstairs, swiftly followed by a thump.

31

Silence followed.

It was freighted. Frayed.

All the blood drained out of my head and pooled around my core. I stood so still I seemed to be vibrating, listening to the jagged echo of Bethany's yelp in my mind.

Or was it a scream?

I replayed it in my head.

The sudden yip. The fractured ending.

There was shock and surprise in it, definitely. But was there anything else?

Like fear? Or hurt?

I couldn't say.

She could have tripped in her heels, or stumbled, or over-reacted to some other harmless incident in some way.

But my instincts said otherwise.

So did my hard-won knowledge. The burden of it.

A coolness spread over my skin. My throat burned. My nerve endings seemed to have been stripped and exposed like bare electrical wires.

And then there was the silence.

It persisted.

There was no call from Bethany afterwards. No shout of

'I'm OK!' or 'Whoops!' or 'Sorry about that!' No bolt of giddy, nervous laughter.

Thump.

The noise was louder this time, reverberating down through the floorboards above the living room.

I whipped my head sideways.

The ceiling light trembled.

My lungs felt as if they might burst from the breath I hadn't taken.

There was still nothing from Bethany or Donovan. No explanation at all.

And I was listening for it, straining for it, all my senses lit up.

My vision had a sharp and unusual clarity. My hearing was pure and intense. I could smell the fresh lilies on the coffee table and the scent was suddenly sickly and cloying.

'Bethany?'

My own voice shocked me. Not just the sound of it, but the fear wrapped inside it: the dry, nervous rasp.

'Is everything OK up there?'

I was craning my neck because I still hadn't moved away from the kitchen island. I wasn't sure I *could* move.

But now my feet were drifting forwards, mounting the three small steps into the living area with a stiff and awkward unfamiliarity as if I'd never traversed them before.

My phone felt as heavy as a brick in my hand.

Perhaps Bethany had fainted. Maybe that could explain the thump I'd heard.

But you heard two thumps. You know you did.

And I hadn't heard them all at once, either. There'd been

119

one thump, and then a pause, and then a second thump several seconds later.

And why hadn't Donovan said anything?

'Bethany?'

There was still no answer.

Was this going to be like the basement, I wondered? Was that what they'd been laughing about? Were they *both* now messing with me?

I stopped and contemplated the front door for a moment, doubt tugging at my insides.

I could step outside. I could refuse to participate in whatever this was and wait for them to come looking for me.

But what kind of person would that make me?

—click.

And in my mind I was instantly back in that bathroom again with the man with the metallic voice. I was alone with nobody coming to help me.

There was no possible way I could do that to somebody else.

I moved towards the stairs and started to climb. It seemed to take me a very long time to reach the top.

I didn't call out this time. Somehow, I sensed it would be the wrong thing to do.

When I stepped onto the landing my own blood raged in my ears.

Turning painfully slowly, I started towards the main bedroom, my feet dragging across the carpet as if my ankles were shackled.

The door was hanging partially closed.

I reached it and exhaled faintly, pushing it fully open.

Donovan looked up as I entered.

He was stationed near to the sofa with his back to the middle window, his backside and hands perched on the windowsill behind him.

A long, awful moment of waiting.

'Where's Bethany?' I asked.

32

Sam

'You have to do your best to step back and analyse the situation you're in,' Sam told the Boxer. 'You need to try and stay calm, where you can. Take some deep breaths. That always helps. Then you need to look at the facts in front of you. Not what you *think* you might be seeing or *think* you know, but what you *are* actually seeing and *do* actually know. You can test your fears against the facts. Are they rational? Could there be another explanation?'

'But often,' the Artist said, 'isn't it what you're *not seeing* and *don't know* that scares you? It is for me.'

'And me,' the Lost Girl agreed.

The Athlete nodded. 'Fear of the unknown.'

'Or of missing something you should be noticing,' the Artist said, and shivered. 'That's what scares me, anyway.'

33

Donovan didn't answer my question.

'Where is she?' I asked again.

He tipped his head to one side and gazed at me, as if he had no clue or didn't care what I was talking about.

'She was just up here with you. She yelped or screamed or – I don't know exactly. And there was a thump or a bang, and then a few seconds later there was another thump and—'

This time he shrugged and rolled out his bottom lip.

'Will you please say something?'

'You've really outdone yourself with this bedroom, Lucy. The more time I spend in it, the more I like it.'

A dull clang of panic.

Something rose up and lodged in my throat. A bubble of air that wouldn't pop or release.

'There's just . . . such a feeling of space.'

I didn't take a step back.

I stayed where I was.

There was a reasonable distance between us. The width of the room. Five or six metres.

And I was close to the doorway if I needed to be.

'Bethany?' I called.

It came out quieter than I'd intended. My grip tightened around my phone.

I stared at Donovan for a perilous moment, noting how contained and composed he appeared, how he wasn't making any effort to come towards me or close the space between us. How he seemed content to simply perch by the window and watch.

Turning quickly, I looked along the landing behind me, then snatched my head forwards again.

Confusion and suspicion fizzed in my veins.

Perhaps this was all entirely harmless. Perhaps Bethany was simply in another room.

Again, the thought hit me that this could be an unpleasant prank Donovan and Bethany had cooked up together. Maybe they believed I'd overreacted about the basement and this was a misguided lesson they were trying to teach me.

Or maybe something else was going on. Some other dynamic that had eluded me before now. Perhaps Bethany and Donovan knew each other much better than they'd let on.

He still hadn't moved.

'Bethany, can you please say something?' I called. 'Where are you?'

How could silence be so loud?

My head throbbed as I listened for a response that failed to come.

I was staring at Donovan, but I was acutely aware of what I could see in my peripheries and I was listening hard for any noises from behind.

Despite its generous dimensions, our bedroom was lightly furnished. There were the bed and the beside cabinets, the small white sofa next to Donovan, a faux fur rug, the shutter blinds, the fireplace and the walk-in wardrobe.

I thought about that.

A buzzing in my temples.

The walk-in wardrobe was just to my left but I couldn't see inside it from where I was standing.

'Why are you doing this to me?'

'I'm just here for a house viewing, Lucy.'

'I could ask you to leave.'

'Then ask. Go right ahead.'

He stood up and casually slipped his hands into his pockets.

But of course there was a problem with asking him to leave. Because to leave he'd have to come past me. Or I'd have to move away from the doorway.

'Stay where you are,' I said.

'You know, you're really sending me conflicting signals here, Lucy. I thought you wanted to sell me your house? First you were pretty funny about the basement. Now this.'

I lifted my phone in my hand and thrust it towards him, showing him the screen. I'd unlocked it with my thumb. My fingers and hand were shaking.

'Do I need to call the police?'

'Why would you need to call the police?'

'Where's Bethany?'

He shook his head mildly, as if I was making a fool of myself.

'I could scream.'

'Really? Doesn't that strike you as an overreaction?'

'There are neighbours around.'

'I should hope so. It's a popular neighbourhood. Very desirable. That's why I'm here, *remember*.'

I tapped a nine into my phone. Followed by another nine.

'Quick question,' he said. 'If you do call the police, what are you going to tell them? I'm here to view your house.'

'Not like this you're not.'

'OK. Then allow me a follow-up question. How long do you think it will take for them to get here?'

He said it as if it was nothing – barely a consideration – but I caught his meaning. He was telling me that he could get to me before the police could.

'You're scaring me.'

'I think you're scaring yourself, Lucy. Like with the basement. What have I actually done?'

I shook my head even as a slight, unwelcome doubt festered inside me.

Maybe I *was* overreacting.

Maybe my imagination was getting away from me.

My *thoughts*.

I tapped a third nine into my phone, making sure he saw me do it. I then rested my thumb over the call button and gestured towards the walk-in wardrobe.

'I'm going to take a look in there now.'

'Your house, your rules.'

I edged towards it, sliding my left foot across the carpet, following carefully with my right, keeping my gaze fixed on him the entire time and my back to the wall behind me.

If I was fast I could still get back to the bedroom door and out onto the landing before he could get to me.

If he came for me.

And if I could get to the landing then I could get to the stairs and on down to the front door and out, out, out and—

'Take your time, Lucy. I'm not going anywhere.'

Another slow step.

Now or never.

I did a fast half-turn with my head. A there-and-back glance that allowed me to see that the walk-in wardrobe was unoccupied.

He still hadn't moved.

I stared at him with my thumb hovering over the call button.

'I don't understand what's happening. Where is she?'

I jerked my head to my right and my skin seemed to contract, pulling taut against my bones.

That's when I sensed it.

The lure of it.

The cosmic inevitability.

Another bathroom.

But not the main bathroom behind me.

The en suite.

34

'Are you going to move?' I asked him.

'You tell me.'

I peered hard at him, brandishing my phone. 'If you move, I'm calling the police.'

'OK.'

'Don't move.'

He used a finger to slowly draw an imaginary cross over his heart.

I glanced towards the en suite, nerves scattering across my shoulders and back.

There are two ways in and out, I reminded myself. *If he comes through one way, you can leave by the other. You can still get out. There are no doors.*

I checked on him once again, trying to gauge what exactly he was up to, and then I rushed forwards, threading my way along the right-hand side of the bed, darting through the gap beside the privacy wall.

The moment I stepped off the carpet onto the marbled bathroom tiles, I whipped my head to my left and took in everything in one breathless scan.

I'd polished the floor tiles earlier and they gleamed in the light.

I saw the walk-in shower and the wall-hung toilet and the freestanding copper bath and the double sinks.

I saw the window shutter that was closed for privacy at the end of the space and the white cotton towels on the towel rail and the dressing gowns hanging from the hooks on the wall.

Bethany wasn't here.

It didn't make sense.

I'd watched her come upstairs with Donovan. I'd heard them laugh and giggle and then I'd heard them walk along the landing towards the main bedroom together. I'd heard Bethany's yelp followed by the thumps.

And how long afterwards had I come upstairs?

Not long.

A frantic swarming in my bloodstream. A heady confusion. My fingers began to twitch and curl.

There was something else.

Something out of sync, or misaligned in some way, that I couldn't quite identify.

I stepped onto the bath mat in front of the shower cubicle and squinted.

Whatever I had noticed had been there and gone in the blink of an eye. It was something I was seeing or not seeing, or maybe it was nothing at all, but somehow it felt wrong and—

Get out.

A squirt of fear in my belly.

I turned around too quickly and he was right behind me – tall and broad, silent and looming – and I shrieked and jerked backwards just as the bath mat slipped from under me and then I was falling, my arms flinging upwards, my back arching backwards, the ceiling rotating above me and the floor tilting up to greet me until the back of my skull dashed off something solid yet hollow-sounding and my head was filled with a white-hot pulse of light.

35

Sam

Something quivered in Sam's chest. An unexpected tremor in the muscles around his heart. He felt the hairs on the back of his neck begin to rise and his skin start to cool.

Strange.

Someone other than Sam – someone more susceptible to emotional responses or more prone to superstition – might have said that it had felt as if someone had walked over his grave.

Which didn't make sense. Because the session was going well. The group was bonding and interacting. Yes, they were challenging his ideas but there was no denying that they were engaged, wanting to learn more.

Well, apart from the Librarian, maybe. It would be beneficial if Sam could get him more involved.

Which was when Sam turned towards him and – with a queasy spasm in his throat – finally understood that he should have listened to his instincts, after all.

36

I groaned, my eyelids fluttering, lying prone on my side.
Footsteps.

Coming closer.

I flopped onto my back.

Mistake.

I groaned louder as a wave of sickly pain sloshed around inside my skull, crashing against my temples.

Donovan crouched next to me, his outline rimmed by a glaring light.

'What happened?' I mumbled.

My mouth was filled with cotton.

'The sink,' he said. 'You hit your head on the sink.'

He touched gloved fingers to the back of my skull and I braced against a spike of pain.

'Here.'

Cupping a hand under my neck, he lifted my head, then reached out to his side and a moment later set my head down on something soft that I guessed was a towel.

I seemed to be sinking into the ground.

Melting.

'How many fingers am I holding up?'

His voice sounded cold, echoing.

'Two?'

'That's what I thought,' he said grimly, as if I'd got it wrong, and then he took my left hand, rolling up my sleeve.

A sharp scratch on the inside of my elbow and a few seconds later he slipped something into the inside pocket of his coat that caught the light briefly.

He then removed a glove, took hold of my wrist and checked my pulse, timing it against his wristwatch.

Doctor, I thought. *He is some kind of doctor.*

Heat flushed through me. I was sweating terribly, shaky, spent.

Donovan hazed in and out of my vision, his features becoming blurred and indistinct, and then, in a clutch of panic, he seemed to morph into another man in another bathroom again.

No.

I tried to push myself up, but the pain sloshed against my temples and I sank back down as he pressed firmly on my shoulder.

His features gradually realigned, coalesced. His expression was sober. A concerned and contemplative look.

'Don't try to get up.'

A lost moment.

A pulse of swirling darkness.

When I jolted awake – perhaps a second or so later – Donovan released my wrist and rubbed his thumb against his lips, thinking.

Another lost moment.

Another pulse of black.

Time must have stalled or slipped or stopped for a second

133

– an incomprehensible blip – because the next thing I knew he was standing above me, looking behind him over his shoulder, his body tense and alert as if he'd heard something from downstairs.

'Stay here,' he told me.

'What—? Where are you going?'

A roar of white noise filled my head.

I groaned again as Donovan leaned forwards into my field of vision, looming above me, his face a pinkish smear.

'Just wait,' he said, and then he was gone.

37
Sam

The Librarian was bending forwards on his chair with his arms crossed over his stomach, rubbing his hands up and down his upper arms as if he had a chill. He was murmuring to himself. Whispering. Agitated.

Sam took a lightning-quick glance at the rest of the group. The Artist appeared worried. The Lost Girl was shaking her head and pushing back her chair. The Boxer and the Athlete were trading looks as if asking one another if they should stand up and intervene.

'It's OK,' Sam told them, calmly raising a hand in the air.

The Librarian whined and raked his nails down his jumper, clawing at the material. His mouth drooped.

'You're safe here,' Sam told him. 'You have nothing to fear.'

But the Librarian just moaned and shook his head in a distressed and agonized way, as if Sam was missing something crucial, and then he reached a hand up under the sleeve of his sweater and slowly removed a pair of scissors.

38

I lay alone with the strange roaring and hissing sound getting louder and closer.

It made no sense.

Nothing did.

It was as if the wiring in my head had all shorted. None of my thoughts would quite connect.

Closing my eyes against the stabbing sensation in the back of my skull, I was grateful for the soft towel underneath me.

I felt groggy. Sluggish.

You fell, I reminded myself.

Then I opened my eyes as I remembered something else.

Donovan had been behind me. *Immediately* behind me. And—

The pain flared again.

I lay there helpless in the roaring, hissing confusion.

Until a new sound reached me.

A dim chime.

Two notes.

The doorbell.

I struggled to focus as I thought about how Donovan had reacted before. He'd been standing over me. I'd seen him looking behind him with his body tensed because he'd heard something.

Could it have been the doorbell?

I levered myself up very slightly on my elbow.

The room slanted and dipped but this time the pain in my head wasn't quite as bad as before. The faint whistling in my ears began to subside.

Twisting onto my side, I stared down at the white towel underneath me, my vision gradually sliding back into focus.

There were a few spots of blood on it.

My heart clenched as I reached up with trembling fingers and touched the back of my head, feeling a patch of sticky dampness amid my hair.

A sudden judder passed through the floorboards beneath me. A familiar tremor.

He's opened the front door.

I strained to hear what was happening. It was difficult to make anything out over the roaring, hissing sound in the room, but I thought I could hear muffled voices.

They sounded low and conversational, modulated and polite.

I couldn't tell what was being said.

What *was* that hissing noise anyway?

I turned as carefully as I could.

Steam.

It was billowing out from the shower cubicle, curling against the ceiling, spilling across the floor in misted clouds.

The shower was running.

Why was the shower running?

Lifting the towel, I pressed it to the back of my head.

'Ow, fuck!'

Getting to my knees, I reached above me for the sink my head must have struck – there was a faint smear of blood on it – and pulled myself up to peer into the mirror.

Steam had condensed on the glass but I could see a hazed outline of myself. My hair was tangled and in disarray. My eyes looked wet and dazed. But at least I didn't feel as if I was going to pass out again.

A fresh cloud of steam wafted past me and I squinted at the reflection of the shower cubicle to my left. Donovan must have been letting the water heat up. He must have been planning to soak a towel, clean my wound. Then the doorbell had rung and he'd gone to answer it.

Had he called for an ambulance?

I looked around for my phone, realizing that I could check the doorbell app, see who was down there and—

That's when it came back to me.

Bethany.

I'd been searching for Bethany.

Where *was* she?

39

And where was my phone?

It had been in my hand. I could still feel the shape and the weight of it. But it wasn't in my hand any more.

I must have dropped it when I'd fallen. It must have skidded across the floor and—

I gazed towards the toilet and the tiled flooring, peering at the base of the copper bath.

No phone.

I couldn't see it.

So maybe Donovan had used it. That made sense.

And yes, now that I thought about it, I'd already input 999, so he would just have needed to connect the call. I'd input 999 because I'd been scared because—

An invisible hand reached inside my chest and closed around my heart in a fist.

You'd been scared because of him.

And he'd been right behind you when he shouldn't have been. He'd promised you he wouldn't come near you.

I swung my head in the direction of the landing, the room canting abruptly, the shower hissing in my ears.

I tried to listen to what was being said downstairs but I still couldn't hear very much over the drumming of the shower.

139

Then it hit me.

Was that deliberate? Had he turned the shower on because he didn't want me to hear them?

Or he doesn't want them *to hear* you.

I needed to know who was down there.

Releasing the sink, I took two steps towards the window, then stopped.

Hell.

The nauseating pain in the back of my head blared like a rotted tooth, then gradually steadied and faded a little.

The floorboards trembled beneath me again.

He's closed the door.

I moved forwards more carefully this time until I reached the window in front of me, tilted the shutter blades with my fingers and looked out.

The thickening darkness outside was stained acid yellow by the street lighting.

I couldn't see an ambulance but an old man was standing beside the open gate at the end of our path.

Our neighbour, John.

He had an empty plastic shopping bag hanging limply in his hand. I didn't like the expression on his face. His mouth was hooked downwards, a slash of doubt or confusion scoring a deep line across his brow.

He was only there for the briefest instant, half twisted around, glancing towards our front door. Then he turned and began to walk off, his domed scalp and the wisps of white hair at the sides of his head skimming along past the top of our hedge.

He crossed the road and continued onwards, heading in

the direction of the nearby parade of shops on Upper Richmond Road.

Had he called round to ask if there was anything we needed, as he sometimes did?

If so, had Donovan said something to get rid of him – something that hadn't entirely convinced him that everything was normal and that explained why he'd been looking back at our house with such a conflicted expression on his face?

Or had he been looking that way because he'd watched Donovan let somebody *else* into our home?

John was continuing to stroll away beyond the parked cars and plane trees. He didn't glance back.

There was nobody else around.

My eyes strayed to the 'For Sale' sign in the front of our yard and something inside me tightened and tensed.

Then I lowered my gaze further and peered at my arm for a second. The one with the sleeve rolled up, exposing my familiar, knotted scar, running like a length of hot wire from the inside of my wrist to the crook of my elbow.

I experienced a jolt of fear, icy liquid seeping through my stomach.

Taking hold of my wrist, I lifted my arm closer, staring in disbelief at the inside of my elbow.

No, I hadn't imagined it.

A tiny dot of blood.

I pressed a nail to it, remembering the scratch and the stinging sensation, the way Donovan had slipped something into his pocket afterwards and—

Shit.

In my dazed state I'd thought he was helping me, but what if he hadn't been?

He might have injected you with something.

I remembered what he'd said to me when I'd been lying on the floor.

Just wait.

Why? How had he expected to find me when he got back up here and what was he planning to do to me?

I stared back at the en suite behind me, not daring to breathe as I listened to the maddening hiss and splatter of the shower and beyond it . . . nothing.

Except a taut, silent humming. A soundless note of pure terror.

Which was when a new thought hit me.

Move.

40

I flung myself sideways, scrambled out of the opening to my right and made a grab for the bed.

Knotting my fingers in the pleated throw, I leaned out and stared towards the hallway.

No sign of Donovan.

Sweat poured down my forehead, stinging my eyes. I felt hot and shivery at the same time.

My reflection stared back at me from the full-length mirror opposite. It was as if I was staring at the victim of a sudden road accident. I looked stunned and dazed.

Then I glanced down at my arm and saw the needle mark inside my elbow again, and the horror hit me anew.

I struck out forwards, exiting the bedroom and grabbing hold of the railings overlooking the stairs, sweat dripping in my eyes.

The noise of the shower behind me had receded a little. There was no sound from below, no conversation, no noise from Donovan or Bethany or whoever the mystery caller had been.

I considered going for the front door.

In my mind I mapped out rushing downstairs and grappling with the snap lock and staggering outside.

But I knew Donovan was down there *somewhere* and Bethany could be anywhere.

Were they really a threat to me or was I letting my thoughts run away from me?

I licked my lips. They tasted of salt and oil. A needling pain probed at the back of my skull again.

At the end of the hallway was the bathroom and the back bedroom. I really hated that the bathroom was ahead of me. A wordless danger seemed to emanate from it.

Bad karma. Bad memories.

As if I wasn't freaked out enough already.

Movement to my left.

I jerked my head sideways, gazing down over the railings.

Somebody's shadow was sliding up the stairwell wall from below.

Only seconds until they saw me.

Maybe less.

My heart stuttered.

What to do?

I took a backwards step towards the bedroom.

But the bedroom was where they expected me to be.

Then I glanced sideways and up.

At the stairs leading towards the attic.

41
Sam

'Oh my God!' the Artist gasped, clamping her hands over her mouth.

The Athlete shot to his feet. 'Should I get someone? Who should I get?'

'No, don't do that,' Sam said. 'Please, everyone stay where you are.'

He looked at the scissors that were now pointed towards him. They were a relatively small pair. Translucent plastic handles. Blades perhaps five centimetres long.

They were oscillating wildly in the Librarian's grip. His upper lip was damp with sweat, his engorged eyes bulging. He had started to weep.

'Easy,' Sam said to him. 'Take it easy, it's OK.'

'I'm sorry,' he snivelled. 'I'm so sorry I did this.'

'No, it's OK,' Sam told him again, talking slowly and deliberately. 'Everything is going to be all right.'

The Lost Girl twisted her upper body away from the Librarian, shying from looking, placing a hand on the Boxer's shoulder. The Artist was shaking her head minutely, her skin drained of colour, while the Athlete raised himself up on his toes and looked out through the glazed internal wall of the seminar room as if he was hoping to signal to somebody passing by.

Sam kept his focus on the Librarian, patting the air with his hands.

'I know it's a lot,' Sam said. 'What you're hearing today. But you just need to breathe. Listen to my voice. Take your time.'

'Don't come any closer!'

The Librarian twitched and slashed at the air with his scissors. The Lost Girl shrieked.

'Everybody stay calm,' Sam reminded them.

'I don't know,' the Boxer muttered. 'This doesn't feel right to me.'

Again, Sam kept his focus on the Librarian, blocking everything else out, feeling oddly composed.

This is an opportunity to prove everything you've been saying to the group. This is how you secure their trust.

The Librarian was breathing rapidly, bubbles of saliva frothing at the corners of his mouth.

'You're not going to hurt anyone,' Sam told him. 'You never were going to hurt anyone. Listen to me. Focus on my voice. These are just bad thoughts you're having. Your thoughts are not real. You control your actions. Now, I am going to slowly extend my hand to you, and when I do, I want you to give me the scissors.'

42

I climbed towards the attic with my hands out in front of me, my fingers tearing at the carpet, my shoulder brushing the wall.

A terrible feeling.

Those prickles in my spine again. The sensation of someone looming behind me.

I reached the upper landing, whirled around, stared back.

But the stairwell was empty.

And I knew I had a choice.

Two rooms.

Choose well.

I entered Sam's study at a crouch, bracing myself against the door frame before advancing as far as his desk chair.

Footfall downstairs.

Somebody was striding along the landing. Confident. Fast.

I sneaked on towards the French doors opening onto the balcony, taking hold of the door handles, reaching for the key.

Wait.

A tremor deep inside me.

The key wasn't here. It was missing.

He must have taken the key.

My mind flashed back to when Donovan had stepped in from the balcony earlier. His back had been to me when he'd closed both doors after him. I hadn't paid close attention to what he'd been doing with his hands because I'd been too busy worrying about what to do and say next.

Oh God.

I tugged down on both door handles but they only confirmed what I already knew.

He was locking you in.

He'd planned ahead.

Was Bethany a part of this? What even *was* this?

Fear bulged in my throat.

I scanned the carpet around my feet, telling myself the key might have simply fallen out. The pain at the back of my head spiked momentarily as I looked down, but if the key had fallen to the floor I couldn't see it.

Spinning, my heart thrashing against my ribs, I stared towards the top of the stairs, willing this not to be happening to me, wishing I could be anywhere else.

That's when I heard the shower stop.

The squeak of a tap. A hush followed by a ragged splatter and then silence.

I listened as closely as I could.

Beneath my feet I could picture Donovan or Bethany standing very still and listening for me.

I didn't move. My body was stone.

I wanted to shout or scream for somebody to help me, but I was petrified of letting them know where I was.

The seconds passed like minutes.

When I did gradually turn my head, achingly slowly, I surveyed Sam's study for anything I could use to let myself out.

But all I could see was pens and notebooks, papers and texts.

Then I heard movement again.

Downstairs.

Footsteps.

On the landing.

Hurrying towards the back of the house.

43

They're checking the back bedroom, I thought. *The bathroom.*

I pressed my hands against the French doors. My fingers smudged the glass.

Make a decision.

Think.

Turning quickly, I retraced my steps across the room, accidentally banging into Sam's chair and knocking it aside.

At the top of the landing I paused and looked down the stairs again.

A moment of vertigo.

Of terror.

But whoever was down there didn't show themselves or spot me.

Taking one big step forwards, I crossed into the attic bedroom.

My gaze swept across the skylights, the daybed, the hanging chair and the bookshelves. I was sweating so badly my jumper was sticking to my skin.

I ventured on, making for the small cupboard under the eaves where I'd stashed the vacuum cleaner. I had to duck as I got close because of how sharply the ceiling sloped.

The cupboard was fitted flush against the wall, painted

in the same off-white as the rest of the room. It had concealed hinges. There was no handle. If you didn't know it was there, you could easily overlook it.

I couldn't hide in there.

No way. Not possible.

Not with my claustrophobia.

But inside the cupboard – just past the Hoover and to the right and within careful reaching distance – was a small toolbox.

Sam and I kept it there in case I needed a screwdriver or a pair of pliers when Sam was out because I obviously couldn't go down into the basement for the rest of our tools.

Inside the toolbox there was also a tape measure. Chisels. Hooks and screws.

And resting on the lid of the toolbox was the hammer that I'd used to hang Sam's framed *X-Files* poster.

If I reached inside for the toolbox, I might be able to use the tools to force my way through the French doors. Or I could smash the glass with the hammer if I had to. Defend myself if it came to it.

The cupboard door was secured by a push latch. I knew it squeaked.

Should have oiled it before now.

I looked back across the bedroom towards the doorway. They weren't up here yet, but I was past pretending I could hear any noises they might be making over the crashing of my pulse in my ears.

And once I opened the door, I'd have the hammer. Once I had the hammer—

I pressed the door.

The latch creaked and clunked as it sprang open just slightly.

Then the door swung back as if of its own accord.

And that's when I screamed.

44
Sam

Sam extended his hand towards the Librarian in slow increments. He still felt calm and in control but, even so, he had his doubts. How could he not? It was as if his mind was playing tricks on him.

He understood why, of course. He was familiar with the emotional and logical processing that was going on.

For instance, in one part of his brain some of his thoughts were already jumping ahead to possible future scenarios.

Bad scenarios.

Like the Librarian stabbing him in the hand, or lashing out and thrusting the scissor blades deep into his neck.

'I'm sorry,' the Librarian spluttered again.

'It's OK,' Sam said, focusing all his concentration on the Librarian, trying to quieten his doubts. 'You don't have anything to be sorry for. You haven't done anything wrong.'

Yet.

Sam took a breath and stretched his arm out further.

And in another part of his brain, an old childhood memory stirred. It was from when he was eight, visiting a zoo on a school trip. He could remember how he'd put his hand out slowly, so slowly, towards a glass tank where a Central African rock python was nestled.

The python had been coiled up, unmoving, but although the snake seemed thoroughly uninterested in Sam and his classmates, and even though the inch-thick glass had been between them, a part of Sam had still believed that *somehow* the snake might uncoil, strike, sink its fangs into his wrist.

The power of thoughts.

The irrationality of fear.

Very slowly, Sam rested his tongue on his bottom lip and began to rotate his wrist, turning his palm upwards.

'It's OK,' Sam told the Librarian. 'Just look at me and listen to my voice. I'm going to count to three and then you're going to pass the scissors to me. Understand?'

The Librarian whined at the back of his throat with a sound like a dentist's drill.

'One,' Sam said.

'I don't think I can do this,' the Librarian told him.

'Two.'

Very carefully, Sam turned his head and glanced quickly at the Artist. She was watching him with her face scrunched up as if she was bracing herself for something terrible to happen.

Trust me.

'Ready?' he asked the Librarian.

'No, no, I'm just—'

Sam exhaled again, holding his palm steady, thinking of that big snake behind the glass cage, wondering if he was about to feel its fangs piercing his skin all these years later.

'Three.'

45

My scream slipped out hot and ragged, sharp as a blade in my throat.

I stopped myself as soon as I could, clamping a hand over my mouth, and in the silence that followed there was only Bethany.

Bethany, who had flopped forwards out of the cupboard where she shouldn't have been.

Bethany, whose eyes were shut and whose body was slack and whose wrists had been bound together in front of her waist with the scarf that she'd been wearing around her neck.

She didn't stir when her body hit the floor.

She was completely out of it.

I bit down on my lip so hard it burst inside my mouth with a hot splash of blood.

My scream raged on inside my head, getting louder, more desperate.

I pressed my other hand over my mouth, flattening my lips against my gums. My entire body shook with the effort of holding it in.

But it was already too late.

Footsteps on the attic stairs, thumping upwards, hard and fast.

'Bethany.' I took hold of her shoulders and shook her. 'Bethany, please.'

I whipped my head towards the doorway as Donovan rushed in and skidded to a halt. He eyed me carefully, then swung his head towards the open cupboard door, switching his gaze between me and Bethany, assessing, reassessing.

'You weren't supposed to see that.'

Her, I wanted to yell at him, but instead I hurriedly checked that Bethany's airways were clear, swept her hair away from in front of her face, put my cheek next to her mouth.

She was breathing shallowly. Her chest was rising and falling. I could see a rapid flickering beneath her eyelids.

'What did you do to her?' I asked.

He didn't answer me. I felt around her scalp, tilted her head from side to side.

'Did you hit her?'

'Move away from her.'

'We need to get help. We need to—'

'I said *move*,' he told me, and strode towards me so fast that I let go of Bethany and scuttled backwards until my spine and shoulder blades butted up against the metal frame of the daybed, my backside grazing the floor, my fingers twisting in the carpet pile.

'Stay away from me,' I told him.

He looked at me without saying anything for a few seconds. There was an ice pack in his hand. He must have taken it from our freezer. I'd stocked up on ice packs after Sam had suffered one DIY mishap too many.

'Don't scream again,' he said. 'Don't shout. I can't be responsible for what happens if you do that.'

My chest juddered as I looked at Bethany on the floor in front of him. I couldn't see any obvious signs of bruising or abrasions. There was no blood. No swelling.

He must have drugged her, I thought, and then I looked down at my arm again, at the spot of blood on the inside of my elbow.

A cold shudder rippled through me.

'Breathe,' Donovan said. 'Do not freak out.'

He ducked abruptly from the waist, setting the ice pack aside and slipping his hands under Bethany's armpits.

'What are you doing?' I asked him.

He manhandled Bethany into a seated position, grunting and gasping as he slid her body back inside the cupboard. I could see her handbag in there. Her phone had been in it. I realized too late that I should have tried for the hammer when I'd had my chance.

'Stop this.'

He ignored me, folding her legs in after her, swinging the cupboard door shut against her feet, forcing it closed.

He'd put both his gloves back on, I noticed, and I had an awful feeling about it. Gloves meant no fingerprints, no forensic evidence.

I was still reckoning with the implications as he straightened into an upright position, towering over me.

Too big. Too close.

I didn't look up past his shoes and legs. I shrank back further.

Was anyone outside on the street, I wondered? Had they heard my scream?

I didn't know, but I did know that the houses on either

side of me were currently empty. The Taylor family was on holiday. I'd seen John walking away down the street.

And I was in the attic at the back of the house. *We* were in the attic. Where sound might not travel very far. Where my scream had probably been contained and trapped.

Like me.

I shuddered, looking down at my arm again, at the spot of blood on the inside of my elbow.

Had he injected me with the same drug as Bethany or something different? Perhaps he'd given me a smaller dose and that was why I was still conscious.

'Here.' He dropped into a squat in front of me, reaching for the ice pack and tossing it onto the floor between us. 'For your head.'

The pack landed with a wet crump, the ice inside crackling.

Like the thump I'd heard from downstairs, I thought.

Did that mean Bethany had collapsed immediately or had she tried to fight back?

'She'll be fine in a few hours. Provided you cooperate. I don't want to have to hurt either of you.'

As if he had no control over that. As if hurting us would somehow be *my* fault.

Somewhere inside my mind I could hear the distant rush and gurgle of water. I could feel fast hands grappling with my throat, pushing me down.

It's happening again.

It's happening now.

'Lucy?'

I shrank back even more, feeling a bloom of heat from

the scar running along my arm, worrying what the needle mark might mean, what was going to happen next.

I kept looking at the cupboard door, thinking of Bethany on the other side of it, wondering if I'd be like her before long, if either of us would get out of this alive.

'Stay with me.'

But it was a struggle to marshal my thoughts. They were tumbling into one another. Hazy memories and the present moment were overlapping, duplicating, getting scrambled, mixed up.

I almost choked on the slick of warm blood spilling from my lip.

'Why?' I whispered.

'We'll get to that. I'm going to explain everything to you.'

Everything.

As if there was more to this than what he'd done to Bethany and my own terror and confusion.

'Try the ice pack,' he said again. 'I need you thinking straight. It'll help.'

With what, I wondered?

Not with whatever this was, or whoever he was, or with anything that was happening right now.

And anyway, the pain in my head was one thing. A diminished thing. Whereas Bethany and her well-being were everything.

'She could choke,' I said. 'She could get sick or stop breathing or—'

'She won't.'

He sounded so controlled. So certain.

'You can't just leave her shut in there. You have to let me help her. You have to—'

'Why don't you stop worrying about Bethany and start focusing on yourself?'

Oh God.

'You're going to have questions,' he said. 'I understand that. And that's OK because I have questions too. There's a lot we need to discuss.'

46

Sam

The Librarian squeezed his eyes shut, hissed air through his teeth and then, very gently, placed the scissors in Sam's palm.

Sam's heart flipped over. His hand felt strangely inert, the scissors oddly heavy.

He didn't move as the Librarian cracked his eyes open and stared down in shock and awe, then spat out a mouthful of air and withdrew his hand fast, cradling it to his chest.

'Thank Christ for that,' the Boxer muttered.

'It's OK,' Sam told the Librarian, patting his arm. 'You did really well.'

The Librarian's mouth moved soundlessly. He nodded several times. Then his face collapsed and he bowed his head and he started to sob, big wracking cries that rocked his spindly shoulders and chest.

'It's all right,' Sam told him, reaching down to place the scissors safely on the floor behind his seat, then crouching forwards and resting a hand on the Librarian's upper back. 'Take your time. It's OK.'

He rubbed the area between the Librarian's prominent shoulder blades and looked at the others in the room.

They all seemed to breathe a collective sigh of relief. Some of them shook their heads. Others just blinked.

The Artist had extended a hand towards the Athlete, Sam noticed, bracing it against his upper arm. The Boxer was scrubbing a palm across his bald head. The Lost Girl gnawed her thumbnail.

'How about the rest of you step outside and give us a few minutes?' Sam suggested.

The Artist squirmed. 'We could just go?'

'No,' Sam told her. 'Please don't do that. There's a final exercise I want us to run through before next time. But if one of you could go to my backpack on the desk over there and unzip the top pocket, you'll find some tokens for the vending machine down the hall. Help yourselves to drinks, then come back, OK?'

When nobody moved, Sam rubbed the Librarian's back again and asked, 'Would some water help?'

'I . . . Yes, I think so?' He glanced cautiously at the others in the room. 'Please?'

The Artist pushed her mouth to one side, glancing at the others before shrugging. 'Fine, I guess.'

'I'll get the tokens,' the Athlete offered.

He crossed the room, keeping his attention on the Librarian, then picked up Sam's backpack and reached for the zipped pouch on the front before stopping.

'It's already open.'

'I'm sorry?'

'Your backpack. But . . .' He scooped his hand into the pocket and removed a handful of plastic tokens. 'It's OK, I found them. Are you sure you don't want one of us to stay with you?'

'No,' Sam told him, meanwhile thinking with some puzzle-ment about his backpack. He couldn't remember unzipping the compartment himself, but then again, he hadn't checked it since he'd stashed it in his locker before his lecture. Had he secured the lock on his locker? He couldn't remember. 'There's really no need. It would be better if you could give us a few minutes to talk.'

47

My blood ran cold.

A lot we need to discuss.

As if he'd come here for a reason.

As if it's all about me.

Again, I shook my head. A physical denial. An expression of dismay and disgust.

I told myself he was just messing with me, manipulating me, keeping me frightened and off balance.

Which was working, obviously, because I was beyond frightened now.

I was scared out of my mind.

He was watching me closely. Breathing steadily. Apparently unfazed by what was happening and what he'd done.

He'd surprised and overpowered Bethany. She was right there inside the cupboard next to me. But not only that, he'd done it quickly and efficiently. He'd been brutal and ruthless and eerily calm afterwards.

All I had heard was her fractured yelp and the two quick thumps that had followed and then nothing else. A woman had been attacked in my home, in the middle of my street in the middle of London, and the man in front of me had subdued her, bundled her inside a cupboard and made it back to my bedroom in less time than it had taken me to come upstairs to find him.

He didn't appear shaken or unnerved. He wasn't ashamed or troubled or squeamish. He hadn't *hesitated.*

And something more. He'd obviously paid much closer attention when I'd given him the tour of my home than I'd suspected. I hadn't pointed out the cupboard under the eaves to him but he'd clearly noticed it, logged it, returned to it at short notice.

What else had he seen?

That's when a new horror crashed over me.

The basement.

Was that why he'd spent so long down there, why he hadn't answered me when I'd called down to him? Had he been making some kind of . . . preparations?

No.

A deeper, more primal dread engulfed me.

I'd told him about my claustrophobia. I'd shared my most terrible fear.

I could feel the prospect of it crushing me now. Invisible walls closing in. As if I was trapped in a collapsing Perspex box with no way out, no air.

'Lucy, I'm going to need you to be honest with me. That's the most important thing now. Understand?'

Breath whistled in my lungs, as if I was inhaling through a straw.

Like you've been honest with me? I wanted to ask him. *Or Bethany?*

And then a new thought. A vague but tremulous flicker of hope.

How long would it be until Bethany would be missed, I wondered?

She'd said in her voicemail that her day was 'crazy', so perhaps this wasn't even the last viewing she'd had set up. I knew for a fact that she'd shown our house to potential buyers in the evenings before now. So maybe she was expected elsewhere, or even back at her office. And if she didn't show, then her clients or her colleagues might start to ask questions. They might try to contact her. They'd be concerned for her welfare, surely? The agency she worked for probably had protocols in place, especially when female agents were showing properties to single men.

They'd know she'd been scheduled to meet Donovan. They'd know she was meeting him *here.*

All of this rushed through my mind in a second.

I looked at the cupboard door again, thinking of her mobile phone inside her handbag, digging my nails into my thigh, trying to block out the fear and the confusion and *think.*

How long had Donovan been here? Forty-five minutes? Longer?

He'd told me he wanted to talk. And talking could take time. I could *make* it take time.

Maybe.

Depending on what he wanted to talk *about.*

Plus there was Sam to consider. His support groups usually lasted an hour, give or take. That wasn't definite, things could change, and sometimes he stayed late afterwards – speaking with students, catching up with colleagues in his department, carrying out admin tasks – but if he stayed late, he usually texted me, and if he didn't, he could be home within an hour.

An hour.

My eyes flitted to Donovan's coat, searching for any bulges or bumps where my own phone might be hidden. If Sam texted me, I'd hear it. I hadn't set my phone to silent, unless Donovan had.

Or maybe I can get to my phone or his phone or Bethany's phone.

Maybe I can call for help.

I had to hang on.

As much as I wanted this over, more time was what I needed.

Keep him talking.

'What did you inject me with?' I asked.

48

Donovan looked at me as if I'd said something unhinged.

'You injected me with something,' I told him. 'I felt you do it.'

'I think you may be imagining things, Lucy. It's probably the bang to your head.'

I thrust out my arm, showing him the puncture mark. 'Look.' I pointed. 'What was it? A sedative?'

'You think I drugged you? Why would I drug you?'

I didn't know.

I didn't *want* to know.

But I could feel *something*.

A corrosive heat fizzing under my skin. Contaminating my system. Percolating from cell to cell.

'You drugged Bethany.'

'That was a spur of the moment thing. She wasn't supposed to be here. I'd arranged it so that she wouldn't make it.'

A spur of the moment thing as opposed to what, exactly? And what else had he arranged?

I was so hot my eyeballs seemed to be sweating. My hair was damp and knotted in lank threads that hung before my eyes. My throat raged with thirst, my skin was itchy and blotchy.

Think.

He'd admitted that he'd drugged Bethany. He'd come to my home with the equipment to be able to do that. So perhaps he'd screwed up. Perhaps he'd used too much of the drug on Bethany that he'd planned to use on me.

'Tell me,' I muttered. 'I want to know what you've done to me.'

'I don't understand. You want me to make something up, or . . . ?'

'I want to know what is happening!'

He pushed up to his feet, sweeping back the tails of his coat, plunging his hands into his trouser pockets. His expression was rueful, contemplative, but I could sense something darker lurking beneath it. A focused anger rumbling beneath the surface. I was horrified to think he was reining himself in.

'We'll get to that, but there's something I want to show you first.'

As I watched, he removed his right hand from his pocket and held it before my face with his gloved fingers clenched into a fist, as if he was about to perform a close-up magic trick. He monitored me carefully, eyes ever watchful.

'What is it?'

'Added motivation.'

'For what?'

'For you to follow my instructions and to do exactly what I say when I tell you to do it. No screaming or shouting, remember?'

I waited.

Part of me wondered if he was holding nothing at all. If it was all just a bluff.

But then he opened the bottom half of his fist and – in a glimmer of reflected light – something dangled from his grasp, suspended between his thumb and forefinger.

A set of keys.

Two brass keys. One silver. One a dark, matt metal.

All of them hanging from a simple leather key fob.

One of the brass keys was dulled and oxidized, the other was shiny and new. The silver one gleamed. The dark metal one was thin and flimsy.

I looked closer and something burst inside me, as if a balloon filled with iced crystals had popped inside my stomach.

A tiny Lego figure was attached to the key fob. He was made up of little white and tan plastic components and a blue lightsaber, so that he resembled Luke Skywalker from the *Star Wars* movies.

Sam had a set of keys exactly like it. He'd been a *Star Wars* geek since he was a kid. I'd ordered the little Luke Skywalker figurine over the internet as a gift for him last year.

I backed up against the bed frame so hard that it knocked against the wall behind me.

'That's right. These are Sam's keys. The doorbell before? That was a bike courier. For me. Express delivery.'

The floor dropped away from under me, as if I was trapped in a lift where the cables had failed. I looked again at the

170

cupboard under the eaves, picturing Bethany inside, wondering how much worse this could get.

'Have you done something to Sam? What have you done?'

'Nothing. Yet.' He lifted the keys to the light and studied them idly. 'Sam doesn't even know these are missing.'

He dropped them on the floor in front of me, near to the ice pack.

I reached out for them instinctively, drawing them inwards, cupping them in my palm as I raised them to my face.

I'm not sure what I was hoping for, exactly. I suppose I was seeking some proof that he was lying to me. But the moment I held them, my heart crumpled and turned to dust.

These were definitely Sam's keys.

The flimsy metal key was for the padlock on Sam's locker at work. The old brass key was a spare for John's place next door. The new brass key fitted our front door downstairs. We'd had the lock renewed after I'd selected and installed new brass door furniture. The shiny silver key was for the doors that opened out from our kitchen into the back garden.

The metal of the silver key was untarnished because I didn't think Sam had ever used it. It wasn't as if there was a way into our garden from the rear of the house, so he'd never had any reason to come in that way.

I knew Sam had taken his keys with him this morning because I'd heard him lock the front door when he'd left. He would have zipped them into the front pocket on his backpack, the same way he always did.

'How did you get these?'

'Oh, I didn't,' he said, offhand. 'They were taken earlier today by someone who is helping me. Someone who is with Sam right now. That's the odd thing about his support group, don't you think? He'll let just anyone in.'

49

Sam

Sam was standing with the Librarian over by the windows overlooking the air shaft when the door to the seminar room opened and the rest of the group returned. He'd cracked the window to give the Librarian some air. Talked him down from his heightened state. Assured him it wasn't the first time something like this had happened.

Even if that wasn't strictly true.

Because if Sam was honest with himself, the scissors bothered him.

It had been a close call.

He knew that strictly speaking he should have ordered everyone out and asked them to contact security the moment the situation developed.

Which was probably something the others had discussed among themselves, judging by how they'd fallen into an immediate and awkward hush as they'd shuffled back inside, all of them looking a little shady, a little self-conscious, the Athlete and the Artist seeming to bump against each other because they were standing so close.

'I'm really sorry,' the Librarian said, shamefaced. 'I don't know what came over me before.'

He squinted at them, toed the floor, glanced towards Sam

for reassurance. Sam nodded his understanding, clenching the Librarian's upper arm.

Several long seconds passed before the Boxer grunted an acknowledgement, not giving much away.

The Lost Girl tapped a nail against the can of Diet Coke she was holding.

The Artist looked up at the Athlete, who was holding the door open behind her with his big arm extended above her head.

'Actually, I think we all understand a bit of what you're going through,' the Athlete said. 'Here.'

And he paced across the room to offer the Librarian a bottle of chilled water, clapping him on his other arm when he took it, the Librarian gazing up at him with an expression of gratitude and relief.

'The way I see it, we all came here today for help, right?' the Athlete said, looking around the group. 'We all have our bad moments. So . . .' He shrugged at Sam. 'What's next? Do you want us to all sit back down?'

50

I felt as if Donovan had shoved me backwards into an iced bath. I was stunned.

'There's somebody with Sam?'

'There are five people with Sam, last I heard.' He patted the coat pocket I'd seen him put his phone in earlier. 'It pays to stay updated.'

'They're in touch with you?'

'Well now, it wouldn't be much of a threat if they weren't, would it?'

A threat.

To Sam.

'Who are they? What will they do?'

'Trust me, that really shouldn't be your focus right now.'

'Does Sam know?'

'That's hard for me to say. They're sharing their phobias with him. What do you think? It's their first session. Will he be able to tell one of them is faking?'

I probed my lip with my tongue, the bloodied cut stinging like a tiny voltage.

Cortisol flushed through me.

I had a sudden urge to leap up at him, shove him out of

175

the way, try to get out and contact Sam, but at the same time I knew I had to concentrate.

If it was a lie, it was a horribly plausible one. And if he wasn't lying . . .

'Are they going to hurt Sam?'

'He's not in any more danger than you are right now.'

Not a good answer.

And not a reassuring one, either.

I glanced at the cupboard door again, appalled that Bethany was behind it, crushed by what he'd done.

Then I flashed on an image of Sam in a room with five total strangers. He'd have no reason to suspect that one of them was there under false pretences or that they could be a danger to him.

And Donovan wasn't wrong. I knew that Sam ran an open group. That was the whole point of it. Anybody could walk in and participate.

Sam had shared some concerning stories with me in the past. I knew he sometimes interacted with people who were deeply troubled, not just in his support groups, but for a lot of his private research projects, too. He liked to pass it off as academically interesting, telling me he got jazzed by interacting with people with unusual hang-ups or personality disorders, striving to understand them, but I got that really he didn't want me to worry.

I also knew that he was driven to help people and try to solve their problems, especially if their problems were complex and deep-rooted.

Like mine.

I loved that about him but, right now, it made him vulnerable. Because Sam wouldn't be anticipating any kind of threat and, if a threat came, he wouldn't be skilled at defending himself.

He was tall and gangly, six foot one. Lean, not muscular. Healthy, but not fit. He didn't go to the gym or lift weights. He'd never been in a fight in his life as far as I knew.

He was bookish. Caring. Decent.

He'd been so incredibly patient with me. So understanding. I'd relied on him so much.

And now, just the thought of him being taken from me . . .

I felt my heart rate accelerate. My throat constrict.

'I want to talk to Sam. I have to know he's OK.'

'That's what I'm counting on.'

'You can't hurt him.'

'Then don't make me.'

I felt light-headed. My mouth tasted bitter.

But even as my worries massed in my chest, the thought occurred to me that perhaps the danger to Sam wasn't as immediate as Donovan was making out. I doubted whoever was watching Sam would risk threatening him while four other strangers were in a room with him, would they?

I stared at Sam's keys in my hand, trying to understand the implications of what Donovan was telling me and not telling me.

I was having difficulty with it. There was nothing about my life, or Sam's life, that should have drawn a man like Donovan into our orbit. We weren't the kind of people something like this happened to.

Or are you?

Bad things have happened to you before.

My gaze traced the scar on the inside of my arm until it stopped at the puncture wound close to my elbow.

I couldn't quite fathom what it meant.

Donovan had told me he hadn't drugged me. I had no reason to trust him, but it must have been twenty minutes now since the needle had gone in and I remained conscious and increasingly lucid.

The back of my skull was still tender where I'd banged it. My head hurt with a slow, dull ache. But my vision and my balance were normal again and my nausea had mostly faded.

And the other physical sensations I'd experienced – my shortness of breath, accelerated heart rate, flushes of heat and perspiration – could all be explained by the surplus of adrenaline, panic and fear I'd been subjected to.

But still.

That puncture mark.

I raised the crook of my arm closer to my face, probing my skin. It didn't hurt very much. There was a slight purplish bruising radiating outwards. A reddish halo around the tiny dot of blood in the middle.

Wait . . .

A dangling sensation – as if I was suspended from a thread that was about to snap.

'My toothbrush,' I heard myself say.

'Excuse me?'

I closed my eyes for a second, concentrating. 'I could tell something was wrong when I went into the en suite looking for Bethany. It was something I couldn't quite put my finger on, but that's what it was. My toothbrush was missing.' I opened my eyes and looked at him. 'Why did you take my toothbrush?'

Judders through my chest, radiating outwards, a sudden flush of pins and needles that augured something worse was to come.

And then another thought, cascading onwards.

Logical, but bewildering.

It made a kind of sense, but not the kind of sense I wanted to confront.

'You didn't inject me.'

'I already told you that.'

'But I felt the needle. I felt it sink in.'

This time he said nothing, and I knew I was right.

'Because you weren't injecting me,' I said. 'You were extracting something. You took my blood.'

51

There was a warped soundscape in my ears. My own emergency siren.

My mouth was dry, my pulse tachy and erratic.

I didn't want to ask Donovan the next question but somehow I did. 'Why did you take my blood?'

'Oh, please. We both know the answer to that.'

But I didn't. Truly, I didn't.

Or was that a lie I was telling myself? Was the actual truth that I just didn't want to face up to something horrendous?

I gazed at the cupboard door again and the swirling in my head became louder, more shrill.

Had he taken blood from Bethany, too, I wondered? Were my blood and my toothbrush – what? *Trophies* to him?

My fear cranked up by several notches.

I clenched my fist around the keys in my hand, feeling the metal teeth dig deep into my flesh, a vibrant red flashing at the corners of my vision in tandem with my auditory alarm.

Donovan spread his arms at his sides in a mock-placatory gesture. 'I don't have them any more, if that helps.'

'I don't—? What did—?'

But again I stopped. Because again it hit me.

'The courier,' I said. 'You gave them to the courier.'

Because the courier was the only person who'd called at the house since Donovan had been here. He'd given Donovan Sam's keys. And Donovan had taken my blood and tooth-brush not long before the courier had arrived.

Did that mean Donovan had summoned the courier, or had it all been prearranged, pre-planned?

I wasn't sure which would be worse.

'You gave my blood and my toothbrush to the courier,' I said, staring into the middle distance, as if the answer to what was happening to me was hidden somewhere in this room. 'That's why you were down there so long.'

Donovan watched me struggling to order my thoughts, then he seemed to grow impatient and he twisted at the waist and spun on his heels, flinging out his arms and arching his eyebrows as if he was appraising the space we were in.

'You want a lot of money for this place, am I right?'

'What?'

'I'm saying, you're asking a lot of money for this place.'

'Is that what this is about? The *house*?'

'No, you're not listening to me. I'm making an analogy. I'm painting you a picture.' He reached out and spread his fingers on the sloping ceiling above him. 'You told me you've done most of the renovation work yourself, yes?'

'We did,' I said quietly, confused.

'Right. And let's say I wanted to buy this place. Let's imagine *for just a moment* that's really why I came here today. I don't want to disappoint you, but I have to tell you. A house in London. This borough. Wow, that's a major investment. So even if I liked it and made an offer that you and Sam could accept – and, cards on the table, I really do like what you and Sam have done here – I'd still want to do some checks before my lawyers were ready to exchange and complete. You understand?'

'No.'

'I'm talking about a survey. A thorough one. I'd want my surveyor to check the foundations of this place, search for subsidence, damp, dry rot.' He stamped on the floor as if to demonstrate. 'I'd want them to tell me about anything I should be concerned by. And suppose my surveyor gives me the thumbs-up, well then I'd want my lawyer to do some additional digging. I'd want them to check the title deeds. I'd want to be certain I was really buying what I thought I was buying.'

He shrugged and looked at me again, as if I really should be getting it by now.

'Buyer beware,' he said. 'It's only prudent, right? And you wouldn't have a problem with that. You're the seller. It's what you would expect.

'Well, it's the same with me. I don't want any mistakes, either. I want to be absolutely certain I'm getting exactly what I came here for today. I want my survey to ring all the bells. Hence your toothbrush. Hence your blood. I'm getting an exact DNA match.'

52

Sam

The group all took the same seats as they'd occupied before.
They sat and waited without speaking.

But even though nobody said anything, Sam could tell
that something had changed.

Had he lost their confidence?

Maybe.

Perhaps the incident with the scissors had shaken them
too badly.

Perhaps he should never have broken the continuity, sent
them out of the room, given them an opportunity to bond
without him.

And yet, as disturbing and bewildering as it was to admit,
he felt oddly shaken as he looked at each of them in turn.

The Librarian.

The Athlete.

The Artist.

The Boxer.

The Lost Girl.

What was it?

What felt so . . . off?

It wasn't as if any of them were looking at him strangely
or suspiciously.

They were all sitting there expectantly, even the Librarian, who was rubbing his palms up and down his trouser legs, seeming somehow cleansed and relieved now that the worst had passed.

So Sam couldn't necessarily explain it. There was nothing tangible he could point towards in order to rationalize why his mouth was suddenly tacky, his underarms damp, a clot of invisible phlegm rising up and lodging in his throat.

But it was there.

A negative vibe.

A latent threat.

Almost as if one of the five people sitting around him – or perhaps *more* than one of them – shouldn't have been here at all.

53

'This is insane,' I said. 'None of what you're saying makes any sense.'

'I'm confident your DNA will prove otherwise.'

I grabbed hold of the bed frame, hoisting myself up.

'You're not listening to me.'

'But I am, and meanwhile you're not listening to *me*. We both know this isn't a mistake.'

I cradled my forehead as a crushing weight seemed to press down against me. It was something other than the bang to my head or my fear. I'd begun to sense the hopelessness of our interaction. The futility of trying to talk to him.

Because whatever this was, whatever miscalculation or mix-up he'd made, there was no doubt in my mind that he believed it absolutely.

As I considered that, a new and much more disturbing thought occurred to me.

We both know this isn't a mistake.

But I didn't. I had no clue.

But if he believed it . . .

'Do you know Sam? Have you worked with him?'

He scoffed and studied me with disdain. 'Oh, that's good.' He wagged a finger. 'That's really insulting, actually.'

'Have you?' I pressed.

He leaned back and assessed me from a new angle, then rasped air from his lips, as if whatever patience he'd been holding on to was being stretched dangerously thin. 'And by work with him, you mean at LSE? As what, a colleague? A fellow lecturer?'

'Maybe.'

'Or are you suggesting I'm one of his research subjects? Is that what you're driving at? One of his . . . "special projects"?' He made air quotes with his fingers. 'Because I know what Sam does, Lucy. I've read up on his work. His papers. His areas of expertise. It's all very impressive, if disturbing. There are the support groups, obviously, but that's just the vanilla stuff. I get that he has access to some pretty messed-up people. That he likes to study them one-on-one. So now what you're suggesting is that you think I'm one of those people, is that it?'

He flapped his hands around suddenly, as if he was having a wild seizure, his eyes bulging and then darkening with a burst of anger as he stepped closer and jutted his head towards me.

'And what about Bethany?' He pointed at the cupboard. 'Do you think I did that because I forgot to take my meds? Come on. I know exactly what I'm doing here.' He paused. When he spoke again, I could detect a slight modulation in his voice as if he was struggling to maintain his cool. 'Enough, OK? You want me to spell it out to you? Fine, here it is: I found you. I looked for you and I found you, simple as that.'

'I'm not lost.'

'No,' he said, in a tone that was so subdued he sounded even more dangerous than before, 'but you've been hiding. You've been hiding for a really long time.'

I reached out behind me for the bed frame. Felt my brow tangle.

Before I could say anything more, he plunged a gloved hand inside his coat and removed his phone.

'I texted this earlier.'

He tapped and swiped at the screen aggressively, then rotated his wrist and extended his phone towards me.

'The person with Sam? They recognize you.'

Something inside me lurched.

He was showing me the photograph he'd taken of our main bedroom. I could see myself in the middle of the frame.

Not much of the bedroom was visible around me. The image had been zoomed in tight onto my face and upper body. Or perhaps he'd edited it after taking it. Cropped it.

The focus was exact. My features were clear.

I realized then that he hadn't been interested in taking photographs of our house at all. It had all been about this one picture.

'But that's not going to be enough, is it? Not after two years.'

A sudden threat leaped into his eyes. A predatory hunger.

Two years.

I felt myself teeter.

'That's right, the party, Lucy. We have time. Why don't you tell me what happened? *Make me understand.*'

54

The party.

Somewhere in my head I could hear the music again. The rapid *thrash-thrash-thrash*. People laughing and shouting. Drinks being poured. Lights pulsing and whirling.

And then the lock on the bathroom door.

—click.

The violent shove and the shower curtain that had tangled around me as I'd fallen backwards into the bathtub and the blurred figure who'd cornered me, pressed me down, held me under the water rushing out of the tap.

It had happened so fast. Been so unprovoked.

But staring at Donovan, it was as if the water was filling my throat again, spilling out of my mouth.

I squinted at him until his face became smeared and indistinct.

Oh God.

I almost doubled up and retched.

I knew how quickly he'd overpowered Bethany.

'No.'

I tried stepping back but I had nowhere to go. The bottom of the daybed was pressing against my legs and lower back. I was in danger of tipping backwards over it.

'No, you don't want to talk about it?' he asked me. 'Or no, you won't?'

I raised a hand to cover my throat, my other hand tightening into a fist behind me.

In my head, a part of me was under the bath tap again, snared in the shower curtain, the water pummelling down, strong hands on my shoulders, pinning me there.

'Was it you?' I asked him.

'Was what me?'

I raised my voice. 'WAS. IT. YOU?'

His nostrils flared as he canted his head to one side, a threatening expression forming on his face as he slowly waggled his phone in the air.

'I told you to keep the volume down, Lucy. I'm pretty sure I explained that Sam's life depends on it.'

'Don't you come near me.'

I was shivering. Quaking. A rushing noise in my ears.

My fist tightened behind me, nails digging into my skin.

'Why don't you start by telling me about the roof?'

'I don't—'

'The roof. Start there.'

I shook my head again, faster now.

'I have no idea what you mean.'

'The roof, Lucy. Enough bullshit.'

I peered upwards, groping for the right thing to say. 'I already told you. We had it replaced. We—'

'Not *this* roof. At the party. Tell me what happened when you were up on the roof.'

'There was no roof.'

I stared at him.

The gurgling sounds receded, overlaid by a single, discordant note – a single key played on a mistuned piano.

'Just tell me what happened.'

'Stop fucking with me!'

He glowered and raised one finger, shaking his head in another irate reminder that I needed to be quiet.

I noticed that he'd adjusted his stance, spreading his legs apart, bracing one foot behind him, one in front of him, his coat open and parted around his thighs.

His front foot was perhaps two metres away from me. The toe of his loafer was almost nudging the ice pack that was down on the floor.

I glanced at it, thinking of how he'd tossed it down in front of me, and then his eyes tracked mine and he looked for himself, the skin around his eyes contracting for a fraction of a second, and in that moment I sensed that he was remembering something else and that if I didn't act now then—

I launched myself forwards.

Acting on impulse.

On instinct.

And desperation.

Pushing off from the bed frame, springing forwards from my toes, diving towards him in one fast, explosive leap with Sam's house keys clenched in my closed fist, the new brass key carefully positioned so that its jagged teeth were protruding from between my fingers.

Like a serrated dagger.

A blade.

That I punched down deep into his thigh and—

No.

I was moving inexplicably sideways, spinning around, the room spinning with me.

He'd reacted so fast it took me a moment to recognize that he'd seen my move coming – had anticipated it easily – and had blocked me before I could stab him, forcing my arm to one side, snatching at my wrist with his hand, using my own momentum to twirl me around and draw me into his chest with practised ease.

Like a dance move.

A tango.

Only hard and uncompromising.

A trap.

His arm held me firm as his hand compressed the bones of my wrist. Squeezing harder. Tighter. Remorselessly on.

'Drop the keys,' he said, his breath a hot puff against my face.

I didn't.

He ratcheted up the pressure.

I gurgled in pain.

If I'd thought he was squeezing my wrist badly before, it was suddenly so much worse.

It felt like my bones might disintegrate. I could feel my tendons compressing, bones grinding.

'I said, drop them.'

Still I resisted.

He squeezed even harder again, exerting an impossible force, as if my hand was trapped in a machine vice, my fingers throbbing.

And meanwhile, he pressed his knee into the small of my

back, coiled his other hand around my shoulders with his phone still clenched in it and jerked me backwards and off balance.

I flailed, pushing up onto my toes.

Was this what he'd done to Bethany, I wondered? Was this why she'd yelped?

I still didn't drop the keys.

On one level, I understood that they were useless to me now. He was holding my wrist so securely, and he had my upper body at such an awkward angle, that I had no chance of stabbing him with them.

But I held on anyway.

My stubborn streak.

After what had happened to me in that bathroom I'd sworn to myself I'd never let another man hurt me again.

'You're going to give me answers,' he told me. 'An explanation. I told you I don't want to hurt you and I meant it. But don't push me because that would be a big mistake.'

I cried out as he squeezed my wrist even harder again.

His leather glove twisted my skin until it burned. My bones ached as if they were being heated from within.

Then he squeezed *even harder* and this time I released the keys before I'd made a conscious decision to do it.

They bounced off the floor.

But he didn't release me.

He put his lips to my ear.

'When are you going to get it into your head that this is over for you now? I found you. I swore that I was going to find you and I did.'

'Let me go.'

I stamped on his foot.
Kicked his shin with my heel.
It made no difference.
'I said—'
And that was when the doorbell sounded.
The friendly two-note chime.
Coming from downstairs.

55
Sam

Sam cleared his throat. It wasn't like him to be unsettled or nervous.

'We have five minutes left,' he said, aware of an unfamiliar huskiness in his voice. 'And we've covered a lot of ground today. Plus we've had one or two unexpected moments, I know.'

He risked a smile as he glanced at the Librarian but somehow even this simple expression eluded him, feeling fake, forced.

An awkward silence in the room.

A cough.

Sam looked at the faces in front of him and felt a flutter of disquiet in his thorax.

The moment could only have lasted for a couple of seconds but it seemed much longer. Inside his head he imagined he could hear a faint hissing – the sound of his authority leaking away like air from a balloon.

What was it about today?

'There's just one last thing I'd like to try with you all before you go.'

The Boxer scratched at his ear.

The Lost Girl picked at her nails.

'It's a simple exercise, really. Although you might think it's a bit silly.'

Great. Way to undermine yourself, Sam.

'But it's worked before, I promise. I like to have my groups do this at the end of every session.'

Who was he trying to convince?

Not the Athlete, apparently, who wrinkled his nose as he glanced down at Sam's shoes, as if Sam had trodden in something unpleasant.

And not the Artist, who was surreptitiously checking her watch, as if wondering if she could sneak out early.

'I'd like you to repeat something after me.'

A teetering stillness.

Some embarrassed shuffling.

He might as well have asked them to remove all their clothes.

'It's a sort of mantra that I want us to share as we move forwards as a group. Because I'm really hoping you'll all come back next week. I'm hoping you can support each other as you confront your phobias and push through them together.'

No response.

'So . . . I'll go first and then you can all go afterwards. OK?'

He scanned their faces but none of them gave anything back.

'Actually, it sort of works better if we all hold hands.'

Now they looked at him as if he was a crackpot.

But eventually it was the Athlete who shrugged, sat forwards in his chair and offered his hands to the Librarian and the Artist on either side of him.

Slowly – too slowly – the others joined in, leaving Sam to complete the circle by taking the hands of the Librarian and the Lost Girl, whose hand was very cool in his.

'OK then, here goes. Everyone repeat after me.'

He cleared his throat.

'I'm here for you. You're here for me.'

And then he waited, gripped by the excruciating, unfamiliar certainty that he was completely on his own.

56

We both froze.

Donovan's breath scoured my cheek.

I could feel how still and tense he'd become.

He isn't expecting this.

'Not a word,' he told me, and then he withdrew his hand from around my shoulders while still clenching my wrist, pocketed his phone and ducked down briefly to scoop up Sam's keys before standing again and raising my wrist way up behind me with my elbow straight, forcing me to pivot forwards from my hips, and walking me to the top of the stairs.

He held me there, suspended above the stairwell as I looked back towards the cupboard where Bethany was trapped, my wrist and arm stiff and aching, my hair dangling in front of my face. Could it be Sam at the door? I didn't think so. Not unless his support group had finished early for some reason.

'Down.'

I was leaning so far forwards I would have fallen without Donovan holding me up. His grip on my wrist was relentless. I was scared my arm might break if I stumbled. As I awkwardly negotiated the stairs, I had to strain to look out of the tops of my eyes at the way ahead, the pain thumping absently in the back of my skull.

At the bottom of the stairs he used the same technique to steer me through my bedroom towards the middle window closest to the sofa, where he finally released my wrist and braced me against the wall with his hand on my upper arm, his arm straight, elbow-locked, before reaching out to separate the blades of the shutter blind.

I rubbed the tender skin of my wrist as he looked down towards the front of our house.

My arm felt strangely weightless, numbed, my bones rubbery and weak.

'Are you expecting anyone?' he asked me quietly.

I didn't say anything.

'Answer me,' he said, pinning me harder against the wall.

'No.'

'No, you're not expecting anyone?'

'That's what I said.'

He rose up on his toes, peering downwards.

The doorbell sounded a second time.

I listened for the sound of the doorbell app on my phone coming from his coat, but I couldn't hear it.

Then he adjusted his grip, pulling me sideways until I could see what he was looking at. 'Who is that?'

I could see John – or rather, the top of his head and his angular, bird-like shoulders, the tan raincoat he had on and the pale moon of his scalp where his hair had thinned. There was something in his shopping bag now. The opaque plastic was stretched and weighted down by it.

'It's our neighbour, John.'

'What does he want?'

'I don't know. Maybe he heard me scream?'

'No, that's not it. I saw him before. He was outside when the courier came.'

I didn't say anything to that. Obviously I'd seen John, too. I'd also seen the confusion and concern that had crossed his face.

'Sometimes when he's on his way to the shops he asks if we need anything?' I suggested.

'He has a shopping bag already.'

Donovan thrust his face next to mine to get a better angle on John.

Was Sam's phone still off, I wondered? Because he had the same doorbell app as me. Perhaps he'd answer on his phone and start wondering why I wasn't answering the door myself.

'He's not leaving,' Donovan muttered.

I swallowed with some difficulty.

'The lights are on,' I told him. 'He knows I'm home.' I hesitated. 'He's ex-police.'

Donovan leaned back from the window and gave me a sideways look.

'It's true,' I told him quickly. 'John worked for the Met before he retired.'

'Well, isn't that just perfect.'

The doorbell rang for a third time.

'He's not going to give up,' I said. 'John won't. He's not the type.'

Donovan growled and spun me around, then marched me across the room towards the landing, meanwhile fumbling his phone from his pocket and juggling it in his hand, tapping it with his thumb, clamping it to his ear.

'Pick up,' he muttered. 'Pick—'

His call was answered and he immediately began to speak in a low voice.

'Are you still in the room with him?'

It took several seconds before I heard a muffled response. *'I'm here for you. You're here for me.'*

The delivery sounded off and it took me a second to realize that I was actually hearing more than one person talking. And there was something unusual about the reply, too. The cadence and the flat, forced tone of it. It sounded like the people in Sam's support group were repeating a chant.

'Keep listening,' Donovan said. 'This line stays open. We have company. If you hear anything you don't like, you know what to do.'

'Sam?' I shrieked. 'Sam, can you hear me?'

Donovan swore and snatched his phone away, slamming me against the wall.

Pain lit up across my side.

The breath was knocked out of me.

'He can't hear you.' His pupils were two dark orbs, sucking in any light. 'The person on the other end of this call? They're wearing a concealed earpiece. Sam won't even know they answered my call. But they're listening very carefully to us. Understand?'

A chill permeated my torso.

I nodded.

I understood.

I also sensed that I'd pushed Donovan about as far as I dared for the moment.

'Good,' Donovan said. 'Then let's go and answer your door together. And don't try anything stupid because I guarantee you it won't just be Sam who suffers if you do. Remember, there's plenty of space upstairs in that cupboard next to Bethany for your neighbour, too.'

57

He rushed me down the stairs with his hand gripping the sleeve of my jumper up by my shoulder, holding his phone ahead of us, the screen angled our way. The information on-screen included the number he'd called but no name.

I listened hard, hoping I might catch a scrap of what was being said, hear Sam, think of some way to warn him.

But there was nothing.

Just silence and the faint crackle of the speaker and the sticky thudding of my heart in my chest.

Until I heard the chant again. Louder this time, more composed.

'I'm here for you. You're here for me.'

I almost wished it was anything else.

Then we reached the bottom of the stairs. The front door was ahead of us, the hallway mirror to my right.

I wanted to sprint for the door, haul it open, burst through, flee.

But one glance in the mirror – at the shock and horror on my face, and the determination and intensity on Donovan's – made me push that instinct deep down inside me.

I believed him about the danger Sam was in.

I believed his threat about John.

I'd seen what he'd done to Bethany.

'Listen to me,' he said. 'You're going to open the door and get rid of him. Keep it simple. Make it fast. Because I promise you this: if he comes inside, what happens next is on you.'

He measured me, watching the impact of his words land, then he urged me forwards and took several paces to my left, adopting a position just inside the threshold of the living room but out of sight of the bay window, where he wouldn't be seen from outside, raising his phone towards his mouth.

'Opening the door now,' he said to the unknown person who was watching Sam.

I glanced at the mirror again, tugging down the sleeve of my jumper so that both sleeves matched. I straightened my hair and shoulders, wincing a little as my hair snagged on the cut to the back of my head.

I still looked a mess. No use pretending otherwise.

'I don't know what to say,' I said.

'Think of something. Improvise. Act normal.'

How, I wanted to ask him?

Because nothing about this situation was normal. Not one thing about what was happening to me was normal in any way.

I'd been this scared before. Once. But the episode in the bathroom, jumbled and fragmented as it was in my mind, had been over in seconds. It had been horrifying, disabling, inexplicable. And yes, its impact had lingered and haunted me, but it hadn't been like this. There hadn't been the sustained fear, the open threats. Nobody else had been at risk.

And it hadn't happened inside my own home.

I think that's what was scaring me more than anything else. I'd invited this danger in.

And now he's making you keep it inside with you.

Movement outside.

John had shifted to his left, as if he was trying to peer in through the frosted glass panel at the side of the front door, backlit yellow by the street lighting.

'Open the damn door,' Donovan told me.

I took three steps, reached out a hand that seemed to belong to someone else and touched the lever on the snap lock.

To my side, Donovan retreated a step further, thrusting his phone out towards me in his gloved hand, the call counting relentlessly onwards.

Part of me almost wished John would simply go away. I was scared of him getting hurt. Afraid he might make things worse.

But more than that, I dreaded being so near to a way out and denying it to myself. I wasn't sure I could be that brave.

I levered down the snap lock and parted the door from the seal.

A slight sucking noise.

The wisp of a breeze.

Then I swung the door fully open.

Opened my mouth.

And didn't say a word.

58

Sam

'Thank you, all,' Sam said, clapping his hands once, then rubbing them together. 'Unless anyone has anything to add, I think we're done for today.'

Everyone released the hands they were holding, meanwhile also exchanging fleeting, abashed smiles, glancing down to gather up their bags or rucksacks, standing, patting their pockets as if they might have somehow left something behind, none of them quite looking at Sam or acknowledging him, but all of them clearly uncomfortable and awkward and unsure about the session and how it had concluded.

Perhaps he should have ditched the mantra.

Or maybe he was just having a bad day.

Was he losing his touch?

And then another, more seismic worry.

Would one of them report what had happened with the Librarian to the university?

It was the last thing Sam needed right now because he was convinced there was a whispering campaign against him in the department. He knew for a fact that several colleagues had voiced concerns about his support groups and some of his research subjects. The incident with the Librarian and the scissors could give his detractors just the ammunition they needed to make his life difficult.

Murmurs in the room. A hesitant cough.

The Librarian was mumbling something next to him, another watery apology for his behaviour, his body hunched, shifting his weight between his feet as if he needed to pee, but Sam's attention was drawn to the Athlete and the Artist, the way they were chatting with their heads close together as they lifted their bags onto their shoulders and moved towards the door.

'Um, Professor?'

A tug from behind.

'Do you have a few minutes? There's something I'd like to talk to you about.'

59

John peered at me with dazed and milky eyes. His lips squirmed. His mouth opened wide.

Then he took a step backwards and said, 'This isn't my house.'

My heart plummeted. I suppressed a groan.

Close up, the cuffs and tails of his raincoat were torn and stained. He was wearing old, discoloured plimsolls beneath his suit trousers. His cheap plastic shopping bag rustled in the wind.

He hadn't shaved. Or if he had, he'd shaved badly. There were tufts of whitish hair spiralling out from his cheeks and ears.

'This is not my house,' he said again, gruffer now, his tone edging into belligerence as if his mistake was somehow my fault.

My eyes stung as I shook my head.

I looked at John and wished it had been one of his good days. I wished he hadn't shown up like this, bewildered and lost.

'No,' I whispered. 'You're right, John, it's not.'

'Where is my house? What have you done with it?'

I didn't answer him. I just stayed quiet, still, only too aware of how closely Donovan was studying me.

My skin speckled with gooseflesh as he stepped slowly out from his hiding spot, his head at an inquisitive angle as he came to stand next to me at the door.

He kept his phone up at his side, relaying our conversation to his accomplice.

A long, awful moment as he looked at John. He took his time over it, absorbing and evaluating the situation. Then he leaned very close to my ear and said, 'Ex-Met?'

'It's true,' I snapped.

But that had been a long time ago.

'So . . .' Donovan paused. 'What do you suggest we do now?'

I didn't answer him.

I didn't know what to say.

I felt as lost and adrift as John appeared.

This was crazy.

This entire situation was crazy.

I was standing in the doorway to my own home, tethered by a phone call to a stranger who'd been tasked with watching Sam and harming him if I made a wrong move.

The street I lived on was right in front of me.

If I leaned out and looked to my right, I would see some of the builders working on the home renovation across the street. I could hear the stereo they had blaring from the scaffolding.

Directly opposite was the shadowed hump of the Dutch bike with the cargo box on the front of it which a dad who lived across the road used to transport his kids to and from school.

It was all so familiar to me, so tangible and real, but right now it seemed oddly distorted and fake, even staged.

My eyes flicked to Donovan's phone. Its screen was still lit, the call still live.

'What do you think?' Donovan was speaking quietly from the corner of his mouth. 'Should I invite him in?'

John's feet scuffed the path as he stared at us in turmoil, the plastic shopping bag he was carrying hanging limply at his side.

I wanted so badly for him to snap back into a moment of clarity. I wanted him to sense how very wrong this all was.

'No.'

'You're sure?'

'John,' I pleaded. I could hear the desperation in my voice. 'John, your house is next door.'

I waited for him to move, but he didn't. He looked at me as if he hadn't heard me at all.

'John, please.'

Still nothing.

I glanced behind him and scanned the windows of the houses opposite, some lit, others not, searching to see if anyone else was looking, if anyone could see.

People around here would know John. Not well, perhaps – not as well as Sam and me – but if they were observant they'd probably know enough to be concerned if they saw him wandering about in circles, angry, upset.

'Tell you what,' Donovan said, interrupting my thoughts. 'I think it's best we help the gentleman home, don't you? That would be the neighbourly thing to do.'

60

There was something in his voice. Something I didn't like.

I spun towards him, a sucking contraction in my chest. 'You can't hurt him.'

'Me? You involved him in this. You're the one who said he wouldn't go away.'

'You've seen him,' I said, lowering my voice. 'You can tell what he's like.'

'And he's seen me inside your house. That doesn't change.'

I whipped my head around, checking on John.

Time seemed to lag.

John blinked back at me, his lips and brow twisted, his jaw slack, his pupils dulled and mired in his own tragic mental loop.

I ached for him.

This wasn't the first time he'd turned up like this. Sometimes he was worse. He could be agitated or angry or frightened. Sometimes I was the one who helped him home, but usually it was Sam.

Sam was just naturally good with John. He was patient and understanding. He was never patronizing. His academic expertise wasn't in dementia but he'd read up on it following John's diagnosis and he'd learned enough to help.

You have to sense that something's wrong, I thought, staring imploringly at John now. *You have to get that Sam isn't here and somebody else is. Can't you see the state I'm in?*

But if he did sense it, he didn't show it. Or more likely he was locked in his own bewildered angst.

'Outside,' Donovan said, pushing me forwards onto the damp concrete. 'Stay close.'

The world seemed eerily hushed. Full darkness had almost fallen and the temperature with it.

A loud clatter made me jump and I looked to my right to see that one of the builders had tossed a tool bag into the back of his van, slamming the cargo doors closed. They would be nearing the end of their working day and leaving soon.

'Guess I'd better lock up,' Donovan said. 'You can't be too careful these days.'

He fished in his coat pocket for Sam's keys and fitted them into the lock on the front door.

The tumblers tumbled. The snap lock engaged.

—*click.*

The sound seemed to snap something inside me and I didn't speak as Donovan spun away from the door, pocketed Sam's keys and showed me his phone again. The call remained live. It had already lasted for more than four minutes.

Somebody is definitely listening in.

They're paying close attention.

'Same rules as before,' he told me. 'No shouting. No running. No bullshit. No tricks.'

I prodded at the cut on my lip with my tongue. My sweat had dried across my forehead, cooling on my skin.

'Break the rules and you'll get other people hurt.'

Leaning sideways, he made a show of looking past me at John, then he raised his phone towards his chin and cupped it in his palm under his mouth.

'We're outside,' he said, to whoever was on the other end. 'Do not let him out of your sight.'

I tried – and failed – to hide the shudder that passed through me.

Then I started.

The doors on the cab of the builder's van had slapped shut with a sound like gunshots. A few seconds later there was the throaty rasp and blurt of a diesel engine before the van swung out from the kerb and pulled away.

I tried not to let it bother me. Tried not to feel abandoned and alone.

Other people would be coming home soon, I told myself. But secretly I knew that wasn't true. Many of the people who lived here had demanding jobs in the City that often required them to work late into the evening.

'Do you know where my house is?' John asked me.

'It's next door, John,' I said. 'I'm Lucy. Your neighbour. I live with Sam, remember?'

He stared at me blankly.

'It's just next door,' I said again. 'I'll show you.'

I reached out stiffly and guided him by his shoulders towards the gate at the end of our path. His bones felt brittle under my hands. His steps were palsied. His plastic shopping bag banged repeatedly against his shuffling legs.

Even though I couldn't run away or shout for help, I was aware that every step I took was being recorded by the doorbell camera. As Donovan followed me along the path, I wondered if he knew that, too.

Somehow, the metal gate seemed to burn my hand as I pushed it aside and then we were out on the pavement together.

'Wait.'

Donovan signalled for me to stay put as he carried out a quick sweep of the street.

While he did so, I glanced down at the pavement to my side.

And stopped.

'No cracks,' I heard myself say.

He peered at me as if I wasn't making any sense.

'No cracks.' I pointed. 'And no uneven flagstones. No tree roots poking through.'

'What are you talking about?'

But I didn't reply.

I was thinking. Remembering. Reinterpreting what I'd seen earlier with what I now knew.

I thought of how the schoolgirl who'd fallen off her scooter had been crying when I'd come outside and found her with Donovan kneeling next to her. How her breath had hitched and her eyes had brimmed with tears when she'd pulled her wrist free of his grasp. I'd thought he was helping her, but—

'She was afraid of you,' I said, seeing it clearly for the first time. 'The girl on the scooter. I thought she was crying because she'd fallen and hurt herself, but that wasn't it, was it?'

Because I hadn't actually seen it for myself, had I? I'd seen the before and after.

There had been the footage of her scooting along on our

doorbell camera with her mother following after her with her attention on her phone. And then when I'd come outside I'd seen Donovan tending to the girl.

But I'd only heard her shriek. I hadn't seen her fall.

'You pushed her,' I said.

'Did I?'

'Why would you—?'

But I stopped myself because I knew the answer to that question.

When I'd come outside, I'd seen exactly what he'd wanted me to see. I'd seen him caring for a helpless schoolgirl.

I'd immediately thought he was kind and considerate. I'd half convinced myself he was a doctor. Someone who wouldn't present any threat if I invited him in.

He'd played it very carefully, very skilfully.

When I'd told him that Bethany was running late, he'd allowed me to believe that he was prepared to wait for her. But then he'd implied he had to be somewhere else and that he didn't have long before he needed to go.

Which was obviously a lie.

So much of it was a lie.

I felt as if someone had kicked my legs from under me.

'What if I'd seen you?'

'Seen me?' He pouted and glanced back at the doorbell for a moment. 'Funny thing about cameras. Once you know they're there, they'll only see what you want them to see. Word of advice: you and Sam should really be a lot more careful with your passwords.'

As I watched, he toggled his phone from the ongoing call to his contact to an app showing the live feed from our doorbell camera. It was the same app I had on my phone. I could see real-time footage of myself, Donovan and John at the end of our path. He must have logged into our system using our username and password.

'Amazing how simple they make it to delete recordings,' Donovan mused, meanwhile thumbing a menu option and opting to delete all footage from the previous two hours. 'Probably best if I switch it off for now, wouldn't you say?'

I shuddered, trying to ride out the hit he'd landed.

'She saw you,' I said. 'The schoolgirl. And her mum. They'll remember you. They can describe you.'

'Maybe I don't care if they do. Seems to me we were still out here on the street when they left, weren't we?'

'There's Bethany, too.'

He hummed. 'For now.'

And then he strode on along the pavement, leaving me staring back towards the outside of our home.

I felt numb, powerless.

The indoor lights were glowing from behind the shutter blinds and through the fanlight window above our front door. Oblongs of warm yellow shone out from the French doors of Sam's attic study, throwing the topiary on the balcony into sharp relief.

To an outsider, it probably looked like a perfectly pleasant, perfectly blameless house.

'Lucy?' He swung open the gate leading towards John's property. 'Shall we?'

61

Sam

The Lost Girl stayed behind with Sam after the others had left the room. As Sam looked at her, he sensed a strange, nervy tension coming from her. And now that it was just the two of them he began to see that she was a few years older than he'd taken her for. Twenty-three or twenty-four, he guessed.

What possible events in her past could have caused her to postpone coming to university until now, he wondered? Could they have something to do with her sleeping phobia?

'How can I help?' he asked.

'Right.' A breath. 'The thing is . . .'

She scrunched up her face and bit down on her pierced lip, adjusting the strap of the heavy bag on her shoulder with her purple nails. As she did so, he noticed a small, amateurish tattoo on the inside of her wrist for the first time.

'Yes?'

'I was wondering, with my sleep deprivation and everything.' She dipped her head and he caught the shimmer of something plastic in her ear, beneath her hair. Another piercing, he supposed. 'Being so tired is definitely impacting my studies. And I have this essay due next week that I'm not sure how I'm going to get done with being so exhausted all the time. So I wondered, do you think you could write my tutor an email for me? I just thought it might sound more credible coming from you.'

62

John's keys were in his coat pocket. Donovan watched me closely as I fitted them in the lock and shouldered my way in through his door.

Today's unopened post collected in a drift by my feet.

The hallway smelled of dust and mould and heat from the radiators. John had a habit of setting the thermostat too high.

When I flipped on the hallway lights, an old patterned carpet and faded wallpaper sprang out of the darkness.

I stepped aside as John trudged past me, seeing a little of the tension go out of his body as his surroundings became familiar to him again.

But when I turned to leave, Donovan stepped forwards and blocked my way, moving in behind me, closing the door.

'Oh, I think we should both make sure John's properly settled, don't you? You can start by helping him with his shopping.'

I clenched my jaw, shaking my head.

Donovan acted surprised, raising his phone towards his mouth, hoisting an eyebrow.

'Sure you want to say no to me?'

I glared at him some more, feeling my anger churn inside,

until I turned away and caught up to John, gently easing the plastic shopping bag from his grip, the bag straining, its contents banging dully. John turned his face towards me, a lost and searching look in his eyes.

'It's OK,' I told him quietly. 'I'm going to take care of you.'

'We both are, John,' Donovan said.

He waited until I looked at him again, then made a show of speaking into his phone.

'I'm going to hang up now,' he said. It was clear he was talking for my benefit as well as for whoever his accomplice was. 'You can let him leave but follow him home. Message me when you're close.'

Slowly, he moved his index finger to hover over the icon to end the call. When he pressed down, the phone emitted a low auditory chirp.

I felt hollowed out.

Foolish, maybe, because on one level I should have been relieved that the immediate threat to Sam had subsided, but it still felt as if a link that had been tethering me to him had been abruptly severed.

I was on my own again, at least until Sam got here, which I now understood was something Donovan wanted to happen.

Why was that, I wondered? What did he have planned for us both?

It normally took Sam around forty minutes or so to get home. I honestly couldn't tell, in the moment, if it would be a good thing or a bad thing if he got here sooner or later than that.

'You know,' Donovan said, 'if you keep staring at me that way I'm going to start thinking you don't like me very much.'

'Go to hell.'

He pocketed his phone, then stepped up behind John and removed his coat.

'John, why don't you take a seat? Make yourself comfortable. Leave us to put these things away.'

John looked at me again with the same misted, faraway gaze. I reached out and squeezed his arm, nodding for him to go ahead and do as Donovan suggested, feeling a pang deep inside as he turned without protest and shuffled off into his front room.

Once he was gone, Donovan immediately searched through John's coat pockets, removing a wallet that he flipped open and scanned – he only seemed interested in John's ID – before pausing when he discovered a boxy Nokia mobile, then breaking it apart, removing the SIM card and battery with deft efficiency.

He returned the useless handset to John's coat and draped it over the banister at the bottom of the stairs. The SIM card and battery he tipped into an umbrella stand by the door.

I felt horrible.

First there was John, who had no idea how dangerous Donovan was. Then there was Sam, who had no clue what was happening and what he might be returning home to face. And finally there was Bethany.

I was aware I was physically shaking again. I seemed incapable of controlling it.

'You go after him,' Donovan said, pointing behind me towards the room John had entered.

'No, I want to leave.'

I stared at him, holding my ground.

Donovan didn't seem impressed or perturbed, preferring to gaze up the stairs towards the landing instead.

'You said he lives here alone?'

'Yes.'

'Not lying to me again, are you?'

I felt my nostrils pinch. A squirmy throbbing at the back of my head. I resisted the urge to reach up and cup my hand over the cut to my scalp.

'I already told you. There's nobody else here. We should go.'

'No,' he said. 'Not yet.'

Then he seized my elbow and dragged me on.

63
Sam

Sam exited through the foyer of the main university building, the Lost Girl hurrying alongside him.

It was dark outside, a swirling breeze picking up and the temperature low enough for him to pause to fasten his jacket.

'Thank you again,' the Lost Girl said. 'For everything.'

He wondered why she was still following him. Was even starting to wonder if she was hanging around for other reasons. He doubted she had a crush on him. She could be one of those students who wanted him to *think* that she had a crush on him, but if that was the case, he couldn't understand her angle. The colleague she'd asked him to email was in the Department of Geography and the Environment, not his own. Perhaps she'd ask him for more emails down the line.

'You're welcome,' Sam told her, not just distracted by disabling the airplane mode on his phone and surveying the traffic that was already beginning to slow and coagulate on the streets around them, but also needing her to see and appreciate that he was distracted, had other priorities, reasons to move on with his day.

He had to be careful about this. He didn't want to upset her, not when she was vulnerable.

'I'm starting to wonder if I might actually sleep tonight, thanks to you.'

'That's great,' Sam said. 'Truly.'

As he scanned the square in front of him, he was surprised to find that the rest of the group were more or less arrayed around him, too.

The Librarian was sitting on a stone bench off to his left, vaping aggressively and talking on his phone.

Over by a coffee cart that was being closed up for the day, the Athlete and the Artist were engaged in casual conversation, the Athlete standing with his feet shoulder-width apart and his big arms folded, the Artist toying with the strap of her bag as if she was shaping up to leave but making no effort to actually go.

Behind them was the taxi rank, where the Boxer was resting his palms on the roof of a black cab, talking through the open window to a driver he seemingly knew. Noticing Sam, his expression became guarded and he returned his attention to what the driver was saying to him, apparently wary that Sam might approach him and give away his dark secret.

'Do you have any phobias?' the Lost Girl asked. 'It just occurred to me, you heard all of ours, so I was thinking—'

'I'm sorry,' Sam told the Lost Girl, jerking a thumb over his shoulder with an apologetic grimace, setting off in the direction of Temple station. 'But I really have to run to get my Tube. My girlfriend's expecting me. I need to get home.'

64

Donovan let go of me when we entered the living room.
John's shopping bag banged against my hip as I stepped
clear of him.

John was already seated in his favourite armchair, his
bony hands clutching the armrests, staring fixedly ahead.
He seemed only vaguely aware of our presence and he
showed no signs of interest when Donovan crossed the room
and drew the heavy curtains, the brass curtain rings clinking
sharply, everything becoming dim and indistinct until he
clicked on a floor lamp.

A strange second of dislocation.

In some ways, it was like travelling back to how our place
had looked two years ago. There was a lot of dark-brown
furniture and a wall-to-wall carpet. A threadbare three-piece
suite and full-length fabric curtains. A boxy television in the
corner and a low coffee table scattered with a newspaper,
dirty cups, John's magnifying glass.

I twisted the handles of the plastic bag around my fingers,
feeling increasingly uneasy.

'That's enough,' I said. 'I've done everything you asked
me to do. Let's go.'

But Donovan didn't respond. He was too preoccupied

carrying out a fast survey of the room, running his eyes and fingertips over the fireplace and a glass display cabinet, craning his neck to peer behind a chair, tilting a low bookcase away from the skirting board as if he was a spy searching for hidden listening devices or a miniature camera.

I didn't know what he was looking for, or why, and I was almost certain I didn't want to know.

'What's in the bag?' he asked me, without looking my way.

I ignored him, which prompted him to puff air from his cheeks, as if I was exhausting his patience.

'Sam takes the District Line, right? Those trains can come in pretty fast. You do understand I can call my contact back any time I like?'

'Is that supposed to scare me?'

'It does scare you. It should scare you. So just tell me what's in the bag.'

I delayed a moment longer, then raised it and looked down.

The bag was moderately heavy. I parted the handles and peered inside.

Not that I needed to because I already knew what I'd find.

'Well?'

Donovan had progressed to tugging the curtains away from the wall and scanning the skirting board beneath the bay window.

'Cat food,' I told him. 'Two tins.'

He absorbed that for a second, then allowed the curtains to flap closed and crossed towards John, crouching in front of him, peering into his face.

'Where's your cat, John?' He waved a gloved hand in front of John's glazed eyes. 'Where is your cat?'

'Barnaby?' John's voice trembled. 'Oh, he'll be back before long. Barnaby is always hungry.'

Donovan turned, snatching up the television remote and switching on the TV.

The volume was loud. An early-evening quiz show. The hosts and the contestants were too happy and smug for the moment, the colours too vibrant.

'This way,' Donovan told me, tossing the remote aside. 'Bring that bag with you.'

He swept out into the hallway without waiting for my response, and after glancing at John one last time, I followed him, watching as he stepped into the former dining room that was now John's bedroom, finding a light switch on the wall.

I edged inside after him, watching as he went through a similar routine to the one he'd carried out in the front room. First, he ducked down behind the old hospital bed Sam had sourced for John, with its painted and scratched metal railings, and the primitive electrical control panel that allowed him to raise and lower the bed. Then he closed the curtains, nearly upsetting the tray table with a framed photograph and some of John's meds on it as he completed his sweep of the room, again paying close attention to the skirting boards and the area behind the door while ignoring the framed picture of a cricket scene on the wall, before taking the shopping bag from me and moving on into the kitchen.

He opened the bag as he entered, reaching inside for one of the cans and then barking, 'Christ!' and raising his right foot in the air as he almost stepped into a bowl of cat food down on the floor. Inside the bowl was a congealed mix of paste and kibble.

'Stinks in here.'

He looked around him until his gaze zeroed in on the landline phone fixed to the far wall, close to the yellowed, freestanding fridge.

Based on his reaction, I gathered it was what he'd been hunting for in the other rooms he'd been searching, and I watched with a deep sense of trepidation as he set the shopping bag down on the small Formica table and crossed towards it, snatching the handset off the wall, trailing a springy spiral cord, then looking all around him before spying a pot of kitchen utensils from which he removed a pair of scissors that he used to snip through the spiral cable and then through the phone line connected to the wall unit.

There was a pedal bin close by and he stamped on it until the lid flipped open, then dropped the handset inside and, after a moment's thought, added the scissors, too.

He took his foot off the pedal and the lid clanged shut, but already something else had attracted his attention.

He was peering curiously at the many tins of cat food stacked on the kitchen countertop on the other side of the room. There had to be twenty or twenty-five tins altogether.

Donovan strode towards them, then snatched open the doors of a cupboard above the counter.

He stepped back.

The cupboard was filled with yet more cat food.

'He goes every day,' I explained. 'It's his routine.'

Donovan nodded slowly and picked up the shopping bag again, removing the two new tins John had just purchased and stacking them on the counter alongside the others. He then scrunched the empty bag into a ball in his hands, passing it between his palms as if it was a thinking aid.

'Tell me about the rest of his routine.'

If he was impacted by the reality of John's dementia, he didn't show it.

'I don't understand.'

'Where else does he go? Who else does he see?'

'Nobody.'

He frowned, unconvinced.

'Nobody except Sam,' I told him. 'And me, sometimes.'

'What about a cleaner? Or a carer?'

I hesitated.

'Don't lie to me. Not again.'

'We get a cleaning agency in,' I told him carefully. 'About once a month.'

'When are they next due?'

My eyes travelled to the calendar on the wall behind him. Sam had circled a date a couple of weeks away in red. I didn't like these questions. I hated to think where he was going with them.

'A fortnight.'

'Doctor?'

My voice dropped. 'John hasn't been in a while.'

'Kids? Other relatives?'

'No.'

'His wife's dead?'

I stared at him, a cold sensation streaking up my arms and legs.

'There are photographs of them together,' he explained

with a jerk of his chin. 'In the living room. On the tray table next to the hospital bed. On the fridge here. Did you think I wouldn't notice?'

I glanced at the portrait shot on the fridge. It was an image taken from decades before, of John in his prime in his police uniform, his chest puffed out, Mary at his side, beaming.

'Plus you told me earlier he was retired and lived alone, there's no evidence of a woman's things in that living room, and from the state of his clothes and this place generally . . .'

He left the rest unsaid but it was clear he hadn't missed much.

That worried me. Because he'd also studied the photos of me and Sam in our home. What had he deduced from those, I wondered? What conclusions had he drawn from touring our house?

'When did she die?'

'About a year and a half ago,' I told him quietly, glancing behind me over my shoulder. But I needn't have worried about John overhearing us. He was in his own head right now. And the TV was too loud. I could hear the quizmaster joking with his co-presenter. 'She had a fall on the stairs. Broke her hip. There were complications with her recovery in hospital. She never made it back home.'

'So who looks after him?'

'We do,' I said. 'Me and Sam.'

But mostly Sam.

Sam's grandparents had been good friends with John and Mary. They'd lived next door to one another for most of their lives. And John and Mary – perhaps because they'd

229

never had kids of their own – had taken a shine to Sam. They'd sent him birthday cards and Christmas gifts. Sam had been fond of them in turn.

It had been rough for Sam when he'd lost his grandparents. His parents had been killed in a car smash when he was only a teenager and so, when his grandfather and later his grandmother died, he'd felt properly like an orphan for the first time.

Like me.

I understood that was one of the bonds that had connected us, but it was also why Sam spent so much of his time caring for John. He'd call round most mornings before work and every evening to make sure everything was OK, which is why he had a key to John's place. I'd got into the habit of cooking meals for Sam to bring over for him, too.

I loved Sam for doing it. I liked that he was so kind. But I think we'd both known for a while now it had been nearing the point where John was going to need more support than we could give him. I'd mentioned it to Sam several times, as considerately as I could. He'd nodded glumly and told me I was probably right, but he hadn't acted on it yet.

I got that it was part of why he'd been so stressed about putting our place on the market. Once we had a buyer and the prospect of selling became truly real, everything with John would come to a head. I suspected Sam carried a lot of guilt about that.

'Now can we go?' I asked.

Donovan passed the bag between his hands some more, tilting his head from side to side as though he was running through the pros and cons of my suggestion. He pressed his lips together and made a small noise in his throat as if he'd reached a decision. Then he unfurled the bag and snapped it in the air so that it billowed and expanded.

'Afterwards,' he told me.

'After what?'

But instead of answering me, he rushed out of the room with the bag.

65

'Hey!' I called.

Donovan ignored me.

I darted out into the hallway after him.

'Hey!'

He didn't slow. If anything, his pace increased.

Everything about his body language – his speed, his contained movements, the way his gaze was fixed dead ahead of him – scared me.

A streak of electric horror forked downwards from the top of my skull, branching out through my torso.

'What are you doing?'

He circled one wrist with a fast movement, cinching the handle of the plastic bag around his fingers.

'Don't!'

He circled the other wrist. Snapped the bag taut between his hands. Then he swerved right through the doorway into the front room without looking back.

I ran down the hallway and in through the doorway after him.

And stopped cold.

Fear fluttered in my stomach.

Donovan's eyes flashed my way from where he was

standing behind John's armchair with the bag – held taut and tight – above John's head.

John's glazed attention was on the television, light flickering across his docile face.

'No,' I breathed.

Donovan watched me.

There was the slightest contraction of one eye, as if he was assessing my response.

Then he lowered his hands.

I sprang forwards – my shin barking off the edge of the coffee table – and launched myself at him.

I made a grab for his arm. His chin.

My fingers scrabbled against the stubble on his jaw.

But before I could get a proper grip, he hunched his back and ducked his chin down against his chest, then spun tightly around, shaking me loose, sending me sprawling towards the hearth and the fireplace.

I slammed down hard.

Pain lit up across my elbows, knees and chin.

I braced my hands out ahead of me and was able to arrest my momentum before I crashed into the fireplace.

Just.

Then I turned.

Donovan was staring at me with a thoughtful, analytical expression.

Behind him, John had bolted to his feet, though Donovan seemed not to care.

John was treading one way, then the other, his body language agitated, his eyes wide and afraid as he looked between us.

I had no idea if he was really seeing us or if he was actually seeing the muddled component parts of a scene that didn't make any sense to him.

He scratched at his neck.

'I'm going to feed Barnaby,' he muttered. 'Barnaby. I have to feed him now.'

As he stumbled from the room, disappearing along the hallway, Donovan kept his focus on me.

I said, 'He doesn't have a cat.'

'Excuse me?'

I shifted onto my side, my upper back braced against the marble mantelpiece, needing him to understand.

'Barnaby's dead. He was put to sleep two months ago.'

Donovan eyed me as if from afar, suspicion clouding his features.

'He doesn't remember,' I continued. 'He goes to the shops every day. *Because that's his routine.* But he doesn't remember about his cat. He won't remember you. He won't remember us being here. He won't remember calling at the house, or seeing you inside, or going to the shops, or when his cat doesn't come home tonight. He won't remember any of it.'

'Well, that's too bad,' he said, turning to go.

'If we leave now, I'll talk to you,' I called. 'I'll tell you what you want to know.'

He stilled. 'You're going to have to do that anyway.'

'Not if you kill John, I won't. I swear to you I won't.'

He seemed to consider it.

'I mean it,' I pressed. 'Leave here with me now – leave John safe – and I'll tell you everything. All of it. But don't, and I won't cooperate. Not willingly. I don't care what you do to me, or to Sam or Bethany.'

He remained motionless for a second more, then swiftly walked out of the room without looking back.

I scrambled to my feet, streaking after him as far as the kitchen, but he put his arm out to stop me when I got there.

John was sitting at the kitchen table, staring with a confounded expression at the tin of cat food and the can opener in front of him. Gradually, he looked up and proffered them to Donovan in a wordless appeal for help.

I watched in a state of slow horror as Donovan started forwards, approaching him with the bag in his hands.

'If you—'

'Relax.' He set the bag down on the table, took the can opener from John and fitted it to the tin. He cranked it purposefully as he looked my way.

'Two conditions,' he told me.

'Anything.'

'The first is that John stays in this house.'

'That's normal. John will be here until tomorrow now, won't you, John?'

Donovan finished opening the tin and set it down on the table, then rested a hand on John's shoulder before stepping away to pick up the cat bowl. After selecting a fork from the cutlery drawer, he placed a foot on the pedal bin and scraped the congealed cat food out of the bowl. I could hear it splattering down against the plastic liner and on top of the landline phone he'd dumped inside earlier.

'If I hear someone call round, or the front door opens—'

'You won't.'

He placed the cat bowl onto the table, upending the tin of meat paste above it. He then forked a clump out, mashed it with the fork, slid the bowl in front of John.

He was still holding the fork, and this time, when he placed his hand on John's shoulder and angled the tines of the fork towards his neck, it was clear to me it was another warning.

'You understand that I can get back in here any time I like?'

'Yes.'

'Doesn't have to be today.'

'I said I understand.'

He reached forwards and poked at the plastic bag with the fork. 'You understand what happens if I do?'

I nodded.

I understood what would happen.

I also understood that Bethany's life was in jeopardy.

I knew he had someone following Sam home.

'Good. Then ask me what my second condition is.'

I glanced at John. He didn't seem to be getting any of this. Mostly, I think, he was just relieved that the cat food was where he wanted it to be.

'What's the second condition?'

'You tell me about the roof. Everything you remember. Every single detail of what happened that night and leading up to it.'

I stared at Donovan, a sickly effervescence in my bloodstream.

'I can do that.'

'Good.' He tossed the fork down onto the table, wiping his gloved hands clean. 'Then we should get back next door. Sam will be home soon.'

66

Donovan led me into the hallway, stopping behind the front door, taking out his phone.

'Another neat thing about the District Line. They have a phone signal or Wi-Fi at all the stations.'

He prodded a button, dialling on speaker.

A few short purrs of near silence were followed by a faint hissing and then a recorded, standardized message in a computerized male voice: *'The number you are dialling is currently unavailable. Please leave a message and—'*

He hung up, studying me.

'Average time a train spends at a District Line station is fifty-eight seconds. So here's what's going to happen. When this call connects, we're going outside together. And then we're going to get inside your house as fast as possible. You have thirty seconds to make it to your front door or Sam never gets off that train.'

He dialled again, jabbing at his phone.

I heard the same things as before.

The same short purrs of near silence, followed by the same faint hissing and the same standardized message: *'The number you are dialling is currently—'*

'Once we're on the other side of this door, you don't speak, you don't scream, you don't even think about trying to get away. Understood?'

I just looked at him, feeling trapped and constrained. A new form of claustrophobia.

'Understood?' he repeated.

'Yes,' I whispered.

He dialled a third time.

As before, I heard the same short purrs of near silence and the same faint hissing but this time they were followed by a longer, more somnolent droning, some static clicks, and then another recorded, standardized message, only this message was different. Female. Polite. Laced with a tannoy quality.

' . . . *next station is Sloane Square.*'

'We're moving outside,' Donovan said, into his phone. He was talking in a hurry, sounding focused and tensed. 'Wait on confirmation from me. If you don't get it before you leave that station, move in.'

He snatched open the front door, grabbed my hand and led me outside, quickly locking the door behind him, removing John's keys and then tossing them sideways into a darkened corner of the yard.

I could hear a raucous commotion coming through the speaker of Donovan's phone.

The thunder of moving air.

An iron screeching.

The lurch and shuffle of who knew how many bodies packed tightly together.

'This is Sloane Square. Please mind the gap between the train and the platform.'

'Thirty seconds,' Donovan reminded me.

He strode forwards, tugging me alongside him.

My entire focus was on the buzz and crackle coming from his phone speaker followed by the hiss of compressed air as the train doors parted.

But it was punctured by something else.

Clipped footsteps coming from my left.

I swung my head and saw two women striding our way as Donovan pulled me to a halt.

The women were deep in conversation, dressed in denim jackets and scarves, their heels striking the pavement in a rapid percussion.

A hot and nervous trembling worked its way up my legs.

I could hear the scuffed background noises coming from Donovan's phone. The sound of passengers shuffling and moving and trading positions.

Nothing was said by whomever was watching Sam, but I didn't doubt they were listening as closely as I was.

The women hurried nearer.

Donovan clenched my hand. A signal and a warning.

They passed the end of the pathway and one of them glanced my way – a brief, neutral look – too fast for me to begin to think how to react or signal to her.

My stomach twisted.

The phone speaker crackled.

The women continued without looking back at us.

'Move,' Donovan said under his breath, pulling me forwards again.

My legs were rubber. I stumbled and looked after the women. They weren't looking back. They hadn't sensed anything wrong or amiss. They were totally preoccupied with their conversation.

'I want to talk to Sam,' I said.

'You'll talk to him when he gets here.'

'Before that. I have to know he's safe.'

'He isn't.'

He steered me ahead of him through John's gate, swinging me left and left again, stiff-arming his way through our gate and on towards the light spill shining out from our home.

'This is a District Line train to Wimbledon. The next station is South Kensington.'

'Faster,' Donovan urged.

Fear tangled in my chest. My feet scuffed the ground.

He hadn't backed me into a bathtub. He hadn't locked a door behind him, snatched me by the hair, seized me by the throat.

But still I felt choked.

The pathway to our front door was just a narrow ribbon of tarmac, maybe three or four metres long, with a square of gravel to the right and a band of more gravel to the left.

I'd walked along it countless times in the past without thinking very much about it.

Not now.

I was rushing onwards, barely breathing, but at the same time I seemed to be moving infinitely slowly, infinitely painfully.

The 'For Sale' sign to my left slid by as if in slow motion. I could remember how the guy from the estate agency had turned up to install the sign, how he'd cable-tied it to the railings after ramming it through the gravel with a mallet.

Clang.

Clang.

Clang.

In the moment, in the horror, it was as if I could feel the blows vibrating through the ground beneath me.

'Please mind the doors.'

Donovan hurried me on, digging his fist into his coat pocket for Sam's keys.

I could see the pinpricks of light glimmering around and through the shutter blinds behind the bay window to my right, but I couldn't see inside.

And nobody else can, either.

On the phone, there was another pneumatic hiss of the train doors closing.

A tinny squeal.

A low, shuffling commotion.

Donovan withdrew Sam's keys and stabbed them at the lock. They slipped inside and a fraction of a second later the phone line went dead, snapping away to nothing.

Stasis.

Donovan looked at me.

I looked at him.

My brain seemed to be processing a million thoughts all at once.

Then I leaned to one side, staring after the two women moving along the pavement, and I sucked in a lungful of air to scream.

67

Donovan pressed his gloved hand over my mouth before I could get any noise out. My split lip squeaked against my teeth. He clamped down harder and the back of my skull dashed off the brickwork behind me.

I mewled with pain.

I tried screaming but it was hopeless. I couldn't inhale or exhale. All I could taste was the leather of his glove.

The seconds crawled on.

He watched me dispassionately.

My eyes were wild with terror and panic.

I was horrified by what might be happening to Sam, desperate to shout for help.

Donovan checked quickly behind him.

The women who had walked past us hadn't heard anything. They were still hurrying on.

Using his free hand, he quickly worked Sam's keys in the lock, pushed the door open, then tugged the keys out, guided me forwards and shoved me inside, kicking the door closed behind him.

The snap lock engaged.

—*click.*

I gasped air. My skin had turned clammy.

I raised one hand to my chest and took a slow and crackling inhalation as the lights in the hallway seemed to grow brighter above me.

Everything felt strange.

What had previously been comforting and welcoming about our home now struck me as somehow staged and insincere.

I could smell the scent of the lilies I had arranged in the vase on the coffee table but their aroma seemed sickly, fake.

Only the threat of Donovan was real. It was as immediate and tangible as the ache in my lungs.

His phone was ringing.

He'd dialled out again as soon as he'd closed the door, got no connection, then immediately tried again.

Now he was staring at me with a kind of rueful anger, cupping his phone beneath his mouth.

My mind flooded with thoughts of Sam. Donovan had told his accomplice to move in if Donovan didn't give them the all-clear before they lost signal.

I hated to think what he'd meant by that. He'd told me Sam wasn't safe.

I had visions of a killer closing in on Sam in a packed Tube train, armed with a blade or a poisoned umbrella or a hundred other things I didn't want to be imagining at all.

The call connected.

A swirling, strained hush.

'This is South Kensington. Change here for the Piccadilly—'

'We're inside the house,' Donovan said, watching me keenly. 'Give me your status.'

Silence.

A crackle.

An electronic shushing.

I needed to breathe but I didn't.

Then a voice, sparse and digitally altered. Neither male nor female. Not young or old.

'There were too many people. I couldn't get next to him but I'm closer now. Tell me what you want me to do.'

Donovan held my gaze, nothing at all in his face.

The moment lengthened and stretched.

'Stand down,' he said.

He cut the call and stared at me for a beat longer.

'OK,' he told me. 'Now we talk.'

68

I didn't feel an immediate sense of relief. I didn't really know *what* to feel.

Sam was alive, for now, but he was coming home to this, to Donovan, to the horror and violence that had invaded our sanctuary.

The station announcement had said his train was at South Kensington. So call it, what, twenty minutes on the Tube? A five-minute walk after that?

And then Sam would be here.

I knew I had to do something, but I didn't know what I could do.

My body was bent and bowed, my teeth hurt, my lip stung, my skull was throbbing and I was so anxious I felt as if someone had stamped on my chest.

But I was concentrating as hard as I ever had. I was desperately looking for a way out.

Which is when Donovan brushed past me into the living area, closing Sam's keys in his fist and then slipping them into his right trouser pocket.

Not good.

When Sam got home, he wouldn't be able to let himself

in. He'd have to ring the doorbell, the same as John, and Donovan would be ready for him.

Which I guessed was his intention.

I stared at the door, wondering if whoever was following Sam would come in and join Donovan, too. Then I turned and looked up towards the landing. Bethany was up there in the attic. Alone. Was she OK? Would she *be* OK?

'Sit down, Lucy.'

'I want to check on Bethany first.'

'No. Enough delaying. Sit.'

He took up a position in front of the sofa facing the coffee table, gesturing at the statement chair to the left of the fireplace.

The chair was an accent piece with cream bouclé fabric nestled next to a potted cheese plant. Sam and I had chosen it together from a furniture shop on Tottenham Court Road, close to the shop where I'd been working when we'd first met. Sam hadn't been sure about the colour to begin with. He'd thought it might stain too easily.

Coldness rinsed through me as I imagined the sticky bleed at the back of my skull mingling with the cream fabric.

I looked up towards the landing one last time, hating the idea of leaving Bethany up there alone, then turned and walked stiffly into the living area, moving past the chair Donovan had suggested and perching on the arm of the chair closest to the bay window instead.

Donovan stared at me flatly, as if my minor rebellion didn't surprise or bother him a great deal.

'So, the party. Tell me about the roof. The details. Everything you remember.'

Everything I remembered.

I drew another cramping breath, running my tongue over my aching teeth, a sudden, dizzying lightness filling my head the way I sometimes get if I skip lunch.

For a while now I'd tried never to think about that night. I'd done everything I could to move on from it.

That was when a digitized *ping* cut through the air.

I stiffened as Donovan raised his phone and checked the screen.

'What is it?' I whispered. 'Is that a message about Sam?'

'The lab I sent your DNA to confirming receipt. They're going to run a rapid test.'

I stared at him.

I could feel my blood draining out from my extremities, pooling around my heart.

My mind flared momentarily, the same way it had when my head had hit the sink.

'Why are you doing this to us?' I asked.

'Talk,' he said, sitting down on the green velvet sofa across from me. 'About the party. Start now or you and I are going to be taking a trip back next door to see John again before Sam gets home, and this time I won't be nearly so civil.'

69

I delayed for a moment longer before speaking. Not just because it was difficult for me to talk about, but because I was trying to wrap my head around everything he'd just said and what it could mean.

'You're talking about the party in Farringdon?' I asked him.

'Of course.'

'There's . . . a lot I don't remember.'

A lot I didn't want to remember.

'Tell me what you do remember.'

I blinked at him, aware of my breathing growing quicker, shallower.

It wasn't that easy.

And not just because I was in denial, or because remembering anything about that night was painful for me, but because there was so much I genuinely couldn't recall.

I knew I had to tell Donovan *something*. I believed him when he said he would go back next door and harm John if I didn't.

But it was hard.

'I have a lot of blanks.'

'Then fill them.'

'It's not like that. It's not as simple as you're making out.'

I could have told him some of the things Sam had told me. About how the brain is wired for self-preservation. About how I wasn't blocking, as such, but rather my memories had been absorbed, stored away until I was ready to process them fully.

I knew it was possible that as time went on – as I healed – the complete picture would come back to me, maybe even abruptly, like the flip of a switch, but until that time there was nothing I could actively do to force the situation and access my memories.

It wasn't as if I wanted them gone. Not deep down. In many ways it would have been a lot easier if I could have remembered the assault and my attacker more clearly because that might have given me a shot at understanding why it had happened to me. Perhaps even closure.

I think that was the most difficult part. Not the things I *couldn't* remember but the fragments I could, and how they were out of sequence and incoherent and refused to make sense to me. Whenever I had tried to put them together – *really* tried – it was as if my mind just . . . whited out, like a television that was on the fritz.

'It was somebody's birthday,' I heard myself say.

He flinched. It was only subtle but I noticed it.

'Or I think it was their birthday?' I squeezed my arm, closing my fingers around the scar under my sleeve, thinking of how I'd been marked, branded by what had happened to me, and meanwhile looking over my shoulder towards the window, thinking of Sam coming home.

I could hear traffic outside. I could hear the wind stirring the leaves of the trees.

'It wasn't anyone I knew,' I continued. 'I don't know how I got invited or why I was there. There were a lot of people.'

'People you knew?'

'No. I don't think so.'

He seemed dubious. 'You had to have known some of them.'

I shook my head, feeling the frustration build, gnawing at my insides.

'I don't know how to explain it. I can remember music and smoking and I guess I was drinking – I must have been drinking – because even the memories I do have are blurry. But I don't drink to get drunk like that. Not usually.'

I looked down again at the way my hand had closed around my forearm. I was pretty sure I'd been left with the scar when I'd been pushed into the bath. Maybe I'd nicked my arm on something. Perhaps it had been something sharp my attacker had been holding. But again, I couldn't remember for certain. All I knew was that I hadn't been scarred before that night.

'I think I had a meeting with a potential client not too far from where the party must have been. The meeting was at a bar somewhere near Farringdon. But I can't remember which bar, or who the client was, or how they contacted me. I've walked around there since. Nothing seems right. Things had been going badly for me. My business was in trouble. I must have ordered a drink. A couple of drinks. But after that . . .'

Again his brow furrowed, as if what I was telling him didn't fit with any scenario he'd anticipated. 'Are you saying you think you met somebody in the bar who was going to the party?'

'Maybe. Or maybe my drink was spiked.'

That stopped him. I could see that on some level he was

having to reassess his assumptions, that what I was telling him was troubling him.

'It would fit,' I told him. 'With what happened later.'

'What did happen later?'

'I—'

I winced and raised a hand to my head.

Pain again, though this time it had nothing to do with the blow to the back of my skull.

This pain was older, more ingrained, located to the left of my frontal lobe. I'd had it before when I'd flashed on that night, especially if I'd tried to force my memories, push my way through the blinding white glare. It was another reason why I'd shied away from trying to remember too much.

I heard Donovan's bodyweight shift on the sofa cushions to my side and I squinted out through my fingers to see that he'd moved towards the edge of the couch, his elbows on his knees, hands clasped loosely together.

Was that concern on his face?

I watched as his gaze became distant and thoughtful, before he turned his head and looked away from me through the kitchen towards the basement.

Oh God.

My heart started galloping.

Not that.

The basement door was still open.

Was he thinking of bundling me down there and scaring me until I told him what he wanted to know? Maybe holding me down there until Sam got here?

'I went to the bathroom,' I said in a rush, feeling a spike of relief when Donovan returned his attention to me.

'Go on.'

I swallowed. It felt like a peach stone was lodged in my throat.

I wished I could move the vase of lilies out of the way from between us. Their scent was making my sinuses sting like menthol.

I rubbed my aching temple but it didn't help to soothe or ease my discomfort.

Nothing could.

Not the meditation exercises I'd practised, or the anxiety meds my GP had prescribed, or the therapy sessions Sam had run with me.

Sam had made it clear to me that he wasn't a qualified therapist. He had friends he'd suggested referring me to. But I'd resisted. My trauma had been inflicted by one stranger. I'd been reluctant to relive it with another.

'I really hate talking about this,' I said.

'Too bad, because I have to hear it.'

'Please.'

'Just tell me the rest. Now.'

I glanced at the door, imagining Sam getting home, picturing Donovan pulling him inside, attacking him . . .

'Someone followed me in,' I said, and the pain flared again in my temple, sickly and acute.

'OK, someone followed you into the bathroom. How does that tie in to the roof?'

'There was no roof. I keep telling you. There was—' I broke off again, grimacing, clutching my head in my hands. 'They locked the door behind them.'

—*click*.

'Who did?'

And then I stopped.

I froze.

Because a new thought had struck me. A fresh and horrible idea.

'Is that who is working with you?'

'What?'

'Whoever did this to me. Attacked me. Are they the one you've been calling? The one watching Sam?'

Because maybe they were afraid I'd come after them, go to the police, or – I don't know – sell my story to the press or try to sue them.

I tried to concentrate, to *think*.

Could my attacker have been wealthy or high profile in some way? Were they afraid of a scandal? A #MeToo revenge?

But why now?

Again, I peered out through my splayed hands at Donovan. My eyes felt scrubbed and swollen.

He stared back at me with one eye half closed in a thoughtful squint, his head angled slightly to the side, mouth opening as if I'd finally said something that had connected with him.

'Wait.' He shifted further forwards on his seat. 'Let me get this straight.'

I ducked lower under a fresh onslaught of pain. It was difficult for me to pay attention to what he was saying right now because my discomfort was too raw, the trauma too embedded.

'Just . . . listen to me, OK? What you did is not something you can just get away with. It's the whole reason I'm here.'

'What *I* did? I didn't do anything. This was something that was done to *me*.'

He leaned back, confounded, his eyes dimmed and searching. He looked a lot like someone who couldn't tell if he was being duped or not.

'What about what *he* did?' I pressed. 'What you've done? What—'

I hissed, bared my teeth.

White-out.

The pain in my head was overwhelming.

Blinding.

'Hey,' he said. 'Hey, look at me.'

He clapped his hands as if he was trying to snap me out of it but it was much too late for that.

'Focus. Talk to me. The bathroom. Someone followed you in and they locked the door and—'

—*click.*

And I was there in my mind again.

Just as I was always there in a part of my mind.

Just as I could never let it go.

The door locking and the stranger closing in on me and me falling and the shower curtain wrapping around me and my arm singing in pain and—

'Stop this.' I clamped both hands to the sides of my head, squeezing, cringing. 'Stop this. Stop it, please.'

70

'Hey,' he said. 'Hey.'

I must have lost time.

It had happened to me before.

Blank spaces during my days.

Voids I had fallen into.

'Hey.'

It frightened me.

I knew I had to stay with him. Be present. Protect myself.

I'd sunk to the floor. Puddled into a ball.

'Hey.'

He waved a hand in front of my face. He'd been sitting across from me with the coffee table between us. But now he was down on one knee in front of me. I wasn't sure how long had passed. It could have been five seconds or five minutes.

'Hey.' He gently shook my shoulder. 'Where'd you go? What just happened to you?'

I trembled.

My mind flashed on the schoolgirl who'd fallen outside. Donovan was talking to me in the same soothing way that he'd talked to her, using the same caring tone.

It made my skin crawl.

'Hey.'

My forehead and the back of my neck were burning hot. My scalp ached as if someone was pulling my hair.

I kept my face down. Stared at my hands curled up in front of me.

My sight was blurred. My fingers were doubling.

'Listen to me. Focus on my voice.'

I shuddered. It was the wrong thing to say.

I got what he was trying to do. I understood that he was trying to bring me out of my panic attack.

But the last thing I needed right now was to listen to Donovan's voice. Because it brought back *his* voice. The figure in the bathroom. The man who'd attacked me.

'I've been watching you.'

'Don't.'

I squeezed my eyes tight shut. Felt the backwash of pain against my temple.

I heard Donovan move back a little, but his hand remained on my shoulder and I didn't want it there. I didn't want to be touched at all.

'Let go of me.'

He withdrew his fingers but I could still feel their imprint afterwards, aching like sores.

'Time to get you up,' he told me.

I didn't respond.

'Come on, I'm going to help you into this chair and then—'

He reached for me again but this time I leaped up and away.

Too fast.

Too unsteady.

The floor rocked and dipped.

I reached out for the armchair I'd been sitting on, but my hand passed right through it, and meanwhile he grabbed for my other wrist, holding me up.

My scar burned fiercely under his grip. It was roaring hot.

The rest of me felt wet and limp, as if I'd been drenched in a storm.

Hold on.

'Just so you know,' he told me, 'you were completely out of it for a few seconds there. I mean, totally out of it.'

I snatched my arm away from him and this time he let me.

'Like you care.'

'Maybe I do,' he said. 'Now. And you really don't remember the roof?'

'I told you, I wasn't on any roof.'

'Listen—'

'Stop saying that! You don't want to help me. You drugged Bethany. You were going to suffocate John. You have someone following Sam.'

I raised a hand to ward him off. I was perspiring copiously. My saliva was hot and oily. I thought I might pass out again.

'Look,' he said. 'Sam will be here soon.'

Sam.

Anxiety knotted in my stomach.

He couldn't walk into this.

I didn't want him in danger. I didn't want him to get hurt.

'Please,' I begged. 'Leave him out of this.'

'Just . . . sit down for a second, OK? I'm going to fetch you some water. Let you catch your breath.'

71

Donovan turned and took a step away from me, but I didn't do as he suggested and sit down.

I wasn't going to do *anything* he wanted me to do.

Not again.

Not this time.

No more.

I was stooped over, weak and juddery.

And I was very, very scared.

For Sam, and for me.

Which must have been something Donovan was relying on because he took another step forwards without looking back.

That's when I lunged for the vase of lilies.

It was right there on the coffee table between us.

A white ceramic jar with a curved handle and a thick base. The ceramic was weighty and solid. When I'd set it down on the coffee table earlier it had made a low *thunk*.

I seemed to be moving towards it much too slowly, as if I was moving through water.

It was taking an age for my fingers to curl around the handle.

And I was clumsy with fear and haste.

The backs of my fingers bumped against the cold ceramic. The jug toppled. Then I cupped my left hand around the side of the vase for support and gripped the handle properly and lifted it up.

With a strangled exhalation. A half-gasp of shock and surprise.

Partly because I'd really done it.

Partly because it felt enormously heavy.

And partly because he'd heard me and was starting to spin.

I was still raising the jug. The lilies were bouncing and splaying outwards, their pollen rising in a hazy puff, the water slopping and sloshing around.

I was intending to strike him over the head. One hard blow. A wild swing. Knock him unconscious. Knock him down.

But already I was starting to see the difficulties with that.

Because the jug was too big and too heavy.

Because he was too alert and too fast.

I couldn't move quickly enough.

I was going to have to raise the jug up, and then stop, and then reverse my momentum and bring it downwards again.

On top of his head.

Which was always going to be difficult because he was taller than me, and because he was swinging fast at the hips, his coat tails billowing outwards around him, his elbow scything upwards, instinctively protecting his head at the same time as knocking the jug from my hands.

The jug plummeted.

Time seemed to accelerate with it. Everything collapsing inwards in a terrifying whoosh and rush.

I reared backwards on instinct.

The jug hit the floorboards sideways.

It detonated on impact. An explosion of ceramic and water and petals.

Followed by a moment of stillness.

Of horror.

I saw Donovan's face twist with surprise and distaste, as if I'd somehow betrayed him, or as if he was regretting letting his guard down.

But by then I was dropping to my knees.

Not because I'd meant to. Because my legs had collapsed from under me.

And he was reaching downwards. Snatching for my arm to hoist me up.

I pulled my arm away from him but he adjusted and seized hold of my underarm instead, heaving me to my feet as his lower leg nudged the coffee table sideways and his shoe crunched on broken pottery and the spill of water and flowers.

He lifted me as if it was nothing. As if I was made of air.

The room blurred. My mind strobed white.

The stink of the lilies was strong and astringent.

And then he stopped in an instant. And went very still.

As if something inside him had snapped or suddenly failed.

Or as if some unseen film director had clapped their hands and yelled, 'Cut!'

Slowly – too slowly – we both looked down together.

At my fist in his side.

At the jagged ceramic chunk I had dug deep into his stomach – under his coat, through his sweater – and the hot blood that was pulsing out over my hand and wrist.

72

He hissed air through his teeth. His nostrils flared. His eyes drilled into me with a dark and vibrating intensity.

I let go of the sharpened hunk of ceramic and stepped backwards.

I was weightless. Floating.

He pressed both hands to his torso, underneath his coat. The chunk of ceramic had gone in somewhere under his ribs.

I wasn't a doctor. I hadn't studied anatomy. But I wondered if the shard was near to his lungs. Maybe it had severed a vein or an artery.

You did this.

I shivered.

The blood kept coming.

It was pumping out, luscious and dark, oozing between his gloved fingers, seeping through his sweater.

I didn't speak. I couldn't.

The entire situation seemed impossible to me.

He hissed more air. Spit bubbles through his teeth. A judder passed through him and he stared at me, appalled.

Then he sank slowly and agonizingly downwards onto the edge of the sofa, tipping first to his left, bracing himself on his elbow, before leaning the other way, dropping to the ground and kicking the coffee table away to one side.

He was making an awful straining, whining noise. It was obvious he was in a lot of pain and discomfort. He couldn't get up.

I moved as if to go towards him, help him, then stopped and stepped back.

No.

He could still hurt me.

I was sure he *would* hurt me now.

And Sam.

My heart seized.

I back-pedalled. I thought of rushing upstairs to Bethany, but what we needed right now was help, help, help.

'Where are you—? Lucy? What—?'

His words faded into an agonized, keening grunt as I circled around the end of the sofa. He was staring at his hands, his eyes wide and trembling, his lips peeled back.

I ran for the front door.

It was locked from the inside. On the latch.

'Come on, come on.'

I fumbled with it. Flicked it, my fingers slick and greasy, slipping on the mechanism.

The catch gave way.

Night air swept in.

Darkness and streetlight.

I glanced once more towards the sofa without seeing him and then I bolted, running blindly outside.

And slammed into something unseen, ricocheting off violently towards the railings running atop the wall next to the gate.

73

I grabbed the railings before my chin struck the painted barbs.

An arm swooped around me from the side, pulling me upright.

Sam.

He stared into my face, his eyes flickering rapidly with shock and concern.

'Oh, thank God!' I said, throwing myself at him, hugging him, inhaling his scent.

It was such an enormous relief to see him. I felt myself sag.

Then I stiffened and pushed him away, bracing myself against his arms as I rose up on my toes and scanned the street in both directions.

'Lucy? What is it? What's wrong?'

'Is someone with you? Have you spotted someone following you?'

My eyes scoured the darkness and the pools of street lighting, searching for a lone figure watching from the shadows, behind a tree or a car.

'What are you talking about?'

'Someone's been watching you. Following you home. Have you seen anyone?'

'What?'

'They were in your support group.'

He looked at me as if I was making no sense.

His dark hair was gelled and spiked, as always. His face was placid, unshaved. He was wearing his worn corduroy jacket over a dark plaid shirt. His backpack was slung over one shoulder.

I needed him to understand how urgent this was.

'They took your house keys!'

Sam stared at me, perplexed. Then he lowered his backpack from his shoulder, unzipped the front pouch and delved a hand inside.

'But my keys are right here.'

I stared down as he opened his palm and I felt something inside me loosen and shift.

The Lego Luke Skywalker key fob. The four keys.

A roaring static in my head.

A plunge of confusion.

'No,' I said. 'No, that can't be right.'

I stared back at the house, at the open front door and the light shining out and the stillness and silence emanating from within.

A sense of unreality gripped me.

But Donovan had shown me Sam's keys. I'd seen them with my own eyes. I'd held them in my fist.

Donovan could have had Sam's keys copied, I told myself. He could have had a new set cut. He could have matched Sam's Lego key fob.

That *must* have been what happened.

The pain in my head was getting worse. A torrent of synapses firing and shorting.

I looked along the street again. It seemed inert. Empty.

Either the person following Sam was hiding or – was this possible? – there had never been anyone following him in the first place.

Could Donovan have lied?

I thought about it as Sam zipped his keys into his backpack again.

Donovan could have deceived me, I supposed. I'd only ever heard the voice on the end of the phone once. And the voice I'd heard had been digitized. *Faked?*

What about the Tube announcements?

Again, I supposed it was possible Donovan could have pre-recorded them, played them back to me, used them to help create the impression that Sam was in danger and thereby keep me under his control.

It would have required some planning but not too much. He'd already hacked into our doorbell, so he obviously had some tech know-how. And this entire mess was clearly something Donovan had been building up to for some time.

Was any of it genuine?

'What happened to your head?' Sam asked me. 'Lucy, are you bleeding? And your hands!' He took hold of my wrists, angling them in the streetlight, staring in wonder at the blood on my fingers, black and sticky as tar. 'What happened to you?'

'There's a man in the house,' I said.

'What?'

'A man called Donovan. In the living room. He came for the viewing. It was just me and him because Bethany was running late and he said he'd been looking for me, searching for me.'

'Why? I don't—'

'I don't know, Sam!' I bounced on my feet, checking the street again. 'He keeps talking about a roof. It doesn't make any sense. Can you call the police?'

'Shouldn't I just—?'

'He drugged Bethany! He's shut her in the attic cupboard.'

His face fell. He looked horrified.

'Sam, please. Just call them.'

I wrestled with his jacket. Wrenched out his phone. I pressed it into his hand and watched as he studied me in grave silence, swallowing visibly, then nodding fast and unlocking the screen.

He tapped in 999, made the call.

'Ask for an ambulance, too,' I said, as he raised his phone to his ear. 'I stabbed him before I got out. It's bad. I think he could be dying.'

74

Sam stepped away to make the phone call and I doubled over by our front wall, gripping hold of the iron railings, breathless, shaken, the backs of my fingers brushing against the thick foliage of the box hedge.

I felt hollowed out. Unravelled. My skin shimmered in the cold as a biting sense of fright and disbelief took hold of me.

Glancing sideways, I looked towards John's house and experienced a tiny pulse of relief. I'd kept John safe, at least. Perhaps that was something I could cling to in the days and weeks to come.

'They're on their way,' Sam told me, ending his call.

I nodded woodenly. My mouth was swamped by a chemical taint.

I looked up towards the top of our house at the attic windows opening onto Sam's study, picturing Bethany again. I only had Donovan's word for it that whatever he'd given her would wear off after a few hours. But what if he'd lied about that, too? What if he'd done something truly terrible to her?

It was only as I looked down again that I saw Sam venturing towards the front door.

'Sam?'

He didn't answer me.

'Sam, what are you doing?'

'It's OK, Lucy.'

'Come back here.'

'I'm just going to take a quick look.'

'What? No. You can't.'

He raised a hand to me without looking back over his shoulder.

'Sam.'

'You said you stabbed someone, Lucy.'

'He's dangerous.'

'If you've stabbed someone, we need to check if they're OK.'

'There's an ambulance on its way.'

'Yes.' He glanced back, a twinge crossing his face. 'And the police. They're going to want to know what happened here. You could be in trouble.'

'Trouble?' I pushed away from the railings, tramping after him. 'It was self-defence. Sam, please!'

'I'll just stick my head inside. If we can help him, we should.'

Help him.

Sam always wanted to help people. It was in his nature. Fixing people who were broken. But monsters like Donovan didn't deserve his help.

'Sam, you're not getting it.'

A bedroom light came on behind a window in the house two along on our right. A woman appeared behind the glass, looking down at me.

'Sam.'

He set one foot inside the front vestibule where he paused and carefully lowered his backpack to the ground outside on his right.

'Sam.'

He took a cautious step forwards, moving in a slight squat with his arms out at his sides, as if his muscles were tensed and primed to react to anything he might encounter.

I bit the inside of my cheek and peered off along the street again in both directions.

Then I glanced up worriedly towards the neighbour who was watching from behind her window. She frowned back at me for a nonplussed second before raising both arms and drawing her curtains closed.

I stepped up behind Sam, bumping into his back as he wrapped his fingers around the glazed internal door frame on either side of him.

He leaned forwards and looked in.

'I don't see anything,' he said.

'He's behind the sofa,' I whispered.

He took another step and I stuck close to him, knotting my fist in the material of his jacket.

The house wasn't eerily silent. It seemed to buzz and hum. The fridge-freezer, maybe. Or the drone of electricity running through the wires in the walls.

'Hello?' Sam called.

Nothing.

He's dead, I told myself, and the words clacked and settled like stones in my mind. *You've killed someone.*

I tugged Sam back but he took another step forwards,

pulling me after him. By craning my neck, I could just see over the back of the sofa to the coffee table, itself shunted sideways towards the fireplace from when Donovan had kicked it as he'd fallen.

'Careful,' I whispered, and I stepped sideways on rubber legs, pulling Sam with me, steering us around the end of the sofa towards our left so that the kitchen was behind us, the living room ahead, the open door to the street on our right.

I peered over his shoulder as our view fanned out in a slow and steady arc, like a door swinging open.

The fireplace and the slanted coffee table and the shattered fragments of the vase and the flowers and the water and the blood.

Sam stiffened and cocked his head to one side.

A trapdoor swung open beneath my feet.

'There's nobody here,' he said.

75

My vision wobbled.

There was blood and mess where Donovan had been, but he wasn't there now. He wasn't anywhere.

Pressure built around me, squeezing in.

I was scared to turn. Scared to move and break the stillness.

Where was he? Had he gone upstairs to Bethany?

'Will you show me your hands again?' Sam asked. 'Now that we're in the light?'

'We have to go,' I told him.

He didn't respond. He just nodded wordlessly, staring with uncertainty at the shattered remains of the broken vase.

'We have to go right now, Sam.'

It was so cold in the room. Much colder than before. Gooseflesh spread across my skin as I looked at the open door to outside.

Sam moved closer to me, gently taking my hands and inspecting them silently, then nudging my chin to one side and sucking in a draught of air as he saw the cut at the back of my head.

'Tell me again how you did this.'

And that's when I realized. That's when it hit me.

He thought I'd fallen.

He thought I'd whacked my head on the corner of the coffee table, smashed the vase, given myself a concussion, maybe.

He thought everything I was telling him was imagined. A delusion. A catalyst that had transformed my anxieties and phobias into a tale about a rogue intruder.

Something puckered at the base of my spine. A sensation of being watched.

I didn't want to move but I whirled around anyway, staring into the kitchen.

Nobody there.

But the door to the basement remained wide open.

I dropped my gaze to the floor.

There were spots of blood on the steps leading down into the kitchen.

A smear on the edge of the granite countertop beyond the sink.

Another drop close to the basement steps.

Could Donovan have gone down there?

Sam released my hands and crossed in front of me to return to the vestibule, where he stuck his head outside to look for the police and the ambulance he'd called.

Turning back to me, he shrugged awkwardly, then stepped into the living area again, this time moving around the other end of the sofa closer to the bay window, as if to analyse the scene of devastation on the ground from a new angle.

The air tightened between us.

Everything throbbed with an oddly charged intensity.

The atmosphere in the room. The blood in my veins.

Then the darkness shifted and Donovan rose up with a roar of pain from behind the armchair, slipping his arm around Sam's neck.

76

Sam yelped. His eyes went huge. Donovan cupped his free hand over Sam's mouth and his cheeks billowed from behind Donovan's gloved palm as he twisted his body and writhed and groaned.

Donovan didn't release him.

He held Sam's neck compressed in the crook of his elbow.

Sam moaned louder as Donovan pressed his knee into the base of Sam's spine, levering him backwards from his hips.

Dread thudded inside me. Donovan's movements had a rehearsed precision. They suggested a degree of training or expertise. I thought of how he'd restrained me before. I'd experienced for myself his strength and his composure. There was no doubt in my mind that he knew exactly what he was doing.

But his face was sickly and pale. He was sweating prodigiously, his teeth bared in pain.

I started forwards but he told me, 'Don't,' and tilted Sam back even further.

I stopped.

Donovan sucked air through his nostrils. His face was taut and contorted. He contemplated me with a penetrating look.

I noticed that he'd removed his coat and I could see that his jumper was stained red and torn extensively where I'd stabbed him. I couldn't see the wound itself because he'd packed it with a sterile dressing and a bunched tea towel, held in place by strands of duct tape which he'd passed around his midriff in a rough and ready field dressing.

The spots of blood I'd seen in the kitchen made sense to me now. He hadn't gone down into the basement. He'd used the first aid kit I'd left on the side instead.

The tea towel had been hanging over the handle of our range cooker. He would have found the duct tape in a drawer of the kitchen island.

His face, neck and gloves were spattered with blood.

Sam's toes scrabbled for purchase on the waxed floorboards. He reached up and dug his fingers into Donovan's arm, trying hopelessly to prise his grip free.

I could tell that he couldn't breathe. His face was already taking on a purplish hue in the bright electric light.

'Stop this,' I shrieked.

Donovan squeezed Sam's throat harder in response. 'Close the front door.'

I glanced towards it – it was still hanging open – then returned my attention to Sam.

His cheeks bulged. His eyes pleaded with me to comply. His complexion was glossy, the Adam's apple in his throat protruding sickeningly.

I was afraid to move. Afraid not to.

Everything that mattered to me hung from a thread.

'Shut the door now or I'll break his neck.'

Donovan tugged Sam's head to one side as if to demonstrate. I could see the muscles standing out like cords in Sam's neck.

'No,' I begged.

'You've already had your free pass tonight, Lucy.' He nodded towards John's house next door. 'You don't get another one.'

Sam stamped his foot repeatedly. He shuddered. His fingers began to twitch.

'Shut the door.'

I curled my toes in my shoes, craving the wail of the emergency sirens, the spatter of blue lights.

'The police are coming,' I said. 'They'll be here any second.'

'Then you'd better lock it as well. Do it now. I mean it. Three seconds or he dies.'

I finally moved.

The floor felt soft and marsh-like under my feet.

When I reached the door, I stifled a whimper as I looked outside.

No sirens.

No lights.

I shut the door, my hand trembling as I reached up and rested my thumb against the snib button on the deadlock.

Blinking tears from my eyes, I slipped it upwards.

—*click.*

77

'Turn around,' Donovan told me.

I turned and stared at him, my eyes flicking to Sam.

An intense wash of desperate energy coursed through me. Adrenaline. Cortisol. My fight-or-flight response had kicked in but I had nowhere to flee to and no way to fight. The fight was inside me, tearing me apart.

Sam was holding himself rigidly still, clinging on to Donovan's forearm to prevent himself from falling because his upper body was tipped so far backwards from his hips.

His eyes were endlessly darting between us, wild and pleading.

'Go into the kitchen,' Donovan said.

Sam's cheeks quivered. Sweat sprang from his face and brow. His mouth was making fast plosive sounds from behind Donovan's hand.

'Let him go.'

'The kitchen,' Donovan said. 'Now.'

I shook my head at Sam – a wordless apology – and started to move, crabbing sideways and descending the steps down into the sunken kitchen area.

'Sit on one of those stools.'

In the periphery of my vision I could see the open door

to the basement, but I made sure not to look at it directly as I hurried by the end of the kitchen island. The last thing I wanted was to draw Donovan's attention to it or have him think of forcing us down there.

'Sit.'

I lowered myself onto the same wooden stool I'd perched on earlier when he'd gone upstairs with Bethany. It felt hard and unyielding underneath me.

My hands found their way to the granite countertop. I spread my fingers. They were tacky with perspiration and so alive with nervous energy that the little finger on my right hand flickered of its own accord.

'You have to let him go now,' I said. 'Please. He can't breathe.'

He watched me for a second more, a strange curiosity lighting his eyes, then he opened his arms and stepped back as Sam dropped to the ground.

Sam gasped and heaved. His back arched. He immediately coughed and hacked and clambered onto his hands and knees, spit dribbling from his lips, his chest and lungs quivering and his throat making a horrid dry retching noise.

Donovan clutched a hand against the wound to his side, grimacing, then swiped the back of his glove across his mouth, a stripe of blood marking his cheek.

After taking another moment to brace himself, he moved towards the front door and used his duplicate keys to lock the deadlock and seal us inside. He then returned the keys to the right hip pocket of his trousers before bending low with a gruff exhalation of agonized pain and rapidly patting down Sam's clothes until he found and removed his mobile phone.

Once he'd confiscated it, he hauled Sam up by the scruff of his shirt, dragging him forwards as Sam scrambled to get his footing until they reached the top of the steps leading into the kitchen and Donovan tossed Sam down them.

Sam twisted and hit the floor on his flank, skidding sideways, then sprang to his feet and hobbled backwards away from Donovan towards the bare brick wall behind me on my left.

From the corner of my eye I could see him heaving air with one hand on his chest and his other hand feeling for his throat, massaging the bruises and marks on his skin as he contemplated Donovan with fear-filled eyes.

Donovan monitored him coolly, clamping his hand to his side again and labouring down the steps to move to the opposite side of the kitchen island from me, then turning awkwardly towards the units running along the wall.

With one quick movement he opened the door of the microwave.

I could see my mobile phone inside and what I guessed was Bethany's phone, too.

The plastic casing of both phones was bubbled and pocked.

A terrible odour of burnt chemicals wafted out.

Donovan tossed Sam's phone in, slammed the door shut, prodded buttons on the front. They blipped and binged, and then he punched one final button and the microwave whirred to life.

As he turned back to face us, his features contorted in discomfort, our phones flickered and glitched inside the microwave behind him.

There was a fizzing pop. A tendril of smoke.

'Word of advice.' He was talking through his pain. 'Don't ever heat a phone for more than a minute. Ten seconds is normally enough to kill the signal. We wouldn't want to start a fire now, would we?'

The microwave binged a final time and went dark aside from a brief blue fizz from inside.

He then snatched open a drawer on the island unit across from me.

A *thunk* and a clatter and he removed a large hatchet knife that he slapped down sideways on the countertop.

I recoiled inwardly.

The knife had a short rubber handle and a large rectangular cutting blade. It wasn't a utensil we used very often, which was why it had been buried deep in the drawer where the duct tape had been. Sam had purchased the knife on a whim during a trip to a department store several months earlier. He'd prepared a couple of meat dishes with it and after that it had stayed in the drawer ever since.

Until now.

I tried not to look as scared as I felt.

But it was hard.

I knew the blade was fiendishly sharp. From the way Donovan clutched his side and tilted the blade to the light with a quick, appraising gaze, it was clear he understood that, too.

I looked up at him slowly.

I had no idea how much blood he'd lost but he appeared to be in a very bad way. He looked drained and sickly, his face bloodless and drawn, his neck gleaming with sweat. Blood was seeping through the tea towel he'd taped to his side, dripping in slow splotches onto the floor. But something was driving him on. He wasn't going to relent or let us go.

I withdrew my hands from the countertop very carefully and cupped them together on my lap.

Next to me, Sam shuddered as if he'd been doused by an icy shower, then murmured something that sounded like a silent prayer as he bumped up against the exposed brickwork behind him. His shirt was untucked and parted where several buttons had come loose. His skinny chinos had slipped downwards, exposing the tops of his boxer shorts. His hair was matted and sticking up in clumps, his lips slick with saliva.

'Why are you here?' he asked Donovan. 'What do you want?'

But Donovan didn't answer him. He simply lifted the hatchet knife and then wrinkled his nose against a fresh jab of pain as he inspected the wound in his side.

'Didn't have to stab me, Lucy. This really smarts.'

Not enough.

I stole a glance at the front door, listening for the sirens that were coming, the squeal of brakes, the thump of car doors.

'What are you going to do when the police get here?' I asked him.

Donovan paused, studying me with feigned surprise.

'Sam?' He waved the blade of the knife at him. 'Do you want to explain or should I?'

78

Sam didn't respond right away and it worried me.

I got why he might be hesitant. I understood that he was shocked and scared, and I guessed he was afraid that if he told Donovan the police were on their way he might panic and attack us with the knife.

Perhaps he thought that if he delayed until the police got here, they'd know how to handle the situation better than we would.

Or perhaps he was trying to get a read on Donovan, assess him, understand him. Sam had an analytical mind and he had experience of dealing with people suffering from fears and delusions. I knew he'd been in rooms before with individuals who could be unpredictable and dangerous.

But I needed him to speak up.

I needed him to back me on this.

'Sam?'

He shot me a furtive look, then swallowed audibly and peered at Donovan again, searching his face as if he was looking for a secret meaning behind Donovan's words.

Something flitted behind his eyes. Something I couldn't quite interpret.

'Sam?'

He swallowed again and when he spoke his voice was hoarse and afraid.

'I'm sorry, Lucy.'

I stared at him, feeling a rumbling deep inside. A warning quake.

I hadn't moved. My stool hadn't moved. I knew that for certain, but for a crazy second it felt as if my stool was wobbling wildly.

'Sam?'

'Shit. Oh, shit.' He tugged his hair by the roots, ran his hands down over his face. 'I . . . messed up. I didn't call them. I just thought . . .'

He didn't say any more. He didn't have to.

I understood the terrible miscalculation he'd made.

'It's just with the way you've been lately, your panic attacks and your anxiety about the house viewings . . . you know how you spiral and obsess and . . . you were just looking so out of it when I got home.'

I didn't respond.

I didn't say a word.

My mind flashed on the phone call Sam had made outside. I thought of how he'd stepped away from me while I'd bent forwards and clutched the railings as he'd talked to the emergency services.

Except he hadn't talked to the emergency services.

He'd faked the call.

I felt light-headed, glancing towards our front door again, then staring in a ringing daze towards our living area.

I thought of the way Sam had stalked inside ahead of me as I'd gripped his shirt from behind, how he'd contemplated the displaced coffee table and the smashed vase and the blood and how he'd asked me again how I'd hit my head.

He didn't believe you.

He didn't believe you from the very start.

It rocked me.

'Nobody is coming?' I was still struggling to wrap my head around it. 'We're on our own?'

'Well, that's not quite true,' Donovan said.

He transferred the hatchet knife to his other hand as he fished his phone out of his trouser pocket. When he glanced at the screen, he made a small appreciative noise at the back of his throat without explaining why.

'What are you talking about?' Sam asked him.

'Why I'm here,' Donovan told him. 'Why you're here, Sam. And why *Louise* is here with us, too.'

79

It was hard for me to tell if Donovan knew he'd got my
name wrong.

It seemed like an unwitting mistake. A slip of the tongue,
perhaps brought on by his blood loss and suffering. Louise
instead of Lucy. As if he'd misspoken and had failed to
notice. As if his faculties were beginning to dim.

But then when he said nothing more – when he turned
his focus back to me, sweating, pensive, awaiting a reaction
– I began to understand that it had been deliberate. Targeted.

'That's not my name,' I told him.

He didn't respond. He just stared at me and swiped at
the perspiration on his upper lip with his thumb.

'You said Louise.'

Again, he said nothing.

'My name is Lucy.'

I could hear a muted ticking in the room. It was coming
from the wall clock above Sam but it might as well have
been inside my head.

I glanced back at Sam in confusion. He was pinned against
the wall, his body tensed, his face blanched, his eyes huge
and tremulous.

He shook his head at me.

I think we both sensed that we were dealing with someone who was acting increasingly unhinged. Sam would know better than me, but I guessed it was possible Donovan was undergoing a psychotic episode.

But then another possibility occurred to me. A more obvious one.

'You have the wrong person,' I said.

I swung my head between Donovan and Sam, my conviction growing, needing them both to understand.

'Don't you get it? I'm not who you think I am. You've made a mistake.'

The more I thought about it, the more it made a crushing sense.

The blood tests. The DNA analysis. He'd talked about wanting to verify that I was the person he was searching for.

But that implied an element of doubt on his part. It meant he knew he could have made a mistake.

'You have the wrong person. The wrong house. All of it. You're wrong.'

Donovan contemplated me for a long moment, his chin tilted upwards slightly, nostrils twitching, as if he was smelling the unpleasant stink of our microwaved phones on the air.

'You're scared of the basement?' he asked me.

Not this.

I reached out a hand to Sam and he took it.

'She has claustrophobia,' Sam explained, giving my hand a squeeze.

'And you would know?' Donovan said.

'Yes.'

287

'Because you're an expert? I've read some of your work, Sam. Your academic papers.'

Sam gave my hand another squeeze. 'Is that supposed to intimidate me?'

'No.' He gave Sam a hard look. 'But I'd be lying if I said I couldn't tell that it does. You wrote this one piece. It was about how some phobias have a simple trigger and others are much more complex. I'm paraphrasing, but I think your general point was that there could be a real mixture of reasons. A childhood incident overlaid with another trauma, for example. Or layers of multiple traumas. They can confuse the picture. Get jumbled up.'

'That can happen, yes.'

'Interesting.' Donovan returned his attention to me. 'I looked in your medicine cabinet. In the en suite. You have a lot of medication.'

I just stared at him. It was another invasion, and while I suppose it shouldn't have irritated me, it still did.

'For your anxiety?' he asked me.

'That's none of your business.'

'Prescribed by your GP?'

I said nothing.

'You pick up the medicine yourself?'

Sam did. Usually. There was a pharmacy that was convenient for the university. But I wasn't going to tell him that.

'So now what happens?' Sam asked.

'Hmm?'

'I asked, what happens now? What do you want from us?'

'Now?' He assessed me again. 'Now we get Louise to tell us the truth.'

80

My heart sank.

He seemed to be stuck on this. I was scared he was past reasoning with. Terrified we had no way out.

The police weren't coming. Sam hadn't called them. I was furious with him for lying to me; I was wounded, hurt. How could he not have trusted me? How could he not have got that this wasn't all in my mind?

I knew my anxieties had been spiralling lately. I understood it was something I hadn't got a handle on, despite Sam's guidance and help and, yes, the meds I was on. What I hadn't appreciated until now was quite how worried Sam must have been about me. I hadn't realized things had got *that* bad.

Outside of these walls, the only person who had any understanding of our predicament was John, but John's understanding was tangled and confused. He'd been upset and distressed enough to leave his living room when I was fighting with Donovan, but it was a huge stretch to think he might try to raise an alarm now that we'd left his home.

This is on you.

You have to think of something. Anything.

You have to dig yourself out of this pit.

'Oliver Downing,' Donovan said.

'Who?'

He growled deep in his throat, shaking his head ominously, his whole demeanour suggesting he was seething inside.

'Look, we obviously don't know who that is,' Sam told him.

'DNA,' Donovan replied.

'Excuse me?'

He grimaced and adjusted his stance, taking a moment to contemplate the makeshift dressing he'd applied to his wound. I could tell he was concerned by the blood he was losing. I wondered if it would make his actions even more rash.

'I took a sample of DNA,' he said. 'From Louise. That text I just got was a progress report from a lab I'm using. Shouldn't be too much longer now before I get some preliminary results. A rush job, admittedly. Not something that would stand up in court. But it's going to be enough to tell me the sample matches the DNA found at the scene.'

'Scene?' I asked.

He looked up at me. 'The crime scene. On the balcony. Below the roof.'

His face was pinched, his voice tight. I could tell this all meant a great deal to him. I could see how invested he was.

I just didn't know what it had to do with me.

'Somebody fell?' Sam asked him.

'Oliver fell.'

'And you think this has something to do with Lucy?'

'With Louise. Yes, I do.'

'Why?'

'Because of what I do, Sam. Because of who I am. I'm an intelligence officer with the British Army. I just got back from a long posting overseas. I'm skilled in finding out information. Usually information other people don't want me to find. Layman's terms, I'm an investigator. A specialist one. And like any investigator, I follow clues. And on this occasion all the clues led me to one place. Here. To Louise.'

I glanced at Sam. He seemed to be as lost as I was.

An intelligence officer. Could that be true?

In my mind I cycled back through Donovan's behaviour since he'd been in our home. I thought about his attitude. His bearing. There were times when he'd been violent, terrifyingly so, but hadn't I also had the sense that he was holding himself in check, as if he was following some sort of inner rule book or code?

I wondered now if that could be because of military training. I supposed it could also explain how he'd been able to subdue and drug Bethany so swiftly, how he'd disarmed me when I'd come at him with the keys, the restraint hold he'd put Sam in, even the way he'd quizzed and pressured and probed me. But what could any of that have to do with us?

'You have to listen to me,' I said slowly. 'If this man—'

'Oliver.'

'If he fell, that had nothing to do with me.'

'Your DNA will show otherwise.'

I didn't say anything to that.

I was beginning to think it was futile trying to reason with him. My attention would be better focused on other things.

Like the knife he'd taken from the drawer. It was on the countertop and his hand was resting lightly on it.

But he wasn't holding it properly.

He seemed more preoccupied by the wound I'd inflicted. He'd clamped his other hand over it again and he was pulling a face and snorting air, cursing under his breath.

We were only three metres apart.

My feet were resting on the metal crossbar towards the bottom of the stool I was perched on.

I looked again at the knife and rocked my toes forwards, exerting some pressure onto the balls of my feet.

'It was under his fingernails, by the way,' Donovan said, closing his hand over the knife handle, sliding it off the countertop. 'Only traces, but enough. That tells me he scratched his attacker. Hard. When she pushed him. Before he died.'

Something curled up inside me.

I felt a sudden tightening of the scar on my arm.

I knew he couldn't see it. Not right now.

But he'd obviously seen it earlier when he'd rolled up the sleeve of my jumper and stuck a needle in me.

And from the way he was staring at me – through me, almost – I understood he was telling me exactly that.

'He's dead?' I asked.

'Yes.'

'I had nothing to do with any of this,' I told him.

'If what you're saying is true, the police would have investigated,' Sam added.

'Oh, you're right, they did.'

'So?'

'So nothing. Oliver went up to the roof with a mystery woman. Witnesses confirm that. The police got a description but nobody knew who she was. It was a big party. Lots of people.'

A little of my certainty ebbed away.

A big party.

Lots of people.

Discomfort churned inside me. The scar on my arm seemed to shrink and contract.

I thought about the blanks in my memory. The gaps.

One day it will all come back to you.

But I didn't remember a roof. All I remembered, and then only barely, was the music and the lights and the attack on me in the bathroom.

And your arm.

The scratch you can't explain.

And then another thought. A sudden one.

'What did he look like?' I asked. 'Oliver?'

Donovan considered my question. He took his time over it, resting the point of the knife on the countertop, twirling it from side to side. Then he hummed, picked up his phone and tapped it several times with his thumb. He scrolled for a moment, then tapped once again.

He turned it to show me the screen, the same way he'd turned it before when he was showing me the photo he'd taken of me upstairs.

Only this time the screen was speckled with blood and the image he was showing me was quite different.

I found myself staring at a photograph of a handsome young man in outdoor gear. His hair was windswept. His skin was flushed. He was smiling with a moorland scene behind him. I got the impression the photograph had been taken during a hike.

Seeing him increased the churning in my blood.

I didn't recognize him. It wasn't as simple or as concrete as that. But I felt *something*. A stirring. An intangible sense of a connection, somehow.

A pressure was building in my head, like the beginning of a migraine. A strange tingling across my skin.

And then a bright flash behind my eyes. Stinging. Blinding. And . . . *something*.

'What is it?' Donovan asked. 'What's happening to you?'

I groaned. Pressed the heel of my hand against the side of my head.

I didn't want to white-out again.

I couldn't.

But I also sensed I was close to something.

'Talk to me,' Donovan said.

I bared my teeth and squinted at the photograph again.

The man featured in it – Oliver – looked tall and physically imposing. Like the blurred, dark figure who'd attacked me.

With the metallic rasping voice.

'I've been watching you.'

Another painful flash.

And a flicker of darkness behind it.

In my mind's eye I glimpsed a smudged and indistinct vision of a face, of movement, of someone crowding in on me.

Was it possible that Oliver had been the man who'd assaulted me in the bathroom?

'Louise?'

I winced and massaged my temples.

I didn't know if it was possible, but if it *had* been Oliver, then it could explain something else. Part of the reason the attack had been so frightening was because it had been apparently motiveless. But perhaps it had been inexplicable because the man who'd attacked me had been tragically unbalanced. Perhaps he'd lashed out because it had been the precursor to a more terminal crisis.

'How do you know he was pushed?' I asked.

He tensed. 'You're suggesting he jumped?'

'Yes.'

'That's where the police got to. Oliver had some issues. A history of clinical depression. They decided he could have got the blood under his fingernails another way.'

My way, I thought. *With what happened to me in that bathroom.*

'So they stopped looking.' His jaw stiffened as he put his phone away, still gauging me intently as I stopped rubbing my temples and lowered my hands. 'Nobody's been looking into this properly until I got back from my posting.'

He twirled the knife around some more, the blade grinding against granite.

'But I know he didn't jump. I know he was working through his problems. And he had a lot to live for. Everything a young guy could possibly want. He'd just moved into an apartment he shared with his sister. My sister, too, as it happens. That's why I know he had to have been pushed. Because Oliver was my little brother.'

81

I got up off my stool.

I didn't know why.

Maybe I sensed the situation was even more volatile now that it was personal to Donovan.

Or perhaps I instinctively understood that I needed to alter the dynamic. Pull his focus elsewhere.

Which I did by accidentally toppling my stool as I climbed off it.

I slumped and nearly fell, but Sam grabbed me and caught the stool at the same time.

'Sit down,' Donovan told me.

I didn't say no but I didn't do as he asked.

I pulled clear of Sam and reached for the countertop, moving along to my right, away from the end of the island unit where Donovan was watching me from.

My head felt too heavy on my shoulders. My temples were pulsing. I felt sickly and hot.

The apartment.

The party.

The scratch on my arm.

It all made a strange sense until it didn't.

I tried to concentrate. Tried to push past the blockage in my mind and remember what had happened to me more clearly.

But I couldn't.

The blockage remained stubbornly in place.

In my mind's eye, it was a white elastic film. Opaque, with a hint of shadows moving on the other side, but the details remaining too shady and vague for me to decipher.

I could push on the film, poke at it, but it always stretched and held. I couldn't pierce it to see what was on the other side.

One day that film may just snap.

Sam had told me that. What he *hadn't* told me was if I would snap with it when it did.

It felt like there was a crazed whirring in my brain. A febrile energy. A humming like the drum of a tumble dryer spinning out of control.

Oliver. Oliver Downing.

I repeated the name in my head but it made no difference.

It meant nothing to me.

I moved further along the countertop, hand over hand, shimmying backwards to pass the next stool along.

I was getting nearer to the end of the island unit. Closer to the Crittall doors behind me and the garden beyond that.

But when I snatched a look at the doors I saw something that chilled the blood in my veins.

The key that had been there earlier was missing. He must have taken it, too.

I couldn't bolt out into the back garden and scream for help.

And even if I got out there, I couldn't escape to raise the alarm. The fence panels we'd installed on top of the walls were too high.

'You know,' Donovan said, switching his attention to Sam,

'my brother was a student at LSE. Economics, not psychology. You ever meet?'

'No, I don't think so.'

'I just wondered. Because he had some issues, like I said. And that got me thinking: where might Oli have gone for help? And then I found out about your support groups. I actually sent an email about it. Maybe you saw it?'

'We're not able to discuss the support groups. University policy. There are privacy rules.'

'That's pretty much what the reply I got told me. The reply came from an administrator in your department. I tried talking to her on the phone, explaining the situation, even met her in person. She told me anyone who joined your support groups had to sign a consent form but she wouldn't let me see them.'

Sam swallowed. He really didn't seem to get where Donovan was going with this.

'But I'm the persistent type and I waited until one of your support groups finished up. I thought about talking to you directly but not right away. I watched you instead, followed you home. No real reason except habit. I'm used to gathering intelligence. Usually a lot of it is wasted. First thing I noticed was your house was for sale. Second thing I noticed was it wasn't just you living here.'

He reached into the hip pocket of his trousers and removed what looked like a crumpled piece of paper. It was light blue with a glossy finish. Folded until it was about the size of a credit card.

He flung it towards me.

It twirled through the air, over the sink, hit the countertop and bounced and skidded my way.

'What is this?'

'Take a look.'

I exchanged a lingering glance with Sam.

He was still holding on to the stool, a little absently, almost as if he'd forgotten he had caught it. I saw a deep line form in the middle of his eyebrows. A flicker of disquiet at the corners of his mouth.

I reached for the piece of paper and carefully unfolded it with shaking hands.

'That was in Oliver's bedroom,' Donovan told me. 'His things got boxed up after he died. I was the first one to pay attention to it.'

It was a flyer for a business.

The stock was high quality. The font was simple but elegant.

It had been folded over so many times there were multiple creases. The edges were scruffy and furred.

Louise Patton Home & Interior Design

There was a photograph of . . . *me* on the front.

A headshot.

Only I looked quite different. My hair was long and tied up in a ponytail. I appeared to be wearing a businesslike blouse and blazer, a broad and confident smile.

'I don't understand.'

'What is it?' Sam asked.

I held it up between my fingers and thumbs and showed him. There was also a website address and a telephone number on the front.

The reverse was blank.

After looking at it for a few seconds, Sam gave Donovan the same confused look that had formed on my face.

'Did you do this?' I asked him.

Donovan simply watched me. His lips had thinned. I couldn't tell if it was because he was concentrating on something or if he was suppressing another dose of pain.

'Is this supposed to convince me of something?' I continued. 'Because it doesn't.'

'The URL for that website is dead,' Donovan told me. 'The mobile number is disconnected.'

Sam shifted a little to Donovan's right and Donovan immediately lifted the knife and pointed it at him, twisting the blade sideways in the air.

'How about you put down the stool, Sam?'

Sam looked at it, nonplussed, then slowly put down the stool and raised his hands in a gesture of surrender.

Donovan returned his focus to me, drawing small circles in the air with the point of the knife.

'I did some digging into Louise Patton. I spoke to some of her former clients. One of them was pleased but a little frustrated to hear from me. They said she'd just been starting on a job for them when she stopped responding to their messages. Eventually they gave up and hired someone else.'

'This isn't mine,' I said. 'I don't know where you got this. I've never seen it before.'

'The client also told me they'd gone so far as to look for Louise at her day job. They said she worked part-time at a furniture shop on Tottenham Court Road.'

I didn't say anything to that.

It didn't make any sense.

'I took that flyer to the same shop,' he continued. 'Showed it to the manager. She confirmed you'd worked there. But she said you quit. By text message. She said she'd tried contacting you. Left a voicemail. Never got an answer. She's had staff who have treated her that way before. People can be funny about quitting.'

I shook my head.

I had left my job when I'd moved in with Sam but I'd spoken with Corrine, my manager. She'd wished me well and told me I was always welcome back in the future if things didn't work out for me.

'Ask me when the text message was sent,' Donovan said.

I glanced at Sam again.

There was something else in his face now.

Not just worry but a puzzled look of distress and disquiet.

'No?' Donovan said. 'Then I'll tell you. It was sent the day after my brother was pushed off that roof.'

82

I let go of the flyer.

It fluttered downwards onto the countertop as I retreated further back around the end of the kitchen island.

I didn't understand this.

I didn't know what he was hoping to achieve.

'Lucy?' Sam asked.

There was a different quality in his voice. An uncertain modulation.

I looked at him and immediately felt something inside me begin to disintegrate.

The puzzled and scared expression on his face had developed into something more like panic and doubt.

'Lucy, what is this?' He reached up and clutched at his hair. 'What's happening?'

'It's a stunt,' I told him. 'A lie.'

I stared furiously at Donovan, ignoring the flyer, daring him to say something more.

'Louise,' Donovan said, fixing on me doggedly. 'Her name is Louise.'

Tears filled my eyes.

The humming inside my skull was getting louder, more intense. It wasn't just making it hard for me to hear my own thoughts, it was making it difficult for me to trust them, too.

I didn't like the way Donovan was watching me. He wouldn't look away. He seemed to be using every trick he could think of to apply more and more pressure, the same way he'd relentlessly squeezed my wrist upstairs.

'Sam, he's lying.'

But another piece of my heart seemed to crumple and flake away when I saw the way Sam was looking at me.

He was clearly anguished and upset and scared.

But it was also apparent that he was having difficulty trusting me.

And he was glancing between myself and Donovan repeatedly, as if he was asking himself why – if I was really who I said I was, if I really didn't know what was happening here – Donovan had ended up inside our home.

'Lucy?' He stopped himself, closing his eyes for a second, as if he couldn't believe what he was about to say. 'Look, if you have something to tell me, if there's any truth to this at all . . . Jesus.' He lowered his hand from his hair and cupped it to the back of his neck. 'I mean . . . he has a knife.'

Four small words but they said so much more.

Because it wasn't just Sam's way of reminding me Donovan had a knife. It was also his way of saying that he didn't want Donovan to use that knife on me, or on him.

Especially if I'd been deceiving him.

Particularly if, by telling the truth, I could somehow lessen the danger we were in.

He has a knife.

And that was the whole point, wasn't it?

Donovan had the knife so he had the power.

He could say what he liked about me, no matter how outrageous, and the knife would lend credence to his words.

It could turn me into a liar in Sam's eyes.

A murderer.

A fake.

Which is why I reached down, opened the wine cooler in front of me and removed a bottle of white wine by its neck.

83

I raised the wine bottle up next to my shoulder like a club and stepped out from behind the end of the kitchen island. One long pace until I was facing Donovan with nothing between us except two or three big strides.

'That's a bad idea,' Donovan told me.

It probably was.

If I was thinking logically, if I was calm, I probably wouldn't have done it.

But I wasn't thinking logically. I wasn't calm.

I was exhausted.

And frightened.

And I couldn't take a second more of this.

'Put the bottle down. Take a moment to think about everything I've been telling you. Think about Oli.'

I didn't put the bottle down.

The green glass was beaded with moisture. It was cool and slick in my fist.

And I'd done too much thinking already.

Donovan sized me up for a careful moment, then slowly held the knife out in front of him. He was favouring his right side, using his other arm to cover up his wound.

'You don't want to do this,' he told me.

Tremors coursed through me. I felt spent and exposed, as if I was standing in a gale.

The open door to the basement was behind me. I could feel the darkness oozing out from within, coiling around my ankles, dragging me back.

I took a small step.

'Lucy, be careful,' Sam warned.

His voice was tight and pitchy. He looked very unsure and very afraid.

Donovan half twisted to face him, the knife moving with him, an appraising cast to his face.

Sam slowly reached out for the kitchen stool again. Fitting his hands around the wooden seat, he jerked it a few centimetres off the ground and held it warily, angling the legs towards Donovan as if he hoped to use it like a shield.

'I'm sorry about your brother,' I said. 'I'm sorry for what happened to him. But you need to get out of our house.'

The wine bottle was wavering in my fist. My arm radiated a shimmery energy. I took another small step forwards and watched as Donovan gauged me again, peering at me as if he was looking through a thick mist.

'I can't do that,' he told me carefully. I hated how he was talking to me. As if he was the calm and reasonable one and I was badly overreacting. 'I go when you go. We'll be leaving here together. You're coming with me.'

How, I wondered? Where? Because people would see if he tried to take me away from here. Even if he waited until the middle of the night, he'd be risking a witness spotting us. And I was not going to leave with him willingly. Not if I could help it. I'd rather shout and scream and take my chances.

And what about Sam?

I go when you go.

Did that mean he thought he could leave Sam behind? And Bethany, too?

'All day, every day, my mother torments herself,' he told me. 'She asks herself why Oli jumped. What did she do wrong? What did she miss? She's suffering, too. It's killing her. I've seen her shrink away from life, grow so fragile. Oli wasn't the only victim of what happened that night. So you're going to come with me, you're going to look her in the eye, and you're going to tell her the truth. That's what I want. You're going to give her the answers she needs.'

'I don't have the answers you want,' I told him.

'You do. You will. We're going to go soon.'

'No.'

I lunged towards him, swinging for his face.

The bottle flitted through the air.

He ducked backwards with a bark of pain.

Then impact.

An explosion of glass and wine.

I'd missed him and hit the hood over the range cooker.

Wine doused the stove top. It foamed and fizzed.

Chunks of glass clattered down.

My arm went light.

I was still clutching the bottle neck but now all that was left was a short, jagged curve.

I stared at it.

Donovan looked at it, too.

I saw the anguish cross his face.

I was pretty sure he was thinking of how I'd stabbed him

with the shard from the jug, maybe also calculating that his long arms and the blade of the hatchet knife would give him much more reach than the broken snub of the bottle would give me.

'Listen to me,' he said. 'You're making a mistake. You need to—'

I screamed.

Donovan's head had shunted violently sideways, his shoulder and torso following a split-second later, as if he'd been blindsided by an onrushing car.

A shout. A roar.

It took me a second to understand that Sam had charged forwards with the kitchen stool out in front of him, ramming into Donovan's neck and upper body with the metal legs.

Sam was still screaming. Donovan had been spun around on his heels and now he was falling backwards, his upper body slamming down against the stove top, pinned by the legs of the stool, his head mashed up against the tiled splash-back.

One of the metal crossbars at the bottom of the stool – the footrest – was crushing his throat.

Sam yelled louder, terrified, out of his depth, and pushed down harder.

Donovan spluttered and tried to rise up but he couldn't.

He couldn't breathe, couldn't shout. His airways were being crushed.

But the knife was still in his hand and it was still dangerous.

He swung the blade towards Sam. Scything at his thigh.

A wet ripping noise as he slashed through Sam's jeans.

Sam cried out, tipping to one side as Donovan began to swing the knife back the other way.

No.

I released the bottle neck, rushed forwards and made a grab for Donovan's wrist.

I banged his wrist against the handle of the oven.

Banged it again.

Dug my nails deep into his skin.

I was still holding on, still fighting for the knife with Sam leaning over me and mewling in fear and fright, his feet skidding backwards desperately on the floor as he pressed down even harder on the legs of the stool until Donovan's hand and arm went gradually floppy, the strength left his body and the knife fell to the ground.

84

I took a step backwards, staring at Donovan.

A ripple of horror made me physically buck.

Donovan's eyes were closed. The crossbar of the stool was embedded in his throat. His body was limp, his arms splayed at his sides. Blood from his dressing was dripping slowly onto the stove.

'Sam?' I whispered.

Sam stumbled as he readjusted his footing. His mouth was gaping. I could see blood staining the fabric of his jeans where he'd been cut on his leg.

He cringed and eased up on the force he was exerting down through the stool, but only by a fraction. He looked scared and horrified by what he'd done.

When Donovan still didn't move, I swallowed thickly and reached towards his neck, my hand moving slowly, slowly, until my fingers touched his jugular.

His skin was warm and clammy.

He didn't respond to my touch.

I pushed gently on Sam's arm with my other hand until he eased off very slightly more on the stool.

A terrifying second.

I gulped as I probed Donovan's neck, wary of the slightest movement.

A flicker beneath my fingertips. His pulse was sluggish, but there.

I felt a trickle of relief in my stomach mixed with more uncertainty.

Now that I was nearer, I could see the tremor of his pupils beneath his eyelids and, when I raised the back of my hand to his nostrils, a faint exhalation washed against my skin. It reminded me of Bethany. We needed to get to her.

'I think he's unconscious,' I whispered.

'Are you sure?'

'I think you can ease off. I think it's OK.'

Sam looked terrified as he lifted the stool away in shaky increments, poised to stab down with it again if Donovan stirred.

'It's OK,' I said again. 'He's not moving.'

Very slowly, Sam lifted the stool clear and set it down sideways on the kitchen island, snatching his hands away from it as if he wished he'd never touched it, but keeping it within reach.

I could see how freaked out he was. There was a wash of tears in his eyes and he was hobbling from the cut to his leg.

When he looked again at Donovan, he seemed equal parts stunned and appalled by his actions.

'Thank you,' I told him.

He nodded wordlessly but I could tell he was uncomfortable about it. I could tell he still wasn't sure about me.

I placed my hand on his back. I could feel the heat coming through his shirt.

'You saved me,' I whispered. 'You did the right thing.'

His hands were loose at his sides. He wasn't hugging me back.

'But can you call the police now?' I asked. 'For real this time? I have to go up and help Bethany.'

I went to hurry away but Sam reached for my hand, pulling me back.

'Why did you think there was someone else?' he asked me, his gaze flitting across my face. 'Outside. You said you were afraid someone was watching me. You thought they might have followed me home.'

'Because that's what he told me. He made me think he was communicating with someone in your support group. He told me they were faking a phobia. But now I think he was lying.'

'Why?'

I glanced at Donovan again. He still wasn't moving but I was reluctant to waste more time.

'Because if he was working with someone else they would have followed us in here. He would have called them for help after I stabbed him. Just like we should be calling the police.'

A tiny line formed between Sam's eyebrows.

'What is it?' I asked him.

He didn't answer me. His gaze had gone inwards, as if something was niggling at him, a thought he was afraid to voice.

'Sam, what is it?'

'There was someone in the group today,' he said slowly, almost as if he was only now piecing it all together in his mind. 'She stayed behind with me at the end. I noticed she had a tattoo. Inside her wrist.'

He turned my hand over and showed me, smoothing his fingers over my skin close to my scar.

His fingers felt strangely cold. I didn't like the haunted look on his face.

'The tattoo was of a bumblebee.'

'So?'

'Her phobia.' He raised his gaze to the ceiling and closed his eyes briefly, as if he'd overlooked something obvious he should have spotted before now. 'She told me she suffered from trypanophobia.' .

'I don't understand.'

'Fear of needles. She shouldn't have had a tattoo.'

And that's when Sam seized hold of both my arms, spun me around and shoved me hard down the basement steps.

85

Sam

'I'm sorry,' Sam told the Lost Girl, jerking a thumb over his shoulder with an apologetic grimace, setting off in the direction of Temple station. 'But I really have to run to get my Tube. My girlfriend's expecting me. I need to get home.'

Except he didn't go home. Not right away. And he didn't have a girlfriend.

Yet.

He just needed to make his excuses and hurry off from the Lost Girl, then take up a position on the other side of the street, in the doorway to an office block, watching the Athlete and the Artist as his anger and frustration roiled in his gut.

They didn't know he was watching them. They were too preoccupied with one another. And Sam had become an expert at keeping to the shadows.

The Athlete had his thumbs hooked in the shoulder straps of his backpack. He was several inches taller than the Artist, acting chatty and casual, smiling with his perfectly aligned, perfectly expensive teeth.

The Artist smiled coyly back as she reached into her shoulder bag, removed a glossy flyer and passed it to the Athlete, then studied him with an anxious, pensive expres-

314

sion as he held the flyer between his hands, perusing it carefully before pointing to the photograph on the front with a grin.

The acid burn crept up to Sam's gullet, raging at the back of his throat.

He could see it was a flyer for the Artist's interior design business. She used the same graphics and font on her website.

That was how Sam had first found her. Surfing the Web. Hunting for someone with the right potential to help him remodel his grandparents' place, turn the maximum profit, get everything right.

Her website had featured links to her social feeds. A fledgling Facebook page where she had few followers for her business. Twitter, which she posted to rarely. And Instagram, which she used more often but where she almost never interacted with other accounts.

Soon after that he knew almost everything about her.

Her full name.

Her residential address.

The furniture shop where she worked part-time.

The fact she'd moved to London only eight months before.

She appeared to have next to no contact with any family members. Her parents were deceased. If she had close friends from before she'd relocated to London, they didn't stay in touch with her online, and if she'd made new friends since, there was no evidence to suggest it. Outside of the handful of clients she was beginning to attract, she'd made barely a ripple in the city. He sensed she was lonely.

Like most people, she had a set routine and that made her easy to follow. And once he started, it was difficult to stop.

He didn't just like watching her.

He craved it.

But, somehow, she picked up his trace.

She started looking over her shoulder, peering out of her front window late at night, posting even less frequently on Instagram, never on Twitter or Facebook at all.

He knew she hadn't seen him directly.

He was much too wily for that.

But it was obvious she had a sense of him.

A fear.

Which was perfect, when he thought about it.

Because fears and phobias were one of Sam's specialisms.

And with a few well-targeted ads for his support group on Instagram, plus several flyers of his own put up at the stop for the bus he knew she took home from work, and the cafe she visited alone, he felt confident he could lure her in.

Persuasion 101.

Advertisers had mastered the same skills. Know your audience and give them what they want. Make your subject see what you want them to see, believe what you want them to believe.

And then, when it had all come together and she'd arrived in the seminar room this afternoon . . .

The *rush* he'd experienced.

It was hard to articulate.

Harder still to contain.

Because watching her was one thing, but when she'd talked about her fear of being stalked, of having this irrational sense of being watched . . .

It had taken all of his self-discipline, everything he'd rehearsed and learned, not to spring up out of his chair, grab her by her shoulders and shake her, let her know it wasn't irrational at all.

Because there was someone following her.

He was following her.

And now she'd come to him.

86

Being pushed down the basement stairs was like falling in a dream.

Except when I hit the bottom I didn't wake up.

My nightmare had only just begun.

I tried to breathe but when I opened my mouth a great sucking fear invaded my chest.

It seemed to suck the basement walls inwards with it.

They hurtled towards me.

The ceiling slammed down.

I shrank into a ball, cradled my head, closed my eyes, pressed my back and upper body against the bare brickwork of the walls at the bottom of the stairs, in the corner of the room.

The tiled floor was gritty. The air was stale.

Thousands and thousands of cubic pounds of stone and earth and brick pressed down on top of me.

I was scared to look out from behind my arms because if I looked I'd see where I was. I'd know I was really down here.

So my brain switched to other priorities, carrying out a quick inventory of my body, finding the points that were flaring in pain.

My knees and elbows. My ankle. My chin. The heels of my hands, wet with blood.

I'd put my hands out in front of me as I'd fallen – they were grazed and skinned – and somehow thinking of that was worse because I could remember how I'd pushed against nothing but air.

Pushed *through* nothing.

Until I landed with a jolt and all that nothing rushed in at me.

Imagine you're not here.

Pretend you're anywhere else.

But I couldn't do that.

I was incapable of it.

Because the realness of what was happening was inescapable to me.

And that's when I heard it.

Something rooted deep in the marrow of my innermost fears.

—click.

It was the sound of the bolt on the outside of the door to the basement sliding home.

87
Sam

Sam followed the Athlete and the Artist for the rest of the afternoon, into the early evening.

He couldn't let it go.

Even though he knew he should have.

Even when he risked being seen.

Which he wasn't, because he was careful and well practised, and because he maintained his distances, monitored his angles, watched for reflections in windows and mirrors and the glass of passing vehicles.

He didn't move too quickly or too slowly.

He blended in.

But seeing them together, watching how comfortable they were in each other's company, how they talked and laughed and confided in each other, how delighted the Artist was to have company, watching them *connect*, then later stroll into a pub . . .

It savaged him.

More than he'd been prepared for.

More than he could take.

Because he'd lured her to him, for him, not for the Athlete or anyone else.

Plus it was happening too fast.

It shouldn't be happening this fast.

His whole intention had been to take it slow and careful, build her trust, her *reliance* on him, not to see her get swept away by some facile trust fund prince.

And then later, inside the pub, when he'd watched from a distant booth and seen the Athlete take her flyer out of his pocket to talk about it again, when she'd used her phone to scroll through some images demonstrating her work, the two of them crouching together over the table to study the screen, their faces almost touching, eyes locking, he began to feel *the fear.*

That maybe it was too late.

Maybe he'd lost her to him.

Which was clearly unacceptable.

And was why, when they left the pub together a short while later, a little drunk, a little tipsy, he followed them again.

88

I peered out through splayed fingers at the steps leading up to the basement door.

The steps were tall and narrow. Bare timber painted white.

Looking at them, I was engulfed by a powerful sensation of vertigo, but in reverse, as if I was falling endlessly backwards.

As if I'd never stop.

I put my hands out at my sides and clasped the unfinished brickwork around me, deathly cold against my skin.

I was breathing too fast and too shallowly.

The room was starting to spin.

I could still hear the *click* from the bolt on the outside of the door. It seemed to echo against the basement walls, repeating in my mind.

I realized I was picking at the brickwork with my nail.

Strange.

There was something familiar about my instinct to do that. An odd kind of muscle memory.

My exhaled breath seemed to chill the air in front of me as I looked at where my hands were placed.

In the stark lighting of the basement I could see other scratches on the brickwork. They were faint but they were there. Tiny stripe marks scored into the paint.

Exactly where I was scratching right now.

My heart jackhammered.

There was a choking blockage in my throat.

Then a sob funnelled up inside me and burst out.

An involuntary burp of horror and fear.

Sam pushed you down these steps.

Sam locked the door.

And then a new thought, cascading on from the others.

Sam didn't call the police.

What if the reason Sam didn't call the police wasn't because he didn't believe you?

What if it was because he didn't want the police to come?

89
Sam

After the Athlete led the Artist into the modern apartment building in Farringdon, they stepped into a lift together.

They weren't holding hands but they were standing close to each other and trading secret smiles, the Artist blushing and glancing down as the doors shuddered closed.

A fast uptick in his pulse as Sam swept into the foyer, watching the numbers above the lift climb.

. . . 8 . . .

. . . 9

The lift stopped.

He watched the digital panel, making sure it didn't change, then he stepped into a second carriage, rode in it to floor ten and took the stairs down a level.

He could hear the party music before he emerged from the stairwell.

It was loud and percussive. A frenzied pop beat.

And when he stuck his head into the hallway, only one apartment door was open, with people milling around in front of it, vaping and chatting, music and light spilling out. Some of them were dressed in white lab coats. Others in blue hospital scrubs.

He pulled back, strategizing, then the lift binged and a

group of strangers – students mostly, by the looks of it – rushed out, clutching bags filled with bottles of booze.

'Whose party is this anyway?' someone called.

'Who cares?' a drunk girl whooped back, thrusting her fists into the air.

There were enough people, he told himself.

There was enough noise.

And most of them sounded drunk.

Besides, he was a young Assistant Professor. It wasn't totally out of the realms of possibility for him to say he'd been invited if they bumped into each other.

You can do this.

You have to do this.

You know you won't be able to let it go.

So he slipped in through the door, shuffling between strangers towards the main living space, which was a riot of flashing lights and writhing bodies, and where a gaggle of people were gathered on a balcony outside.

He couldn't see the Athlete or the Artist anywhere and when a drunken girl bumped into him he grabbed her arm and shouted, 'Who lives here?'

'Amy,' she yelled back, her pupils glazed, a silly grin on her face. 'It's her flat-warming. We're both studying medicine at UCL.'

She pointed to where a young woman dressed in green scrubs with a stethoscope around her neck was chugging from a bottle of prosecco, the revellers around her chanting encouragement, the foaming liquid trickling down the sides of her mouth.

'Her brother lives here, too,' the girl yelled. 'Oliver.'

She was pressing herself against Sam, her body warm and pliant, but all he felt was a slick of disgust, his eyes scanning the melee, searching for the Artist.

'Which one is Oliver?'

'The hot one. He's a rower. He's—'

But as she peered around, she couldn't spot him, and when she turned back, mystified, Sam was already moving off. He shoved his way back through the crowds, past the kitchen, trying doors in the hallway, interrupting a young couple who were necking in the bathroom. After excusing himself, he entered a bedroom that was empty aside from two young women who were sitting on the end of the bed, one of them sobbing into her hands, the other one rubbing her shoulder.

The one who wasn't crying shot him a warning look as his eyes swept the room. He saw some weights and fitness equipment in the corner, a photograph tacked to a notice-board of the Athlete arm in arm with his sister, the medical student, and what could have been an older brother, dressed in army camouflage fatigues. And then – in a moment of tingling horror – the flyer for the Artist's interior design business crumpled on a desk.

A house-warming, he thought.

For two affluent young siblings.

One of whom might have invited the Artist to the party, perhaps sweetening the offer by saying they were interested in hiring an interior decorator for their new place.

'What are you staring at?' the girl with the aggressive gaze asked him.

'My mistake,' Sam said.

He started to back out of the room, but the music wasn't so loud that he missed what she said next as she hugged her friend close.

'I mean, so what if he takes some new skank to the roof? You said you two were done. It's his loss, babe.'

90

I squinted at the portion of the basement I could see in front of me.

A breathless moment.

My vision jostled.

The walls seemed to be trembling, warping, as if they might break loose and shuttle inwards at any moment.

They were painted white. As was the ceiling.

The floor had been laid with terracotta tiles.

When Sam had shown me the photographs he'd taken, I hadn't expected it to look quite so austere.

We hadn't included any images of the basement in the property details because Bethany had agreed with Sam that it wasn't an area we needed to focus on.

But now I wondered: was that the real reason?

I glanced up the steps towards the door again, my stomach twisting as I thought about Sam on the other side, thinking of the noise – that *click* – the bolt had made and how it had seemed to chime with something inside me.

Like the lock on the bathroom door.

The one that torments you.

I swallowed too quickly.

Almost gagged.

My head was pounding.

I withdrew a shaking hand from the wall, pinched the bridge of my nose and gradually pushed up to my knees, then my feet.

The floor melted under me.

Or seemed to.

I planted my feet wide apart and put my arms out at my sides to keep my balance.

I edged forwards.

The ceiling is not coming down on you.

You're not going to be trapped down here.

I could tell myself that but I wasn't sure I believed it. My instincts screamed at me to cover my head as if masonry was hammering down.

I'd only taken one step but it felt as if a chasm had opened up behind me.

I peered upwards, towards the door, but I had a powerful sense there was something I needed to see down here.

Something I had to confront.

I'd read once that wolves can smell the scent of fear on the air. A musty combination of pheromones and angst given off by their prey.

On some level I was dimly aware that I could smell something similar right now, the aroma intensified and marked by the specific base notes given off by the static cellar air, the low ceiling, the brick walls and terracotta tiles.

It's your own fear, said a voice in my head.

And then another thought.

An instinctive, olfactory warning beacon, far more powerful than any recollection I could conjure visually or access in any other way.

You've smelled this smell before.

91

Sam

There was a strange absence of noise when Sam nudged open the door to the roof of the apartment building. It was as though the city was holding its breath.

Or maybe Sam was.

Only there was no need for him to do that.

Because all that was in front of him was the rust-pitted cylindrical pedal bin that had been holding the door partially open, a short expanse of tarred and gritted roofing felt and a waist-high perimeter wall.

The roofing felt and the brick wall were clotted with moss and bird droppings. The bin was stained in different ways. Water streaks and cigarette ash, mostly. A quick glance beneath the lid revealed a mosaic of spent butts and a puff of stale weed.

The lid squeaked slightly as he lowered it and that bothered him, but not as much as being here did.

This wasn't like him.

It wasn't what he did.

He planned and thought things through.

He waited.

He watched from afar.

But today had changed him.

Seeing her so close had changed him.

And the thought of losing her, from right in front of him, when he'd been so careful, when she was so perfect . . .

A sudden, agonizing pain arced between his temples like a snap of electricity.

He locked his jaw but the sensation intensified, sinking down through his cheeks, invading his gums.

That was when he heard it.

A low, humorous whisper.

A shushed chuckle.

Suppressed giggles.

He remained motionless but inside he was rocking.

More shushing and giggles, coming from somewhere behind him.

He strode forwards, stepping out through the doorway into a darkness that wasn't really dark, in the way no city skyline can ever be completely lightless.

The sodium glare shifted around him like a spectral fog, grit crunching under his shoes, one finger raised in the air as he emerged from the cover of the doorway as if to point, or jab, or admonish them in a futile, teacherly way, which was rendered even more futile because they didn't see or hear him, weren't aware of him, transfixed as they were by one another.

The Athlete and the Artist.

Their bodies close.

Their faces closer.

His hand circling her forearm just below her elbow.

The joint between her fingers.

And their heads tilted just so, lips parted ever so slightly, suspended in that short pause of assessment and appraisal, attraction and lust.

The Athlete leaned in closer.

The Artist leaned towards him in turn.

Sam started to run.

92

I crept forwards into the basement.

Uncertainty seeped through my veins.

Something was forming inside me. Coagulating in my bloodstream. Pressure massing in my sinuses and behind my eyes. The sensation was even more intense and acute than the pain and pressure I'd experienced before I'd whited out earlier.

It felt almost primal.

I took another step past the end of the staircase, my pulse hammering in my temples, the room fanning open dizzyingly to my right.

A scarred old workbench was butted up against the wall. There were some sagging cardboard boxes tucked away beneath it. To the left was a large plastic tub containing most of our decorating gear. Through the opaque plastic I could see the ghostly outlines of paint trays and rollers, plastic sheets, sandpaper, rolls of masking tape and paint-brushes.

Above the table was a pegboard neatly hung with a variety of DIY tools. I'd seen the pegboard in Sam's photos and I'd used nearly all of the tools at one time or another. Some of them – like the Phillips screwdriver with the black and yellow handle or the extendable tape measure – were so familiar to me that I could feel the weight of them in my hand.

To the right of the workbench, tucked away in the corner of the room, was a shower curtain.

93

Sam

It all happened so fast, but it was years in the making.

Years of dealing with students like the Athlete, who turned up to his classes late and entitled, whom life came to so easily, so readily, where even their stories of hardship and grief could be turned to their advantage, leveraged into a seduction, into a kiss.

Years of seeing opportunities flash before his eyes and vanish before he could grasp them – of relationships that evaded him, and research opportunities handed to other academics over him, of promotion proving elusive, even of a house coming his way in an inheritance that right now felt more like a curse than a gift.

And, most of all, years of thinking and pondering and planning and theorizing about a wide variety of psychological quirks and tricks and experiments that were too 'unethical', or seemed impossible, and how he secretly wished he might pursue them anyway, indulge them, cultivate them, *experience* them.

Years of thinking about the perfect partner, the perfect life, the right opportunities and the courage to seize what he wanted for himself.

All of it had built to this.

To him.

Streaking across a rooftop, thrusting out a hand, as if he was a man trying to stop time, hit pause, go back.

They didn't even sense him before it was too late.

The two of them – the Athlete and the Artist – breaking apart and twisting partially towards him, still joined at the hips, the Athlete's hand just below the Artist's elbow, London lit up behind them, and that brief instant of recognition – a freeze-frame of surprise and miscomprehension on the face of the Athlete, a flicker of distress and horror around the eyes of the Artist – before Sam's hands made contact, first one palm on the Athlete's chest, then the other, and pushed.

All that muscle.

All that training.

The Athlete was thick in the trunk and the legs, but his upper body was vastly overdeveloped, his pectorals a broad slab, his shoulders enormous, his biceps huge.

Which was a problem for him because of the waist-high perimeter wall, not to mention simple physics, the pendulum effect kicking in, the Athlete's legs kicking upwards, his hips pivoting backwards, a gargled cry of terror and outrage, and then one fresh, final development, an outcome Sam hadn't foreseen – to the extent he could have foreseen *any* of this, even his own impulsive actions – as the Artist began to fall, too.

A classic chain reaction.

Because the Athlete was still clasping her arm just below her elbow.

Which is when Sam lunged for her waist and coiled his own arms around her and held on as the Athlete plummeted with one abrupt, violent tug, his nail scraping down the Artist's inner arm, scoring a line that was deep and vivid, bleeding instantly in a way that, when Sam saw it, scared him terribly.

Because she was no longer perfect.

Already.

Before they'd even started, she was marked.

94

I peered at the white plastic shower curtain.

It was suspended from a U-shaped metal rail bolted to the wall.

The curtain was drawn and hanging motionless.

It looked new and spotlessly clean and it bore a chemical scent, as if it was fresh from its packaging.

I stared at it for a moment longer, not breathing, the pain in my head swelling and magnifying, a cluster of bright lights firing behind my eyes.

Turning slowly, I allowed my gaze to flit around the rest of the room.

Empty.

There was nothing else down here.

What had Donovan found that could have occupied him for so long?

Most people, if they'd been viewing this space, would have reached the bottom of the stairs, taken a quick glance around, maybe paced out the dimensions, checked the head height, and that would have sufficed.

And all right, I knew now that he hadn't been here for a legitimate house viewing. He'd come here for something other than that. But even so, what could have kept him down here for so long?

I supposed it was possible he could have used the time to check his phone, send a message, place a phone call. Maybe it was while he was down here that he'd summoned the courier.

He definitely could have been lingering to unsettle me.

But perhaps those weren't the only reasons.

He'd said he was an intelligence officer. He was good at following clues. Maybe he'd found something down here that had stirred his curiosity and raised questions in his mind.

He'd already proven to me several times how observant he could be.

'Listen to me. You're making a mistake. You need to—'

Donovan had said those words to me just before Sam had attacked him with the stool.

At the time, I'd thought – if I'd thought about it at all – that Sam had come at him while he was distracted, seizing the chance to spring an attack on him.

But what if Sam had attacked him then because he'd wanted to prevent Donovan from telling me something?

What if he'd been afraid of what Donovan was about to say?

Donovan had told me to put down the wine bottle. He'd told me to take my time. To *think*.

Very slowly, I looked back at the shower curtain again.

The swelling and the pain. The stutters of bright light.

It was just a plain, inexpensive item. It should have been totally innocuous.

Except for two things.

One, I couldn't think what it was doing down here in the basement, not least because Sam had never mentioned it to me. It hadn't featured in any of his photographs of the basement.

And two, just looking at it made me want to shrink back into the corner of the room, drop down to the floor and curl back into a ball.

95

Sam

The Artist's shock was immediate and disabling, but it wasn't until he'd used the chloroform that he could get her safely down from the roof.

The chloroform was in his backpack. For weeks now he'd been carrying the bottle around with him inside a ziplock bag along with a lint-free cloth, imagining himself using it, rehearsing the steps involved in his mind.

She'd still been spluttering and crying and hyperventilating when he'd hurriedly doused the cloth and risen up and clamped it over her mouth and nose.

And of course it wasn't anything like he'd planned because the whole thing was impromptu and rushed, and because he was far more scared and unnerved than he'd been prepared for, and because she'd moaned briefly and writhed and then dropped to the ground before he could hold her up. There was a hoodie in his backpack. He'd dressed her in it hurriedly, pulled the hood up over her head.

The journey down the stairwell was problematic. She was heavy and her body was slack and the stairs were endless and his terror writhed under his skin unlike anything he'd ever experienced before, but it was still better than taking the lift because nobody saw them and there were no cameras.

And all right, it took him an age and the ambulance had already arrived before he reached the ground floor, but that just gave him a chance to gather his thoughts, to steel himself, to administer a top-up dose of chloroform (just in case) before he coiled her arm over his shoulder and walked her swiftly out through the crowds of partygoers that were now spilling out onto the street, and along the road where he hailed the first cab he could see.

Thursday night in the city. Maybe the driver didn't care, or maybe Sam simply sold the whole boyfriend-looking-after-his-wasted-girlfriend routine better than he could have hoped for, or perhaps his vague answers about a possible stabbing or a heart attack were enough to allay the cab driver's listless enquiries about the ambulance and the group of stunned and appalled revellers who had gathered outside the apartment building nearby.

The Artist stirred a few times on the drive home. She mumbled incoherently. Her head rolled against his chest and rested against his chin, and he could smell her apple shampoo, and they were both perspiring unpleasantly, but then the cab pulled up at Forrester Avenue and Sam paid the driver, who pulled away again almost before they were clear of the cab.

And then it was actually happening.

He was finally taking her in through his front door to the tired and smelly hallway. Flicking on the lights.

The drab and withered interior sprang out of the darkness. The old and broken kitchen was in disarray. There was his general mess and clutter in the living room. Piles of student essays and takeaway containers on the coffee table and the sagging sofa and the mismatched armchair.

He would have liked to get her take on it. *Her first impressions.* But all of that could wait.

Because the one thing he'd finished was the basement.

Everything had been prepared for weeks.

Down they went – her feet bumping on the stairs – and then he adjusted his grip and stiffened his back until he was holding her under the arms and she began to stir again as he walked her forwards, a secret, surging thrill buzzing in his head as he reached out for the shower curtain.

96

The shower curtain crinkled when I touched it. The metal rings jostled on the rail.

A pause, and then I steadied my hand and thrust it aside. And fell . . .

. . . half forwards through a flash of white light into the space in front of me . . .

. . . half backwards into my mind.

I was staring at a shower cubicle. A makeshift one. It was formed out of a knee-high slab of white porcelain that had long ago been installed in the corner of the room. There was a removable showerhead fitted to a sliding wall bar above it that looked a lot more recent. A cold tap and a hot tap.

The porcelain tray was chunky and deep, the glaze rubbed bare in patches, yellowed with water stains in others. The once-white metro tiles fitted to the walls were crackled and greyed.

Looking at it, I felt certain it hadn't started out as a shower.

Once, perhaps, it would have been used by a servant as a sluice. Nowadays, I imagined Bethany would have pitched it to a potential buyer as a dog shower.

But I knew differently.

Because what I was seeing in front of me, in *this* moment,

I was simultaneously seeing in snatches from my blurred and shattered memories.

A torturous, disabling sensation.

Instantly impossible.

Indisputably real.

Because I understood instinctively – in the same way I knew how to breathe – that what I was looking at was a bathroom that hadn't really been a bathroom, where I'd been attacked by a stranger who hadn't been a stranger at all.

That dark, blurred figure.

That rasping metallic voice.

'I've been watching you.'

Oh God.

It hadn't happened at the party with Oliver.

It had happened afterwards, here, in this house, with Sam.

97

Sam

The first time he held her under the shower, he was louder and shriller than he'd intended. It bothered him that he lost control but it had all happened so suddenly. And he'd been anticipating it for so long.

'Who are you?' he yelled.

'Louise.'

'Wrong answer. Your name is Lucy. Who are you?'

And then the other questions. Lots of questions.

Some of them planned. Others improvised. Some of them tailored towards what had happened at the party, on the roof, changing her perception, forcing a shift.

Questions about where they'd met and how they'd connected and how long they'd been together.

Questions about her business, about her work, her life.

The questions would get refined over time.

So would her answers.

He didn't expect it to take right away. The process was going to require a lot of patience.

But that was OK because he was going to arrange it so that they had as much time together as they needed.

As much as he could ever want.

98

I put my hand out to the tiles at my side, staring down at the plughole, the shower curtain tangled in my limbs.

I groaned and pressed a hand to my breastbone, breathless, poleaxed.

Your memories will come back to you when you least expect it. You'll see something, or hear something, some kind of trigger . . .

But the trigger had been down in the basement all this time and Sam hadn't wanted me to see it. He'd kept it from me on purpose, carefully maintaining the gaps in my memories.

The gaps he'd created.

My head swam.

The porcelain blurred.

Ask Sam and our first meeting was like something out of a rom-com movie. It was a story he'd told me many times . . .

I thought of something else then, something Donovan had said.

Upstairs, when I'd thought he'd been taunting Sam – which in a way he had been – without realizing he was telling me something, too.

You wrote this one piece. It was about how some phobias have a simple trigger and others are much more complex. I'm paraphrasing, but I think your general point was that there could be a real mixture of reasons. A childhood incident over-laid with another trauma, for example. Or layers of multiple traumas. They can confuse the picture. Get jumbled up.

Just as my thinking had been jumbled up.

Just as Sam had jumbled it for me.

Because my fears about this basement hadn't been a simple case of claustrophobia.

They'd been far more complex and sinister than that.

99

I stumbled backwards from the shower cubicle, scared, horrified.

My head was humming incessantly. My heart thrashed against my ribs.

I knew that Sam had thirsted after research opportunities which had evaded him. I knew that he'd sometimes complained about his department at the university being too conservative for his tastes.

My terror spiralled as I thought of some of the books I'd seen in Sam's study without ever thinking much about them. Books about brainwashing and coercive control; studies of torture victims and kidnap victims and prisoners who'd endured long-term incarceration.

Had Donovan seen them too, I wondered? Had he noticed them and logged them with his quick awareness, the same way he'd logged and remembered the storage cupboard in the attic?

If he really was an intelligence officer, had he seen something like this before on one of his tours of duty? Perhaps he'd joined the dots.

It didn't seem impossible that he might have put things together when I was showing him around our home.

Especially after I'd told him about my issues with the basement and he'd spent time down here, seeing the shower, maybe even the scratches on the brickwork. Particularly after I hadn't been able to answer his questions about Oliver, or his party, or what had happened on that roof.

When I hadn't known my own name.

That shook me on a whole new level – the totality of the damage Sam had wrought.

I'd been living with this man. Sleeping with this man. I—

I was staring at the DIY and decorating equipment in front of me, the sickly vibration growing more intense inside my head.

He'd had me do all the renovation work on his home.

Months and months of it.

I'd stripped his house back to a bare skeleton and remodelled it in the same way he'd broken me down and rebuilt me.

He must have waited to let me out until he could trust me. Until he'd conditioned me sufficiently.

And then he'd pretended he was helping me to cope with the trauma of a random attack that had never been random at all.

I clutched hold of my chest, wishing I could rip all the horror out of me, shuddering as I looked up towards the stairs, thinking of Donovan and Sam on the other side of that door.

Donovan had made a point of stressing to Sam that he was an excellent investigator before Sam had attacked him and I thought that now I understood why. He'd been taunting him. Letting him know what he'd pieced together.

Was that why Donovan had pushed me so hard? Had he wanted me to break through my conditioning and understand for myself, in front of Sam, what had been done to me?

Putting out my hand now, I reached for the handrail at the bottom of the stairs, gulping painfully as I craned my neck and stared up.

That was when I heard a sound from the other side of the door to the kitchen.

Four high and fast electronic chimes.

Beep. Beep. Beep. Beep.

100

The beeps were not particularly loud. They were partially muted by design. And the noise was further muffled by the door to the kitchen and the distance from the door down the basement steps.

But they were still unmistakable to me because I'd heard them numerous times since our new kitchen had been installed.

The beeping was the sound of the buttons on the front of the microwave being pressed.

Four beeps, because whoever was using the microwave had probably selected a function and a power rating, then set the timer and punched *Start.*

The machine would be whirring away.

The light would have come on inside.

I couldn't hear the whirring or see the light, but I knew with a searing intensity what it meant. I remembered what Donovan had said before.

Our phones were inside the microwave and if they were microwaved for more than a few seconds they could trigger a fire.

Nerves scattered across my back like hot sparks. My knees flexed.

You have to get out of here.
You have to get out of here right now.

I streaked up the stairs and tried the door. It didn't open. It was held firmly shut by the bolt on the outside.

I pushed on the door. I banged on it with the heel of my hand.

'Open this door! Let me out!'

There was no response.

I thumped on the door with my closed fist. I put my shoulder to it. Kicked it.

'Sam? Donovan?'

Nothing.

I pushed myself back in frustration and stared at the door for a moment, imagining the bolt shunting back and the door opening, but it didn't.

Spinning around, I hurried back down the stairs, turning at the bottom, marching towards the workbench and the pegboard of tools across the room.

The tools couldn't have been down here with me before. I would have got out if they'd been down here with me then.

But things were different now.

I was different now.

I'd been on the other side of the door.

I'd seen the bolt that secured it. I knew exactly where it was.

When I reached the pegboard, I swiped a hand across my face, scanning the tools on offer.

After taking down a screwdriver and a chisel, I set the screwdriver aside and picked up a hammer instead.

The hammer had a thick rubberized handle, a shiny metal shaft, a dulled and oxidized metal head.

It was much bigger and weightier than the hammer I kept with my small box of tools in the attic for hanging pictures.

With the chisel in my left hand and the hammer in my right, I strode back to the stairs.

I got madder as I climbed, furious, tightening my grip around the chisel, already rehearsing in my own mind what I needed to do next. Because I'd learned so much, fixing this house. And now I knew how to break it.

But before I struck out, I stopped and pressed my ear to the door.

Had I done this before, too?

Listening for hints and sounds.

Listening for Sam.

At first being terrified of him approaching the door and coming down here.

Later, sickeningly, almost aching for it, wanting him to come.

I couldn't hear steps or movement but I could hear other things.

The roar of the blood in my head.

The low bass whirr of the microwave.

Spitting.

Fizzing.

An electrical spluttering.

Wait.

The pegboard of tools wasn't the only thing that had changed since Sam had held me down here.

And he hadn't just had me redesign and redecorate his home.

He'd also had me oversee the tradesmen who'd carried out the work I couldn't do myself.

Including the electricians who'd rewired the entire house.

When they'd installed the new electrical system, they'd recommended moving the location of the fuse box from a cupboard in the kitchen to a spot on the wall just inside the basement, close to where I was standing now.

I turned to it with a plummeting sensation, knowing what I was about to do and where it would leave me but knowing I needed to do it anyway.

Reaching up, I raised the hinged Perspex screen covering the fuses.

Paused.

Then I cut all the power to the house.

101

The darkness was immediate and total.

It swallowed me whole.

I stared into the blackness and told myself to breathe.

Told myself not to panic.

Which was impossible, obviously, because I'd been trained to panic down here. It had been conditioned into me.

An unpleasant, tacky coolness swept over my skin, slick and waxy.

I could hear nothing now except an inexplicable clicking and it took me a moment to recognize it was coming from my teeth. They were chattering.

The blackness could only have lasted two or three seconds but it seemed to last much longer.

Then my eyes began to adjust.

Not to the blackness. That was too complete.

But to the faint glimmer of light around the rim of the door.

It was flaring and pulsing.

Flames, rasped a voice inside my head.

And then the first whiff of smoke.

It was faint but plasticky. A warm scent on the air.

Using the glimmering light, I traced around the outline

of the door with my fingertips until I settled on a spot partway up from the door handle, where I judged the external bolt to be.

Wedging the point of the chisel into the hairline gap between the edge of the door and the door frame, I then felt around with my other hand until I could tell that the head of the hammer was lined up with the bulbous end of the chisel handle.

I pulled the hammer back and tapped it forwards.

And hit my thumb.

I sucked air and adjusted my grip and tapped again.

This time I struck the chisel and the backlit gap widened fractionally with a *crack*.

OK.

I set my feet wide, stretched my neck to one side, drew back the hammer and was about to swing again when a new electronic noise blared out.

It was piercing, shrill, maddening.

The smoke alarms.

They'd been hardwired into the circuitry, but they also had back-up batteries in the event of a power cut.

I grimaced and slammed the hammer forwards.

And missed.

Almost.

But I caught the edge of the chisel with a glancing blow and it pinged sideways, dropping from my grasp and tinkling in the blackness near my feet.

No.

I crouched as the alarms screamed on, scrabbling around.

It took me a few panicky seconds until I found the chisel

again, then I rose up, slammed it into the door frame and held it firmly in place, partly by the handle, partly by the blade.

Another whiff of smoke reached me.

I swung again with the hammer and hit my thumb again.

It hurt but I didn't care.

I was already swinging again.

And then again.

Sometimes hitting.

Sometimes not.

But hitting enough, finally, so that the blade jutted forwards in my hand, slicing my palm.

It stung but it had to.

Because I wasn't going to let go of the chisel again.

I wasn't going to be stuck down here.

'Fuck!' I screamed, my eyes streaming, my ears ringing, and this time the hammer struck harder, plumb on the base of the chisel, and the entire thing drove forwards, spitting fragments of timber, emitting a dull, chinking sound of metal striking metal.

The bolt.

I swung my hips to one side, giving me more space to work with, and I slammed the hammer against the end of the chisel twice more.

A splitting sound.

A metallic spring.

A low clattering, clunking noise of the bolt falling onto the kitchen tiles, jumping and bouncing around on the other side of the door.

Had anyone heard? Had Sam?

After using both hands to wrench the chisel free from the door jamb and drop it behind me, I raised the hammer up by my shoulder and reached for the door handle.

102

The handle was warm.

I turned it quickly, opened the door and immediately recoiled, raising my splayed hand in front of my face.

The flames were concentrated inside the end of the kitchen closest to me. It looked as if an oil or an accelerant had been sprayed around. A slick of liquid on the island countertop was alight. Shimmers of gaseous blue were rippling across splashes and puddles on the countertop running along the wall to my side.

The fire was still taking hold but it was already beyond anything I could put out myself and it would soon get worse. Patches on the wall were beginning to blacken and smoke. I could see more flames inside the microwave.

Using my bent forearm as a shield, I peered into the glare and heat, my ears throbbing from the raucous alarm.

That's when I saw Donovan.

He was no longer collapsed backwards across the stove top. Now he was lying face down on the floor, motionless, between the kitchen island and the range cooker, one arm bent beneath him, the other draped in front.

I couldn't see Sam.

I didn't know where he was.

Everything was in near-darkness beyond the startling flames but I could just make out the front door through the smoke.

Was it still locked, I wondered?

I didn't know.

'Shit.'

I leaned out and glanced to my side. The doors to the patio were locked and even if I broke the glass and got out there, I'd be cornered in the back garden.

Make a decision.

The furore of the smoke alarm was making it difficult to think.

A puff of sparks exploded inside the microwave and I cried out and ducked, my gaze returning to Donovan.

He *still* hadn't moved.

But I remembered how he'd used his set of keys to lock us inside the house. I remembered how he'd slipped them into his front trouser pocket afterwards.

I remained where I was for one more second, hating the idea of going near him, knowing I was going to have to do it anyway.

103

I took off my jumper so I was wearing only my vest top and pressed it to my face as an improvised mask, then ventured out through the din and the flames towards Donovan, stopping two or three metres away, the heat stinging the exposed skin of my face, shoulders and arms.

Donovan didn't move or make any noise.

On the floor close to him was a discarded can of lighter fuel. I remembered that Sam had bought it several months back to refill a culinary blowtorch he'd purchased. Another needless kitchen gadget.

Like the hatchet knife.

I looked for it but I couldn't see it.

It was no longer on the floor in front of the range cooker where it had fallen from Donovan's grip.

I studied Donovan's prone body more closely. He really wasn't moving.

To my left, fire blazed across the kitchen island.

On my right, the flames had begun to climb towards a wall-mounted cupboard.

Ahead of me, the microwave smoked and steamed.

A bright blue light flashed on the smoke alarm overhead.

This was probably a bad idea.

I should just get out.

But I couldn't leave him to be consumed by fire. I thought I understood now that he'd tried to help me, even if that hadn't been his original intention when he'd come here today.

I nudged him with my toe.

Nervous energy streaked up my leg.

No response.

I bent down and reached out tentatively, then shook him by his shoulder.

Still nothing.

He wasn't faking.

He wouldn't be faking.

And not only that.

It had taken me too long, in the darkness, to notice the puddled liquid the toe of my training shoe was resting in.

It wasn't accelerant.

It was blood.

A moment of pure, still terror – of utter disbelief – and then I grabbed hold of his upper arm and rolled Donovan over onto his back.

The front of his sweater was drenched and I could see two or three ragged holes across his torso in the light from the flames. His neck, throat and face were splattered with gore.

Then his eyes sprang open and he inhaled sharply.

A ghastly, rattling noise.

I scrambled back a short distance, fire scorching the countertop of the island unit behind me, the alarm blaring from above.

With an enormous effort he rolled his head towards me and raised his right hand very slightly.

But there was no threat in it and there was barely any strength.

His gloved fingers unfurled to reveal a bar of light amid the acrid smoke.

His smartphone.

The screen was lit up.

'Ambulance . . . coming,' he wheezed.

A call was counting upwards on-screen.

I could see through the glare that he'd dialled 999 just under a minute ago.

He beckoned to me, parting his cracked lips to say more, but this time when I leaned forwards all he managed to do was to let his phone slip out of his hand.

104

I stayed where I was for a second, just staring at Donovan, the alarm screeching away.

I think I was scared to break the moment and confront the reality of what had happened here.

Sam had done this.

He'd stabbed a man repeatedly, violently.

He'd set a fire.

Then I picked up Donovan's phone, pressing it to my ear. 'Hello?' I shouted.

It was hard to hear in the confusion of the fire and the alarms. I dropped my jumper and clamped my free hand over my other ear. A second of static and then a man's voice said, 'This is the emergency services.'

'Oh, thank God! My house is on fire. My boyfriend has stabbed someone. He has a knife. We're at number 18 Forrester Avenue, Putney.'

I missed what the voice said next as I began to cough from the smoke and the fumes, thumping my fist against my chest to clear my lungs, meanwhile searching around me for Sam.

There was still no sign of him.

'Are you in a secure position?' I thought the call handler asked. 'Do you know where you boyfriend is?'

'No,' I yelled.

The next part I couldn't hear.

I looked around me again, then ducked down towards Donovan.

'Where's Sam?' I shouted at him.

He shook his head and rasped, 'Don't know.'

My insides contracted.

I knew I couldn't leave Donovan here but I was afraid to move him, scared of making his injuries worse, petrified that Sam was still in the house.

'How long until someone gets here?' I asked the call handler.

A muffled response.

'HOW LONG?'

Again, I couldn't hear anything, and this time I slipped the phone into my pocket and put my mouth next to Donovan's ear. 'I have to move you.'

I thought he nodded.

Grabbing the hammer, I reached behind me, lifting up my vest top and stuffing it down beneath the waistband of my jeans, then I scurried towards Donovan's feet, fitted my hands around his ankles and pulled.

He grunted in pain but he barely moved. His weight felt immense.

'Go,' he murmured.

I shook my head and pulled again, harder this time, coughing smoke from my lungs.

He moved a bit further, his arms trailing behind him, his

jumper and the makeshift dressing at his side snagging on the floor.

I checked over my shoulder for Sam, my eyes stinging and streaming, then turned back again.

The flames on the scorched granite of the kitchen island were beginning to diminish but the ones gnawing at the cupboard unit on the wall were starting to blister the paint finish.

'Come on!' I screamed, and this time I yanked with everything I had, falling down onto the wooden flooring, then digging in with my heels and pulling again.

I sucked in more smoke but I didn't stop, dragging Donovan further away from the flames, eventually getting as far as the trio of steps leading up into the living room.

Sinking to my side, wincing from the effort and the shrill alarm wail, I braced myself on my elbow for a moment, then pushed to my feet, slipped my hands beneath Donovan's shoulder blades, took hold of his armpits and heaved and twisted him around until his body was propped sideways against the steps.

He grunted and tried to push himself up, rocked his hips from side to side, flapped his arm weakly against the ground.

'Let me,' I shouted.

Climbing the steps and taking hold of his left wrist with both my hands, I pulled with everything I had. Donovan moaned. My lower back screamed. His glove partially slipped off and his body slid forwards in jerks and increments across the floorboards I'd varnished so carefully.

I repeated the process, getting just beyond the bottom of

the stairs and on towards the front door. Another smoke alarm blared and flashed from the landing above me.

Letting go of Donovan's arm, I took two steps backwards and tried the front door.

Locked.

Suddenly I felt watched.

I was terrified that Sam was about to leap out at us. I was scared he was hiding behind the armchair Donovan had been hiding behind earlier.

Whipping the hammer out from behind me, I removed Donovan's phone from my pocket. After flicking at the bottom of the screen with shaking fingers, I thumbed the torch app, then cast the light over the darkened area to my right, briefly illuminating the green sofa and the marble coffee table, the fireplace and the accent chair.

No sign of Sam.

Armed with the hammer, I ventured closer, slowing as I neared the armchair, the blue light blinking from my side.

My entire body was trembling.

I raised the hammer up above my shoulder and took one large step forwards, shouting out in terror and frustration as I swung the torch beam down and around, but Sam wasn't lurking there, either.

That was when I felt it.

A faint, cool breeze behind me.

I turned and parted the hinged shutters from the window behind them.

The sash unit that was nearest to the front door had been thrown upwards.

It was wide open to the night.

Sam must have gone out this way.

Quickly now, I tucked the hammer behind me again and sprinted back to Donovan, dropping to my knees next to his side, pushing my fingers inside the right hip pocket of his trousers and finding his duplicate set of house keys, then using them to unlock and open the door.

Night air swept in. Crisp and dark and black.

I dragged Donovan just outside onto the pathway. His face was wracked with pain. He was braced in discomfort, sweat springing from his brow.

When I straightened, my legs felt heavy, my lungs were scorched.

Looking to my side, I noticed that Sam's backpack was gone from where he'd left it near the front door.

I clutched Donovan's phone to my ear, my breaths coming in wearied pants. Inside the kitchen, I saw the cupboard unit puff into flame.

'Are you still there?' I asked.

'Still here,' the call handler replied.

'How long until someone gets here? Please, you need to help, I think the fire is going to spread.'

'Units are on their way.'

I glanced behind me, but I couldn't see or hear anything that told me they were close.

'I have to get someone else out,' I said, and then I stepped over Donovan with the torch beam held out in front of me and raced up the stairs.

105

The torch beam jolted and slashed at the darkness. It bounced and dipped ahead of me.

I pursued it up the stairs and along the landing towards the front of the house. As I ran, part of my mind was preoccupied with thoughts of Sam, wondering where he'd gone, what he might do next.

Sam had shoved me into the basement and locked the door behind me. He couldn't have imagined I'd get out.

And he set the house on fire with you in it. He didn't want you to escape.

I streaked on into the darkness, the alarm system screeching and flashing around me, then veered up the staircase to the attic, crashing off the walls.

It was only as I neared the top that I could hear shouts over the noise of the alarm.

Bethany.

'HELP ME! HELP!'

I lurched into the attic room, running towards the eaves, lighting up the cupboard door with my torch.

I pressed against the push catch and the cupboard door popped open. But when I grabbed it and swung it fully back,

C. M. Ewan

Bethany reared away from me, covering her eyes from the torch glare with her bound and crossed arms.

'It's OK,' I told her. 'Bethany, it's me.'

Bethany peered at me, bleary, dazed.

'What happened?' she shrieked.

'We have to go,' I told her.

'I heard the alarm.'

I nodded. It was loud up here in the attic. I guessed perhaps it had roused her earlier than Donovan had intended.

'There's a fire. Please, Bethany, we need to move quickly. Can you walk?'

'A fire?'

She tried to get up but toppled forwards, her legs rag-dolling beneath her.

I reached for her arm and lifted her up, helping her out of the cupboard as she slumped against me.

'Don't feel good,' she drawled.

I dragged her towards the doorway. It wasn't easy. Her legs betrayed her again and we slanted sideways, but I held her up.

When we reached the upper landing, I fitted her bound hands around the banister rail and rushed her down, using the torch to light the way ahead of us.

'It was Donovan,' she panted. 'He did this to me.'

'I know.'

'Should have listened to you.'

I shook my head. Now wasn't the time for that.

When we reached the first-floor landing, I cast the light of my torch ahead of us into the darkness and the gloaming.

Sam was standing there.

106

He was blocking our way.

His shirt was torn and stained.

His face was sheened with sweat and dirt.

His body was slanted to the right because he was favouring the leg that Donovan hadn't cut.

The bloodied hatchet knife was in his fist.

I put out my arm and stopped Bethany from going any further.

Sam dropped his backpack onto the floor next to him. The main compartment was unzipped and I could see loose banknotes stuffed inside. He must have had cash hidden up here. Maybe in the main bathroom. He knew I didn't like to go in there.

'What is this?' Bethany asked. 'What's going on?'

'Stay behind me.' I moved her backwards and stared at Sam. 'The police are on their way.'

'We have to get out of here!' Bethany shouted now, trying to get past me.

I pushed her back even more firmly, taking a step forwards.

She stopped then and started yelling at Sam. 'Why do you have a knife?'

He blinked and looked at her with a strange kind of

disconnection. There was something almost mechanical about his movements. A vacant darkness in the hollows of his eyes.

Blue flashes from the smoke alarm spattered his face but most of him was in shadow. Too much of Sam had been in shadow, I realized now.

A slick of molten lava ran down the middle of my breastbone. It spliced me in two. Gone was my fear, replaced with a scorching hot rage.

'What did you do to me?' I shouted at him over the clamour of the alarm.

Sam's face seemed to change. A slight smug cast to it. Amid the flickers of light in the darkness, it felt as if we were truly seeing one another for the first time.

'I think you've begun to work that out,' he yelled back.

'You killed Oliver.'

'You remember that now?'

'Some of it. I remember we met at your *support* group.'

'What else do you remember?'

'Enough.' I reached behind me to the small of my back and tugged the hammer out from beneath my waistband. I held it low by my side, clenching the wooden handle in my palm and Donovan's phone in my other hand. 'Enough to know that you held me prisoner, messed with my brain, scrambled my memories, attacked me, abused me.'

He flinched.

'Fuck your house,' I shouted, lashing out with the hammer at my side, punching a hole in the stud wall and ripping a chunk of plasterboard away with the claw of the hammer as I wrenched it back free. 'Fuck everything you made me do here.' Another blow. The other side this time. The hammer blew a chunk of timber out of the polished handrail running atop the spindles overlooking the stairwell. 'And fuck you, most of all.'

I took another step as Bethany yelped and yanked me backwards from behind.

Sam lurched towards me, swinging his bad leg from his hip, the knife at his side.

I whipped the hammer upwards incredibly fast as I rocked back on my heels, a wild backhand swing, bringing the weighted head up and clipping his chin in one lightning-quick movement, snapping his head back, freezing him mid-stride.

But by then Bethany and I were falling, tumbling, hitting the deck in a tangle of limbs.

Sam lowered his head slowly. A thread of blood trickled from the corner of his mouth.

He loomed over us with the knife.

Which was when Bethany screamed, shatteringly loudly.

It stopped him.

He seemed unsure what to do.

I aimed the torchlight in his eyes, dazzling him.

For a horrifying second, I thought he was going to leap on us with the knife, but then he shielded his eyes with his hand and tottered backwards, grabbing for the backpack, making for the top of the stairs and then hobbling down them.

I scrambled to my feet and leaned out over the handrail, watching him zipping the backpack closed and limping towards the front door, conscious of the glow of flames from the kitchen area to my right.

He moved outside and stepped over Donovan's body.

Then I saw Donovan's hand reach out suddenly and grab for his ankle, holding on to his bad leg.

But Sam barely paused before lashing out at Donovan's head with his other foot, and Donovan immediately released him, groaning, rolling slackly onto his back.

Sam glanced up at me one final time, his expression tight and savage and somehow accusing, then he stumbled away into the night.

107

I helped Bethany to her feet.

'We need to leave,' I told her. 'We need to get out of here.'

Her eyes were frenzied, her cheeks flushed red, strands of hair pasted to her face. Her breaths were coming in shallow pants as she recoiled from the smoke that was drifting around us, covering her nose and mouth with her bound hands.

I linked my arm in Bethany's and pulled her, the hammer in my fist, lighting our way with the phone torch and gripping her tightly when her legs went rubbery and her head seemed to loll.

We paused at the top of the stairs. I could feel the heat from below. The smoke was getting thicker, blacker.

'Stay with me.' I coughed. 'Not far now.'

I almost lost her as we negotiated the stairs down towards the living room. She missed a step and pivoted forwards, but I pressed her against the wooden spindles and the handrail and pinned her there until I could steady myself and lead her on.

Clouds of smoke wafted past. The flames from the kitchen glowed and flared. The fire was advancing towards the living area. The entire house would be ablaze soon.

When we reached the vestibule and Bethany saw Donovan outside on the ground, she stiffened and wailed, 'Oh my God!'

I coughed and spluttered and tugged her past him.

Her legs finally gave out when the cool air hit her and she fell onto the gravel in the middle of our yard.

'Here.' I pressed Donovan's phone into her hands. 'It's 999. Talk to them.'

I crossed to Donovan. There was a fresh and livid contusion across his temple and cheek. Blood pooling around his body. He seemed to be fully out of it, but when I kneeled down beside him his eyelids flickered, his pupils roved and he muttered something incomprehensible.

I thrust my face closer. He reached up and pawed my shoulder.

'Got . . . to . . . find him.'

'You did. And the police will. They're on their way.'

'Had to push you. Needed . . . answers . . . My brother.'

'You could have just talked to me. You could have—'

But his pupils lost focus and his eyelids fluttered shut again. He looked deathly pale.

'Donovan?'

I shook him by his shoulders.

'Donovan?'

I patted his cheek but this time he didn't come round.

Inside the house the flames were twisting and roiling. They were beginning to consume the staircase, billowing against the ceiling.

I coughed into my elbow, then with what felt like the last of my strength I rolled Donovan onto his side until he was lying in the recovery position and pushed up to my feet.

I swayed and choked on a lungful of air, then doubled over and coughed and wheezed, hacking smoke, spitting onto the ground.

The smoke alarms were much quieter outside the house, even with the door open. None of our neighbours had emerged from their homes to investigate what was happening. No one seemed to be aware of the fire.

I swiped the back of my hand across my mouth before asking Bethany, 'How long?'

'He says under five minutes.'

She was kneeling on the gravel with the phone in her hands, the torchlight glaring and winking, a damp glassiness to her eyes.

I turned from her to look off along the street in both directions, coughing again, but I couldn't see Sam.

I was just turning back in the other direction, my gaze sweeping across the front of John's house, when I glimpsed something from the corner of my eye.

John's front door was ajar.

108

The door was only slightly open but I knew we hadn't left it that way.

I'd watched Donovan lock up and toss John's keys into the corner of his yard. But I also knew that Sam had a key to John's place. He'd shown me that he still had his keys and then he'd zipped them inside his backpack.

But why would he have entered John's home?

I felt a tightening across my scalp.

I didn't move. I wasn't sure I wanted to.

It was deathly quiet all along our street.

Five minutes until the emergency services would be here.

I felt a pang as I thought about John. I knew how vulnerable he was, how upset and agitated he'd been earlier.

I checked on Bethany, who looked petrified and spent, then looked down at Donovan.

Sam had stabbed him, kicked him.

And that's when a deeper realization struck home.

Sam was a monster. He'd brutally attacked Donovan. He'd killed Oliver. He'd trapped me here under false pretences for almost two years.

And throughout that time, Sam had visited John every single day.

I'd believed it was because Sam was a kind person. A good neighbour. I'd thought he'd been caring for John.

But suppose I'd been wrong about that, too? Suppose he'd been just as big a threat to John as he'd been to me?

Oh no.

A hollowness formed inside me as I looked from Bethany to the street once more.

There was still nothing to suggest that any of our neighbours were reacting to the fire in our home. With the box hedge shielding our front yard and most of the shutters closed, nobody could see in easily.

I should have yelled, 'Fire!'

I should have let this all be somebody else's problem.

But again, something stopped me.

That molten rage. It was flooding my veins.

If Sam was in there, I wasn't going to let him get away with this.

Bending down, I picked up the hammer from where I'd dropped it.

'Wait here,' I told Bethany, and then I pushed out through our gate onto the street and crept up John's path towards his front door.

109

The lights were on inside but there was silence from within.

I edged forwards, put my free hand on the open door and listened, a soft breeze tugging at my clothes.

I couldn't see or hear any sign of Sam.

'What are you doing?' Bethany hissed.

I looked back at her and pressed a finger to my lips.

Extending my other hand, I wrapped my fingers around the edge of the door, eased it open and placed a careful foot just inside, fighting hard against the need to cough again.

Every little sound seemed magnified.

The rasp of my jeans against my thigh.

The movement of the wind through my hair.

The softest creak of the door hinge, and the settling of the floorboards under my weight, and the muted hush and strange absence of sounds from within.

I eased the door back further until I could see all along the empty hallway towards the kitchen, the staircase in front of me, the open doorways to my left.

The hammer felt too heavy in my hand.

I heard a moan.

It sounded feeble and pained, confused, forlorn.

I almost whispered John's name but I managed to stop myself.

Slipping off my shoes, I shuffled forwards.

The moan had come from the second room on my left, the one that now functioned as John's bedroom.

I took several careful steps, then stopped and listened.

There was no obvious response of any kind.

I couldn't hear Sam.

He wasn't anywhere in front of me.

Maybe I was imagining it, but I thought I could feel the heat of the fire seeping through the wall at my side. The smell of the smoke seemed to be permeating the brickwork but it could just as easily have been coming from my clothes and hair. My lungs itched with the need to cough.

Another moan, this one more dismal and prolonged.

I was certain now it was coming from John's makeshift bedroom.

Swallowing against the dry tickle in the back of my throat, advancing cautiously, I passed silently around the bottom of the stairs and tiptoed towards the room.

110

I stopped again before I entered John's bedroom.

Glancing back towards the front door I'd left open, I could see the faint glow and flicker of flames.

When I turned frontwards again, the vertebrae in my neck creaked and crunched.

I raised a hand up and cupped it over my mouth, stifling a cough.

I readied the hammer.

It felt for a moment as if even the house itself was listening to me. As if my breathing would give me away.

Then I took one large stride into the room.

The first thing that struck me was the odour.

There was the stale, fuggy scent of bed sheets and sleep.

But also something else.

A trace of ammonia. A sweaty back note of something sour and dismal.

John was sitting on the hospital bed with his back to me, facing the old disused fireplace. His shoulders were hunched, his head bowed, his hands in his lap.

He moaned again.

I didn't think he knew I was here. I got the impression he was moaning to himself.

'John?' I whispered.

He hunched up tighter without turning around.

I blinked, my eyes feeling gritty and sore from the smoke, my throat parched and hot.

I checked all about me, but if Sam was here, he wasn't in this room.

John was alone with whatever jumbled thoughts were keeping him company in his head.

'John, what's wrong?'

He quivered but he didn't reply.

I checked the doorway behind me, then took a step to my side, venturing carefully around the end of the bed and moving closer to John.

'John, will you look at me? I need to get you out of here.'

'John mustn't look,' he muttered, shying away. 'John has to stay in his room.'

A squeamish sensation as I stared at the way he was huddled and cowed. As if he'd adopted this position and pose before.

'Oh, John, no.'

A rush of heat blazed up from my toes to my hairline as I thought of all the evenings when Sam had come next door to check on John. All the times when he'd told me how they'd spent their evenings together.

Sam had told me he'd read books or the newspaper to John.

He'd said he'd marked essays while John had watched TV.

But now I suspected it hadn't been true.

Or only part of it had been true.

Because John's hunched posture, his soft, sad moaning, spoke of a wholly different experience.

'Oh, John, I'm sorry. I am so sorry.'

I reached for his hands but he withdrew from me, moaning louder.

I froze and cast a look towards the door, listening hard for a response.

When none came, I was careful to lower my voice.

'Do you know where Sam is?'

'John won't look. John can't look.'

A sudden, desperate cramping.

My greased fingers slipped on the handle of the hammer.

'John, what is it you're not supposed to look at?'

But instead of answering me, he just shook his head and gazed down at a spot on the floor.

I raised my palm to my chest, my aching lungs.

'I won't go upstairs,' he whispered.

'Upstairs?'

Taking three jolting steps backwards, I leaned out into the hallway, craning my neck to look up.

I felt as if I understood several things all at once, then.

Whatever Sam had come here for – whatever had lured him inside – could be upstairs in this house.

Did it also explain why Sam had moved John's bedroom down to the ground floor? I suspected it was about more than simply keeping John safe.

'Mary went upstairs,' John muttered. 'She shouldn't have gone upstairs.'

I spun back.

No.

Sam had been the one who'd found Mary after her fall.

It was Sam who'd called for the ambulance.

But it was also Sam who'd pushed Oliver from the roof of his apartment building.

It was Sam who'd shoved me down the steps to the basement.

And with Mary out of the way, the only person living next door to us in this house was John. He was alone and he had dementia.

Had Mary heard something that had made her suspicious, I wondered? Had I screamed? Banged on the basement walls? Had she confronted Sam?

Another flush of anger.

I needed to get John outside but I didn't want him to become agitated or shout if I tried.

I drifted further out into the hallway, staring up the staircase towards the landing, feeling my spine pull so taut it seemed to lengthen, picturing Mary and the distance she would have fallen, how hard she'd hit the bottom, the pain she would have been in.

She'd been unconscious when Sam had called me in to help. I'd held her hand as the paramedics had wheeled her out on a stretcher.

I reached the bottom of the stairs and rested my leading foot on the lowest riser, taking hold of the banister in my hand, clenching the hammer next to me.

Was I really going to go up there?

A soft *click* behind me.

I swivelled to see Sam pressing his back against the front door he'd closed behind him.

He was sweating, wincing, leaning all his weight onto his good leg, his bad leg propped lightly on his toes.

'Look at us,' he said. 'Alone again.'

111

His voice sounded different, husky and strained. I wondered if I'd broken something in his jaw when I'd hit him with the hammer.

Or perhaps it was just the real him leaking out.

He surged towards me, hobbling grotesquely on his bad leg, the blade of his knife catching the light.

I shrieked and swung the hammer at him with everything I had.

But he was ready for it this time.

He ducked under my swing and barged into me so hard that I dropped the hammer as I fell back against the stairs.

He advanced on me, and I flipped myself over and scrambled to my feet, hauling on the banister rail with my left hand, vaulting up the first two treads.

It felt like I was trying to run up a down escalator.

A grunt behind me.

Something tagged my heel.

I shrieked again and looked back to see that Sam had lunged for my foot, missed, and was sprawled over the stairs with the knife in his fist, gurning from the pain in his thigh.

A spray of saliva plumed from his lips.

He pushed up from his elbows as I scrambled on, my lungs struggling to suck in enough air.

'Bethany!' I screamed.

My heart was pounding so hard it seemed to be beating out of my chest.

I made it to the landing, already breathless, and wheeled left towards the front of the house. Away from the rear bedroom and the family bathroom, because everything was laid out in a mirror image to our place next door.

Or rather, how our place had been before we'd remodelled it.

Stained wallpaper. Threadbare carpeting. Mould spores and patches of damp on the ceilings and walls.

I streaked past a closed bedroom door on my right.

Saw two doors ahead of me.

Unlike in our house, the front rooms hadn't been knocked through to form one large space.

I chose the door on the right, grasped the handle, put my shoulder to the wood.

Mistake.

The door barely moved before it butted up against something hard on the other side.

I shoved it again.

It didn't shift.

I couldn't squeeze through the gap and, when I looked back, Sam had reached the top of the stairs.

He took a rattling breath and used the handrail to swing himself around, grimacing, snarling, limping my way.

My arm jumped with adrenaline as I tried the door on the left.

It opened and I crashed through, my face, hands and upper body slamming into something flat and hard.

The object skidded forwards and toppled at a slant against something else.

I pressed my hands against it to lever myself up.

The curtains hadn't been drawn. Street lighting illuminated the room, enabling me to see that I was surrounded by cardboard boxes and packaging crates.

They were stacked very high, almost to the ceiling, with narrow, maze-like channels in between. I suspected they contained a lot of John and Mary's belongings.

The cardboard smelled musty. The room was cold. I guessed the heating had been turned off in here.

Bending low, I ducked along the channel to my right.

Footfall behind me.

It vibrated through the floorboards.

Sam laboured into the entrance to the room. I could hear his wheezing breaths.

Fear squirmed in my belly as I ran at a crouch to my left, then sprang up just beneath a sash window.

There were tall stacks of cardboard boxes behind me.

I couldn't see Sam.

He couldn't see me.

I looked out.

No ambulance yet.

No police.

The flames had made it to the first floor of our house. They were lighting up the darkness outside the windows of the bedroom I'd shared with Sam. Dark tendrils of smoke were puckering in the air.

Bethany was standing on the pavement outside John's gate, stepping forwards and backwards as if she couldn't decide what to do, looking fretfully between his front door and then off along the street. Donovan's phone was against her ear and she was shouting into it.

I pressed my hands to the window glass and pushed up, ready to yell to her.

But the sash didn't move.

I stared at the bolt.

There wasn't one.

It shouldn't have been locked.

I hit the glass, thumping and shouting Bethany's name.

'I nailed them shut,' Sam said.

I spun to find him staring at me from the other side of the tall box to my right. A chest-high wall of boxes extended beyond it, separating us. Again, he was leaning to his side. He could barely put any weight on his left leg at all.

My chest was rising and falling. My body felt locked with fear.

I seemed to be looking everywhere all at once, sizing up the distance between us, the shadows in the room, the way he was blocking my route back to the doorway, how he was struggling to stay upright.

'What do you want?' I asked him.

'You. You were all I ever wanted, Lucy.'

A jolt of terror straight to my heart.

My entire body seemed to vibrate as I felt around the window unit behind me. But all I could feel was solid wood and glass.

I glanced over my shoulder at Bethany, and this time she was looking up at me, terrified.

'They're almost here,' she shouted.

'What was it like?' Sam asked me. 'The breakthrough?'

I looked back at him slowly and shook my head. I didn't want to talk about it. I didn't want to satisfy his need to know.

But I also understood that I had to stall for time.

'Did it hurt?' he asked.

I nodded.

'It was distressing?'

'Yes.'

'What else?'

A beat.

My head was spinning.

Then I heard the sirens. They wavered on the air.

We fixed on one another.

The sirens grew louder, screaming nearer.

I saw a fast calculation flit behind his eyes.

The muscles in his jaw bunched.

He raised his knife and glanced towards the bedroom door we'd entered through, as if he was asking himself if he could trap us in here together, and that's when I shoved off from the wall behind me, braced my palms against the tall cardboard box between us and pushed.

112

The box toppled forwards, crashing into Sam, its contents banging around inside, the box gathering a momentum of its own.

He swore. Yelled.

I heard him stumbling backwards.

But by then I was already running to my right, towards the second window in the room, stretching out my hand to my left, smoothing my fingers along the tops of the chest-high cardboard boxes between us, then springing up off the floor, digging in with my elbow, rolling over onto the top of the boxes as if I was launching myself over the bonnet of a car.

I leaped for the next row of boxes.

But whatever was in them wasn't solid at all.

I crashed down through a box lid but I was still moving forwards and the box rocked with me, tipping over, spilling me out.

Pushing up to my feet and hands, I was just darting through the bedroom doorway for the landing when he grabbed me from behind, around the waist, and dragged me to the floor.

I tried to get up.

Tried again.

I writhed and twisted, painfully aware of the knife, but he wouldn't let go.

Using my elbows for leverage, I dragged my upper body towards the stairwell leading up to the attic.

There was no carpet.

The stairs were bare wood.

I jammed my upper arms against the treads, gripped with my fingernails and heaved myself forwards as he pulled me back. Then I turned and reached down very far and dug my thumb into the wound on his leg.

He yowled and loosened his grip just enough for me to slip free and kick and kick and kick.

Hitting his arm.

His chest.

His face.

His nose exploded like a crushed fruit.

He roared in disgust and let go of me and I launched myself up the stairs, a bare bulb lighting my way from above the uppermost landing.

I'd almost reached the top when he roared again and I looked back to see him leaping for me, stretching sideways, his face a bloody mess, his eyes and nose smeared.

I fell backwards through the half-closed door into the room on my right, the back room at the top of the house.

I could hear the sirens outside in the street now. They were loud and raucous.

The room was lit red.

There was a single red bulb in the pendant fitting above me.

No ambient light was coming through the windows at all. They were fitted with blackout blinds.

Sam limped and grunted up the staircase behind me as I backed further into the red-lit room, raising my hands and arms in a defensive posture.

He was gargling horribly as he entered after me, his skin rinsed a deep beetroot by the light of the bulb, hobbling badly, his nose and teeth wet with blood.

My eyes were locked on him but I was also acutely aware of my surroundings.

We were in a darkroom, I realized.

There were photographic prints hanging from wires.

The prints were glossy and lush.

Every image was of me.

Asleep in our bedroom.

In the red light, the colours and the contrasts were washed-out, bleached.

Or maybe there hadn't been many colours in the first place.

Because the photographs had clearly been taken at night with some kind of specialist lens.

A terrible, invasive feeling.

Those *clicks* in my dreams.

Perhaps they hadn't just been my mixed-up, nightmare recollections of my time in the basement.

Perhaps they'd been the sound of a camera shutter, too.

Because Sam hadn't sold all his photographic equipment after all. Some of it was still here.

My feet caught on something and I looked down to see his backpack on the floor.

Drifts of photographs were crammed inside it amid the cash.

This is why he came here.

This is what he wanted.

My eyes settled on some of the prints spilling out of his bag.

Again, the colour spectrums were washed-out.

Again, the images were bleached.

I could see photographs of me bound in the basement, sitting in a chair with my head hanging low, limp in the basement shower, huddled by the bottom of the stairs.

But somehow even worse were the other images.

There were shots of me that must have been taken before my abduction, where my hair was longer, my clothes were different.

Photographs where I was sitting in the window of a central London cafe.

Others where I was waiting for a bus, walking along the street.

One where I was clenching a pair of parted curtains inside the window of my old ground-floor flat in Tooting, staring out with a scared and pensive expression.

'I've been watching you.'

I reached backwards.

Oh God.

He'd been watching me for such a long time.

That feeling I'd had. The paranoia that I was being stalked. The one that had led me to his support group in the first place.

It had been real.

It had happened.

It was him.

113

Sam hobbled forwards, closing the distance between us with one hand gripping the knife and the other hand clenching his thigh.

He was sweating, writhing, his clothes and hair grubby and unkempt. Blood coated his nose and jaw. His breaths were ragged and hoarse.

'You're so messed up,' I told him.

'Me. You. Same as everyone else.'

'I'm not afraid of you.' I reached down to my side and felt my fingers splash in something wet. 'I'm not afraid of anything any more.'

Whirling sideways, I picked up the tray of developing fluid and slung it at his eyes.

He howled and arced backwards, snatching his hands to his face.

I let go of the tray and pushed him aside, driving my fist down against his bad leg, then bursting past him and streaking across the half-landing into the other room at the front of the attic.

It was dark but the walls glowed blue in the stutter of emergency lights from outside.

A pair of warped, timber-framed French doors were ahead

of me, opening onto a small balcony that matched our balcony next door.

I could hear Sam blundering after me from behind, his footfall pounding in an arrhythmic tempo.

I didn't stop.

Didn't slow.

I just rushed towards the doors, raised my right foot in the air and stamped my heel against the lock.

The doors split apart like a log struck with an axe.

My heel ached as if I'd stamped on a spike.

I staggered outside, wheeled left, heaved air, grabbing hold of the crumbling brickwork of the parapet and looking down.

My upper body lurched forwards.

The front pathway to John's house spun beneath me.

I could feel the heat raging from next door.

The house was a gathering inferno.

Windows had smashed outwards on the ground floor. Flames were billowing skywards, mingling with the bright flickers shining out from the front bedrooms. Sparks spiralled on the air.

I shielded my face with my hands and peered towards the ghostly outlines of the emergency vehicles that were parked slantways in the road. I could see two fire engines, a pair of ambulances, police cars. A team of paramedics were rushing Donovan towards one of the ambulances on a wheeled stretcher, holding padded medical dressings against his wounds, an oxygen mask over his face. Bethany was shouting at a duo of police officers in hi-vis jackets, urging them towards John's front door.

A short distance back from them, scores of our neighbours

and other onlookers were now gathered in the lighted doorways of their homes, on the pavement, in the street.

Beneath me, a chain of fire officers jogged up our front path wearing breathing apparatus. Two more fire officers were being lifted into the air on a ladder hoist attached to the back of the nearest engine unit. The articulated platform jerked and arced. They had a fire hose propped over their shoulders.

'Help!' I yelled. 'Bethany! Up here! Help!'

People stared. Some pointed. Bethany looked up at me, stricken, then immediately directed the police officers' attention to me as another woman screamed.

One of the fire officers on the platform tapped the shoulder of his colleague and pointed to me, then motioned to an officer on the ground.

I waved my arms crossways over my head.

Stray roofing tiles crunched under my feet. John's balcony was in poor condition. The felt material I was standing on was sagging in places. The brickwork on the parapet was fragmented and loose.

'Help!'

I screamed so loudly it tore my throat. I was choking on the fumes from the fire.

Then I heard a scuff of grit and a grunt from behind me as Sam stumbled out onto the balcony.

His hair and face were drenched. His eyes were red and sore-looking. His nose and mouth were bloodied.

He shook his head and banged his ear with the heel of his hand, as if he'd just dunked his head in a swimming pool.

He then tottered forwards and contemplated the street for himself, the wash of blue lights and vivid flames staining his skin and glistening off the blood on his shirt and trousers.

'It's over,' I told him.

He bit back a sigh and looked up at the sky, the knife dangling from his grasp.

'Sam?' Quieter now. 'I said, it's over.'

He looked sideways at me. 'No,' he said. 'No, Lucy, it can never be over for us.'

As his gaze swept my face, I felt the weight of everything that bound us. It seemed to weave an invisible tether out of the baked air.

This man knew every part of me.

He'd known more about me than I'd known myself.

And meanwhile he'd been a stranger to me.

But not completely.

Because I knew his mannerisms, his tics, the thousands of intentional and unintentional signals he gave out.

So I knew, perhaps only fractionally after he knew, that he'd made his decision about what to do next.

Which is why I was already spinning off my heel with my heart in my throat, already turning from him and driving with my thighs towards our home, striding forwards as he set off after me and dropped the knife, his arms unfurling, extending, ready to shove me off the balcony, the same way he'd pushed Oliver, pushed Mary.

Except I jumped instead.

Into the whirling darkness and the whipping flames.

My legs treading nothingness.

My arms outstretched.

I thumped into the brick parapet on the balcony of the house that had doomed me, my arms scraping stone as I desperately wedged my elbows and upper body over the top lip of the low brick wall, the heat raging beneath me just as I felt a violent tug and a drag on my waist, my vest top stretching, fingers scrabbling, a yell and a rip and a tear, and then a brief startled cry followed by nothing . . . nothing . . . until a ghastly wet thud and then the noise of everything else rushing back in.

I found that I was staring sideways with my face pressed against the heated bricks as one of the fire officers on the hoist snatched off his mask, looking horrified for a second, then thrust out his gloved hand, shouting, 'Hold on, just hold on, we're coming, hold on.'

'Don't let go!' Bethany shouted.

I locked my elbows over the brickwork.

I clenched my right hand over the scar on my left forearm.

I dug my toes into the wall.

I don't know how long I clung on, exactly, but then gloved hands grasped me and hauled me onto the raised platform and laid me down and patted my back and side.

I lay there, barely exhaling, not listening to anything that was being said to me, not able to process it yet, just gazing down over the edge of the platform at Sam's broken body draped over the railings between our house and John's, and nearby, the 'For Sale' sign that had been knocked sideways, snapped free of its bindings, lying crossways on the ground.

114

'Try to stay still for me.'

I squeezed my eyes tight shut as the paramedic probed the cut to the back of my scalp. I could smell the plastic of her surgical gloves. Could feel her hip pressing into me as she raised herself on tiptoes for a clearer look.

I was propped up on a wheeled stretcher in the back of an ambulance with the rear doors open ahead of me to reveal the chaos on the street.

Everything outside flickered blue and black. More emergency vehicles had arrived and uniformed police officers had taped off the scene. A trio of firemen were carrying out a stunned debrief at the rear of their unit, their helmets and masks in their hands, their overalls soaked, their faces smudged with sweat and soot, hair flattened and greasy.

Behind the police tape, some of my neighbours were staring with shocked, blank-eyed expressions towards the charred and smoking remains of Sam's house and the privacy screen that had been erected around Sam's body. One woman was rubbing her upper arms. Another man cradled a sleeping boy in pyjamas, a worn teddy bear hanging from the child's hand.

'I'm so sorry for what has happened to you and for what

you've been through tonight. But just to be clear, you're alleging that this man – Sam – had been holding you against your will?'

This was from the sympathetic, middle-aged detective standing in front of me who had told me her name was DS Sloane. She had streaks of grey in her hair, kind but tired eyes, a considerate manner. She'd been at pains to make sure I was feeling capable of talking before questioning me, and she was the one who'd agreed it would be OK for Bethany to perch on the end of my stretcher as Sloane jotted down notes in her pocketbook.

Bethany had a foil blanket draped over her shoulders that crinkled every time she moved. She'd been checked over carefully by the paramedic before me and now she was resting her hand on my foot, occasionally drawing on oxygen from a mask that she raised to her mouth. I was grateful she was with me. Happy she was safe. Glad to have someone with a strong personality in my corner.

'Ow!'

'Sorry,' the paramedic said, backing off and tearing open a pack of sterile swabs before returning to continue her work.

The paramedic was dressed in a bottle-green jumpsuit, her hair tied back in a ponytail, black training shoes on her feet.

'He brainwashed me,' I said.

I was aware of the paramedic tensing by my side, as if she couldn't quite believe what she'd heard, but Bethany clenched my foot in a show of solidarity as DS Sloane absorbed my words.

'And how did he do that?' she asked.

'He kept me in the basement. Sometimes he held me under the shower, did other things, I think. There are photos, in John's house.' I motioned towards John's attic with my chin. 'I can't explain it completely, but Sam's a lecturer at LSE. *Was*, I suppose. He taught psychology. I met him at a support group he ran.'

'A support group for what?'

'People with phobias and irrational thoughts. I thought I'd convinced myself I was being stalked. But it turns out I *was* being stalked. By Sam.'

'He wasn't right,' Bethany cut in. 'You could tell that when he was blocking our way out of the house with the knife. It was in his eyes. The way he talked. He was giving off a really nasty vibe. I'd never seen him like that before.'

As she was talking, I could see John being guided along the pavement by a police officer and a paramedic who were gently supporting his arms.

'What will happen to John?' I asked.

Sloane turned for a moment, following my gaze. 'He'll be taken care of. We'll be getting social services involved.'

'Can I visit him later?'

'I'm sure something can be arranged.'

'Someone needs to check his bank accounts.'

Sloane raised an eyebrow. 'Why is that?'

'We were running low on money. For the house renovations. And with John the way he's been . . .' I bit the inside of my cheek, trying to stop myself from crying, thinking of the cash I had seen in Sam's backpack. 'Sam was supposed to be looking after him but now I'm worried he might have gained access to John's finances. I'm worried that's where some of the money came from.'

'Do you have any proof of that?'

'No.' But I thought again of John's wife, Mary, and how I suspected Sam had killed her. 'Just a really bad feeling.'

Sloane assessed me for a moment, then nodded and added a note to her pocketbook.

'What more can you tell me about this man Donovan?' she asked me.

'Excuse me, Detective?'

The paramedic had placed a hand on my shoulder and now she was drawing Sloane's attention to the readout on the monitor that she'd hooked me up to. I could see that my heart rate was high and erratic. The readout from the oximeter attached to my finger made it clear that my oxygen level was low. I couldn't seem to shift the scratchy constriction in my chest.

As if on cue, Bethany passed me the oxygen mask and I used it to cover my nose and mouth, drawing a cleansing breath.

'Can't this wait?' the paramedic asked. 'She's in shock. She has a head injury. I need to get her to the hospital.'

'Understood,' Sloane said, flipping her pocketbook closed and giving me a compassionate smile.

I pulled down my mask. 'He told me he was the brother of somebody Sam killed,' I blurted. 'Oliver Downing? It happened in Farringdon. Two years ago. The police thought Oliver jumped to his death from the roof of his apartment building but he didn't jump.' I sat forwards on the stretcher too fast, the interior of the ambulance beginning a slow spin. 'He was pushed. Sam did it. He—'

I grimaced and cradled my temple as a fresh lancing pain tore through my head. The white flickers again. Remembering still hurt.

I returned the oxygen mask to my mouth and inhaled deeply from it as Bethany nodded beside me. 'He confessed to that. I heard him.'

Sloane paused and then looked between us with a stunned expression of deep concern.

I lowered the mask. 'I was still on the line to your call handler at the time. He might have heard us, too.'

'Those calls are recorded. We can check. What else?'

'Detective, she needs a break,' the paramedic said, helping me to return the mask to my face. 'You can see that she does.'

Sloane seemed to think about it for a moment before switching her focus to Bethany. 'I think now would be a good time for me to take a more detailed statement from you.'

'I think so too.'

Bethany reached out from under her blanket to hug me gently.

'You take care,' she whispered.

I nodded.

'You know that you saved my life, right?'

I exhaled into my mask, shaking my head.

'No, you did. And don't you forget it, because I'm not going to let you. You got me out of there. And now I'm going to be there for you whether you want it or not. We're going to get through this together.'

Suddenly, it was all too much.

The tears that had been welling in my eyes began to spill

down my cheeks. I couldn't supress my shakes and I was overcome by a wave of intense, numbing cold.

'Then good, that's settled, then.' Bethany patted my leg and Sloane reached up to help her down out of the ambulance. Once she was safely outside, Bethany spun back to look at me one last time. 'I'll call you. We'll meet up, OK?'

I nodded. I wanted that, more than I would have guessed. I'd isolated myself from other people for too long. If I was going to get past this, I was going to need a friend like Bethany.

The paramedic stepped forwards and leaned out of the ambulance to swing the cargo doors closed, but I had one last question for Sloane first.

'How is he?' I asked, after lowering my mask again. 'Donovan?'

She rasped air through her lips as if she wasn't sure exactly how to answer me. 'Too early to say. He's lost a lot of blood. But I've seen worse cases pull through. We'll get an update to you at the hospital, I promise. In the meantime, I'm going to have two of our officers follow you there.'

115

'Thank you,' I murmured to the paramedic after she'd closed both doors.

'No problem.'

She propped herself against the medical storage cupboards opposite my stretcher with her gloved hands braced on either side of her and her face angled away from me, looking out through the tinted side windows at the scene we were leaving behind.

Forrester Avenue receded as the ambulance weaved between emergency vehicles and then accelerated, pursued by a marked police car with two female officers inside that pulled out from the kerb as we passed. I stared at the smoking remains of the house where I'd spent my last two years, watching it grow smaller, fainter, already knowing I never wanted to see it again.

It was going to be hard to reconcile myself to the idea that Sam had lied to me from the very beginning. I didn't know why he'd chosen me and I had no real understanding of what his intentions might have been for us in the long term. Had he really planned for us to go travelling together, or would he have looked to entrap me in some other way, I wondered?

The ambulance turned at the end of our road, rocking me from side to side, then continued on. The driver wasn't using the blue lights or the siren and I was glad of it. I needed some quiet to try to decompress.

Looking down at my arms, I contemplated the fresh abrasions across my skin from where the brickwork had scraped me, reaching out with my finger and gently tracing the line of my scar.

'Was that true?' the paramedic asked me. I raised my face, a bit surprised by her tone. 'What you just told that detective about Sam confessing to pushing Oliver?'

Her voice choked as she said it and for the first time I saw the mistiness in her eyes, the way she was pressing her lips tight together. A muscle in her cheek quivered as if she was fighting to hold her emotions in check.

Something flipped over inside me, and suddenly I knew.

Angling her head to one side, she flicked her ponytail out of the way and reached up to pluck something out of her ear between her finger and thumb, showing me the flesh-coloured nub of plastic she'd removed.

. . . *They're wearing a concealed earpiece. Sam won't even know they answered my call . . .*

I glimpsed a blurred smudge of ink on the inside of her wrist, just above the cuff of her blue nitrile gloves.

. . . *she had a tattoo. Inside her wrist . . . a bumblebee . . .*

And lastly, I thought about Donovan and the words he'd said to me when I'd escaped from the basement.

. . . *ambulance coming . . .*

I'd thought that he'd been telling me he'd called for an ambulance in the hope of saving his life. But what if that hadn't been the only reason? What if he'd been trying to explain something else to me?

. . . ambulance coming . . .

Because hadn't I wondered how Donovan was planning to get me away from the house without anyone noticing?

'Just tell me if it's true,' the paramedic said, staring at me as if everything that mattered to her hung on my words.

I dug my fingers into the plastic-coated mattress I was sitting on as we veered around a curve. It was only a short journey to the nearest hospital. We would be there soon.

'Who are you?'

'Amy. Oli's sister. I was watching Sam today. I took part in one of his support groups. We were in a seminar room at LSE. I followed him afterwards.'

It was as Donovan had said. She was the one who'd been on the other end of the phone from Donovan. She must have been on the Tube with Sam but instead of coming to our house she'd somehow arranged it so she would be in this ambulance instead.

If she was Oliver's sister, then she was Donovan's sister, too. As a family, they'd invested so much in this.

'Yes, it's true,' I told her.

She hung her head, exhaling bitterly. 'It wasn't supposed to go like this.'

'How was it supposed to go?'

'We were going to take you away under sedation. Take you to our mother's house. Make you look her in the eye. Make you tell her the truth.'

'Your brother used a sedative on Bethany.'

She nodded sadly, conjuring a broken smile. 'She wasn't supposed to be there.'

'But she was.'

She nodded again, as if she felt bad about that. 'I told him to let me come into that house with him,' she said, and thumped her fist off the counter next to her in frustration.

'Donovan?'

'He's my big brother. Oli's, too. Ever since our dad died' – she paused, glancing up briefly at the roof of the ambulance – 'he's always tried to be there for us, protect us. You have no idea how much what happened with Oli ate at him. He blamed himself for being overseas and not being around. Do you know what he told me? He told me it wouldn't be safe for me to go into that house.'

And he'd been right, I thought. It hadn't been safe. Not for any of us.

'I'm sorry,' I told her.

Because I was.

I was sorry any of this had happened. I was sorry he'd got hurt, that he'd terrorized me, that Bethany had been attacked and John had been threatened.

'You got him away from the fire,' she said to me. 'He has a chance now because of you.'

And with that she reached into a pocket of the paramedic jumpsuit she was wearing, taking out her phone. She sniffed and swiped at her nose with a gloved knuckle, then unlocked the screen.

'DNA results came in,' she said with a catch in her throat. 'You're a match with the blood that was under Oli's fingernails. But something you should know. Brainwashing?' She rasped air through her lips. 'As a doctor, I'm not sure there is such a thing. Not how you might be thinking of it, anyway.

But Donovan sent me a picture when he was in there. From your medicine cabinet.'

She turned her phone and showed me the image. It was a photograph of the inside of the cabinet in our en suite.

'Those are my anxiety meds,' I told her.

'Some of them, maybe. But the pills inside some of those boxes didn't match the descriptions on the outside. And it really depends on the quantities you were taking, the combinations, the dosage, but given the right way – or the wrong way, for you – it's conceivable they could have caused retrograde amnesia, affected your reasoning, made you more suggestible. Sam carried out some of his research work with patients in rehab centres and mental health facilities, right? My guess is he somehow got access to the drugs he needed there.'

It was a shock but also a small gift, I realized. Perhaps a way for me to begin to understand and reconcile myself to the horror that had been done to me.

'Did you tell your brother that?' I asked her.

'I texted him something along those lines.'

I thought about that as the ambulance approached the main hospital building. I couldn't help wondering if that was when Donovan's doubts about what had happened to Oliver and to me had begun to take shape. It possibly explained why he'd been so keen for Sam to get home. I also remembered that Donovan had asked me in front of Sam if I collected the medication for my anxiety myself. He must have guessed that Sam had been switching my pills.

As I turned it over in my mind, Amy braced a hand against the rear door, bending her head to look out of the side window. The ambulance slowed and pulled to a halt beneath the lighted canopy outside the Accident and Emergency Department.

'I need to go and find my brother,' she said. 'He's strong. Stronger than anyone I've ever known.'

'He was talking. Near the end. He tried to stop Sam.'

She glanced back at me, seeming to debate with herself whether to say something more.

'Donovan did some digging into Sam. Background stuff. He looked into his career at the university. Eight, nine months back, an ex-student made allegations against him of inappropriate behaviour for events that took place three years ago. She claimed that Sam coerced her into a relationship and used controlling behaviour before she graduated and broke it off. But the disciplinary process didn't go anywhere because she withdrew her allegations almost as soon as she'd made them. No explanation why.'

I felt as if a depth charge had gone off in my chest. I thought about the stress Sam had been under at work, how his career prospects had been derailed, how he'd complained about whispers in his department. I suspected the allegations had been part of that. And with the person I now knew Sam to have been, it seemed entirely possible that he could have threatened or intimidated his accuser until she backed off.

Three years. It couldn't have been too long afterwards before he'd begun to target me.

I was still reckoning with the implications of that, still reeling from it, when Amy reached for the latch on the cargo doors, then paused.

'One more question,' she said.

I waited.

'Sam. When he fell. I heard you say to the police that he couldn't get a grip on you. You said he slipped. I wanted to know. Are you sure about that? Sure you didn't maybe squirm, or kick at him, shake him loose?'

I looked at her for a beat too long, opening my mouth with no words coming out.

'Good.' She nodded. 'He deserved it.' Then she pushed open both doors and jumped down onto the tarmac, glancing over her shoulder as one of the uniformed officers climbed out of the patrol car behind us. 'Tell them about me, don't tell them about me, that's entirely up to you. But one last thing. That party? I didn't get a good enough look at you with Oli, not to be absolutely certain it was definitely you, but he came to talk to me when you first got there. And honestly? For Oli, after all his problems, all his sadness and fears, I hadn't seen him looking as happy and excited as he did that night in a long time. In my darkest moments, I cling to that. And now I think maybe you should, too.'

116

Six weeks later

'So, what do you say?' Bethany asked me.

'I'll think about it.'

I was sitting across Bethany's desk from her in the office of her estate agency. We were the only ones inside. The office was brightly lit with colourful furnishings. Framed property details were displayed in the large picture windows facing onto the street, suspended from discreet wires.

Bethany swivelled her touchscreen computer monitor to face me, swiping through a series of images of an apartment on-screen.

'It's got everything you're looking for. One bedroom. Modern facilities. Middle floor of a really secure building. I can get you an amazing deal on the rent.'

'You've said that about every place you've shown me.'

'Because it's true. I want you to be happy.'

I stood up from my chair, buttoning my coat and looping my handbag over my arm.

'Then make an appointment for a viewing,' I told her. 'We'll go together.'

'Yay.' Bethany stood from behind her desk and clapped her hands. I leaned forwards to kiss her goodbye on her cheek, but as I pulled back she reached up and took hold of both my shoulders, peering into my eyes. 'Are you sure you don't want me to come with you? I'm due a break.'

As she spoke, the door behind us opened and a middle-aged couple walked in.

'No, I'm fine,' I told her. 'You have customers. I'm going to do this bit by myself.'

I smiled to the couple as I passed them on my way to the door.

'Wave if you need me,' Bethany called.

'I'll come back afterwards,' I replied. 'Tell you how it went.'

It was cold and damp outside. Middle of the morning. The rain had stopped, but the pavement was greasy. Water splashed up in fans from the tyres of passing vehicles as I waited to cross the road.

When the pedestrian lights changed, I glanced back over my shoulder at Bethany, who was already engaging the couple in animated conversation and drawing their attention to a property brochure.

I smiled to myself. Bethany was determined to help me get back on my feet, no matter what it took, just as she was absolutely committed to carrying on with her career.

Only recently I'd discovered that she'd designed some business cards for me and that she was getting all the estate agents at her firm to pass them on to any clients they thought might be in need of an interior designer. In all honesty, I hadn't been sure it was something I wanted to contemplate again, but then the first few calls had reached me and I'd started to find that I was intrigued by some of the projects people wanted to discuss.

When I reached the opposite pavement, I skipped on

towards the small independent cafe that faced Bethany's estate agency and then stopped cold.

Donovan was sitting at an outside table beneath the sodden awning. He was wearing a dark padded jacket over stonewashed jeans and leather boots. He was also looking straight at me as he set aside the newspaper he'd been reading, leaving me in no doubt that he'd known I was coming here today.

'Sit down,' he said. 'I won't keep you long.'

I shook my head slowly, fighting against the urge to turn and run, shout for help.

'What do you want?' I managed.

'To say goodbye. After today, you won't see me again. You've had enough trauma. I didn't want that to be a concern for you.'

I felt my face pull taut even as I experienced a pulse of relief deep inside. I had heard he'd survived Sam's attack on him but that it had been touch and go during his surgery. Looking at him now, there were few signs of the injuries he'd sustained. I could see a small scar on his cheek close to one eye as well as a slight stiffness to his movements that he was doing his best to conceal.

'They told me you asked them to drop the charges against me,' he said.

'They told me that would make no difference.'

'It didn't.'

'And yet here you are.'

He raised his eyebrows and parted his hands, as if the assault offences the police had told me they would be issuing were only a minor inconvenience.

'I told you I was an intelligence officer,' he said.

I waited, not wanting to give him the satisfaction of asking how that factored in.

'Let's just say I have influential friends. People who'd prefer for me to be able to do what I do, where they need me to do it.'

'Bethany won't be happy about that.'

Donovan pressed his lips together in contemplation and looked past me for a moment in the direction of Bethany's estate agency. 'No,' he said. 'I don't suppose she will be.'

I was a bit more conflicted. On one level, despite the terror he'd visited on me, I knew that I owed him something that went beyond the truth he'd been searching for. On another, I was painfully aware that Donovan's mother had already lost one son and I hadn't wanted her to lose Donovan to a prison sentence.

'I never told the police about Amy being in the ambulance with me,' I said.

He nodded.

Based on what I was able to gather from DS Sloane, Donovan had denied that he'd ever had an accomplice. To my mind, it would have been relatively simple for the police to prove otherwise. They had the mobile phone Donovan had been using to stay in touch with Amy, and while I suspected she would have been on a burner phone, the evidence of Donovan's calls to her was still there. On top of that, LSE could have assisted them with their investigation, presumably by putting them in touch with some of the other people who had attended the same support group as Sam and Amy who might have identified her. Or the police could have checked CCTV footage from Sam's Tube journey home.

I guessed now I had an answer for why none of that had happened.

'How's John?' Donovan asked.

I shook my head without answering him. Not simply because he didn't deserve to know that John was now in a specialist care home, but because I was certain he already did.

I'd visited John a couple of times. He was doing about as well as could be expected. I don't think he remembered me but that was OK. The care home had their own cat and I knew he liked that.

My suspicions about Sam turned out to be true. The police checked and discovered that he had been siphoning off funds from John's savings over a period of at least a year. Small sums to begin with, then larger amounts when he didn't get caught. Bethany had told me there would be a queue of developers eager to snap up John's house when it went on the market. The proceeds of the sale would cover his ongoing care costs.

As for Sam's house, I was sure that would sell too, in time, despite the fire damage it had sustained. I knew for a fact that Bethany had no interest in marketing the property. Some well-meaning people had told me that I should sue Sam's estate for damages when the sale eventually went through, but I wasn't interested. I was ready to move on.

'How long were you planning what you did to me?' I asked Donovan.

'Not long. I moved pretty fast.' He glanced down ruefully at his torso. 'Too fast, on reflection.'

'And Sam? Did you always suspect him?'

'I knew things about him. I also knew it was possible he was sheltering you, protecting you. Then there was the chance you'd tricked him and he knew nothing at all. That's why I wanted to get inside the house with you. Talk to you without you knowing why I was there. And when I did . . .' He paused to study me closely, as if assessing how much more he should say. 'In my line of work, you see things. A lot of the time you wish you never had. But when you showed me around, the way you talked, some of the things I saw, I got echoes.'

I shivered and he saw me do it. He then twisted to one side, bracing a hand on the back of his chair and levering himself to his feet with some discomfort.

'Still healing,' he said.

'Me too.'

He stared at me a moment, appraising me, then he picked up his paper and gestured inside the cafe with it.

'Better go in. They're waiting for you.'

He walked away without looking back. I stood there, my heart thumping, my throat closing up, waiting until he'd weaved between other pedestrians, then turned a corner until I couldn't see him any more.

When I glanced back across the road at Bethany, I saw that she was still talking with the couple, blissfully unaware of what had happened, and I decided then and there to keep things that way.

My head felt light. My knees were rubbery. But I refused to let Donovan distract me from why I'd come here today. After taking some deep breaths and closing my eyes briefly, I shook the nervous stress out of my hands and arms, cleared my hair from my face, then spun and walked directly through the fogged glass door of the cafe. A woman in a taupe apron looked up from behind a counter as I entered.

'It's OK,' I told her, pointing to a table by the window where three people were gathered around steaming coffee cups. 'I can see my group.'

I wobbled a bit as I approached but I paused to get it under control, then drew back a chair and sat down. I could feel my nerves fluttering against my ribs. Tears pressing against the backs of my eyes. I was very conscious of the empty table outside where Donovan had been sitting, and when I looked at it, I felt undone for a second, then clenched my hands into fists and pushed on.

'Thank you all for coming,' I said. 'How is everyone?'

'Good.'

'Better.'

'I'm doing OK.'

I believed them.

The taxi driver had lost some weight. He was wearing a charcoal suit, a crisp white shirt and a striped tie.

The girl's hair was longer and lighter. I guessed it was her natural shade. She had on a pretty blouse over jeans, and her make-up was much less dramatic than it had been, though she still had the lip ring.

The skinny guy was still skinny. He was still a bit hunched up and nervous. But he met and held my eyes without looking down or away and his smile seemed genuine.

'What about your phobias?' I asked.

'We were just talking about that,' the taxi driver said. 'I'm pretty much over it. I went with hypnosis therapy in the end. It really helped. I jacked in the cab, though. Got a job as a personal driver for a rich guy who lives not too far from here.'

'And I'm sleeping almost normally,' the girl said. 'Some of what we learned at the support group . . .' She broke off, looking uncomfortable for a moment.

'It's OK,' I told her. 'You can say.'

'I'm sorry, but it really helped. And I have a boyfriend now. He holds my hand when I'm falling asleep.'

'I'm glad,' I told her. 'Truly.'

'I'm more of a work in progress,' the skinny guy admitted. 'But it's a long time since I've been as low or as bad as I was back then. I've been seeing a therapist. I know the warning signs to watch out for. My bosses at the uni have been really supportive. And I've confided in some close friends.'

'That's great,' I said. 'You have no idea how good it is for me to hear that. But before we chat more, do you mind if we do one small thing? Can we all just introduce ourselves properly this time?'

'Mike,' the older man said, with a nod and a smile.

'Caroline.'

'Ross.'

'Well, you all know who I am by now.' It had been in the press enough. I knew they would have read the stories. There had been a lot of coverage of the events at No. 18 Forrester Avenue. So I didn't think any of them were surprised or embarrassed when my voice began to tremble and my eyes welled up. 'It's a pleasure to meet you all,' I told them. 'I'm Louise.'

ACKNOWLEDGEMENTS

Huge thanks to the following for all their help and support with this book:

Vicki Mellor, as well as Lucy Hale, Samantha Fletcher, Philippa McEwan, Karen Whitlock, all those in Sales, Marketing and Publicity and the entire team at Pan Macmillan.

Beth deGuzman, Kirsiah Depp, Karen Kosztolnyik and everyone at Grand Central Publishing.

Camilla Bolton, my agent, and everyone at the Darley Anderson Literary Agency, including Mary Darby, Kristina Egan, Georgia Fuller, Salma Zarugh, Jade Kavanagh and Sheila David.

Sylvie Rabineau at WME.

Lucy Hanington, Clare Donoghue and Tim Weaver.

And Mum, Allie, Jessica, Jack and my wife, Jo.

ABOUT THE AUTHOR

C. M. Ewan is a pseudonym for Chris Ewan, the critically acclaimed and bestselling author of many mystery and thriller novels. Chris's first standalone thriller, *Safe House*, was a bestseller in the UK and was shortlisted for the Theakston's Old Peculier Crime Novel of the Year Award. He is also the author of the thrillers *Dead Line, Dark Tides, Long Time Lost, A Window Breaks* and *The Interview,* as well as The Good Thief's Guide series of mystery novels. *The Good Thief's Guide to Amsterdam* won the Long Barn Books First Novel Award and has been published in thirteen countries. Chris lives with his wife and their two children in Somerset, where he writes full-time.